The Quiet Correspondent

The Quiet Correspondent

There's a thin line between a journalist and a spy

Shyam Bhatia

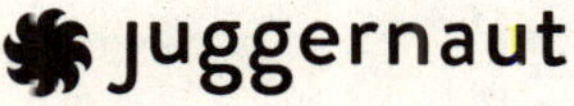
juggernaut

JUGGERNAUT BOOKS
C-I-128, First Floor, Sangam Vihar, Near Holi Chowk,
New Delhi 110080, India

First published by Juggernaut Books 2026

10 9 8 7 6 5 4 3 2 1

P-ISBN: 9789353455446
E-ISBN: 9789353454999

This is a work of fiction. Certain names and events are drawn from the historical record, while others are inspired by real people and places but have been fictionalized. All characters, dialogue and depictions are imaginative reconstructions intended solely for dramatic purposes.

Typeset in Adobe Caslon Pro by R. Ajith Kumar, Noida

Printed at Thomson Press India Ltd

For my wife, my sons, my daughter-in-law and my granddaughters, who remind me every day what truly matters.

Contents

Part I – 1991: London and the Betrayal

Part II – 1978–1990: Fieldwork and the Shadows

Part III : London and the Aftermath

Part I – 1991

London and the Betrayal

1

Naxos

The island was too beautiful for this kind of business. Naxos, early summer 1991, was a paradise hiding a deadly secret. Amol arrived on the second ferry of the day. The sea was flat as blue glass, but his stomach was wired, hungry. Not for food, for a story. For safety. For truth, maybe, though he'd stopped trusting that word.

He needed this story, not just for the byline but also to prove to himself that truth still mattered, that his years chasing shadows hadn't been wasted. Yet doubt gnawed: was there any truth left to find or only versions carefully spun to hide darker realities?

On the dock, a man in wrap-around sunglasses tapped a cigarette loose and looked straight through him. The man's gaze was cold and unreadable, less a look than a challenge. Amol felt it like a warning, a shadow cast long before any words could be spoken.

That was the thing about being half-Indian. To Greeks, he could pass. To Brits, he was a curiosity. To spooks, a useful shadow. He walked past slowly, carrying nothing but a bag and a name in his head.

The island shimmered under the Mediterranean sun, bone-white villages perched on sunbaked hills, olive groves twisted by the dry wind. Amol felt the sea's vast unblinking eye, indifferent to the story he carried and far from the glossy postcards and honeymoon dreams that masked the island's darker truths.

Not this. Not the business of ghosts.

Amol Batty had covered wars, uprisings, famines, but nothing had ever felt as off-kilter as this quiet Greek island, where the ugliness of history had come to roost with the tourists. Amol had once believed journalism was a searchlight in darkness. Now, it sometimes felt more like a spotlight on the performer – careful, rehearsed and often deceived.

The ferry shuddered into dock with a metallic groan. Amol stepped off last, his canvas bag slung over one shoulder, shoes chalked in salt from the Aegean spray. The light was brutal, flat white and indifferent – bouncing off stone buildings, dazzling the sea.

He paused on the quay, letting taxi drivers jostle and call to new arrivals. He wasn't in a hurry. He had time to watch, to think. To look like a man on holiday, even if the weight in his chest said otherwise.

He slotted in here too well. His mother's Indian blood had gifted him dark skin, wide-set eyes and hair that curled too easily in the Aegean humidity. From his English father, he'd inherited a worn-out reserve that made him seem local. Waiters spoke to him in Greek. Shopkeepers waved him past without a glance. German tourists assumed he worked there.

The French girls didn't look at him twice. It was a blessing, sometimes. A curse, often.

For four days, Amol met Sedo Hazan in a dying café – a low-slung ruin behind the tourist strip. Plastic chairs leaned unevenly on sunbaked stone beneath a sun-bleached sign hanging by a rusted chain, its faded red letters barely visible.

The stale coffee sat on the stove since Easter and the old owner, with a smoker's cough and eyes like chipped marble, served whatever scraps he had – over-fried fish, thinly sliced tomatoes, shrivelled olives and warm bottled water. The place was perfect: quiet enough that no one asked questions, indifferent to the heat and the setting sun, as the same two men occupied the same corner table every afternoon.

Each day, Sedo came late. Alone, always watching the door. Moving like a man expecting the bullet. He carried a plastic bag full of papers, plenty of A4-sized blank sheets, sometimes a battered spiral notebook. His clothes were the same – frayed jeans, sweat-stained shirts with sleeves rolled high, open sandals that showed blackened toenails. Kurdish, from eastern Turkey – the kind of man Amol had met a dozen times in the refugee camps and the mountain villages where old wars never ended.

Sometimes, Sedo ate. More often, he didn't. Conversation was scarce. Instead, Sedo sketched.

When they did speak, it was Sedo who asked the questions. 'You write your stories, eh? London newspaper. You know nothing about us.'

'Enlighten me,' Amol said, switching on his recorder.

Sedo smiled thinly. 'What do you know of the PKK, the Kurdistan Workers' Party?'

Amol leaned back. 'Started in the late '70s. Marxist – Leninist roots. Fought the Turkish state for Kurdish independence. The Turks call you terrorists. You call yourselves freedom fighters. The Americans? Depends on the year.'

Sedo gave a humourless laugh. 'Good for a reporter. But you miss the blood. You miss what it means to grow up watching your father dragged from his house, your village burnt. You miss what it means to carry your first Kalashnikov at fourteen.'

Amol said nothing. He couldn't argue. How could a boy from a London suburb understand the world Sedo came from? The weight of Sedo's words pressed down on him, stirring a mix of guilt and helplessness. How could he, safe and removed, claim to grasp the pain etched into every scar Sedo carried?

'Do you know how many of my comrades died in the mountains?' Sedo jabbed a finger at him. 'Do you know what phosphorus does to human skin when the Turkish jets drop it?'

He didn't wait for an answer. Just watched Amol, eyes unreadable.

'I've seen too much blood,' Sedo said, voice low, eyes hard. 'But I still know how to make it flow.'

A pause. Then, not quite looking at Amol, he added, 'I used to dream of being an engineer. The kind who builds bridges. Not bombs.'

Amol wrote that down without much thought, assuming it was a metaphor. Only later would he wonder: was that a confession or a plea?

There were moments – fleeting, instinctive – when Sedo's questions felt less like curiosity and more like calibration.

Meanwhile, the drawings continued. Page after page, lines of ink drawn slowly, carefully: wires, detonators, circuit diagrams dense with numbers and strange, looping symbols. He recognized the posture – head down, fingers smudged with pencil.

His grandfather had looked the same at his Remington in Delhi, writing lines that might tip a cabinet. Except this was another kind of sentence. These sketches were blueprints – not for speeches or policies – but for destruction. They held secrets that could rewrite the rules of warfare and change lives forever.

At times, it felt like Sedo already knew the answers before Amol asked the questions. He wrote in Turkish, sometimes in what Amol assumed was Kurdish .... Sometimes, when the paper ran out, he scrawled on napkins. His hands were steady, his face blank.

When he moved, Sedo carried himself with the quiet precision of someone trained to be invisible, deliberate, composed, his every step measured to avoid notice. There was no nervous twitch, only the steady calm of a man accustomed to shadows. He wore the weariness of a lifetime spent on the run. His presence, a muted echo of danger rather than any show of defiance. He was the kind of man who could pass through an airport with a smile – and a bomb in his bag.

He caught Amol watching him and raised an eyebrow. 'What? You think I do this for fun?'

There was almost a smile there – not quite, but close enough to catch Amol off guard. He was too careful, Amol thought; not like a man hiding, but like one already rehearsed.

On the table, Sedo had left behind a matchbox – ordinary, unbranded, probably nothing. He turned it over once in his palm, then slipped it into his pocket. He didn't know why. Just a reflex. Or maybe insurance. There was something almost childlike in how Sedo had left it behind, an unspoken offering, a footnote in place of farewell.

Amol wanted to argue with himself, but the words caught in his throat. And in that moment, he couldn't deny it – not entirely. Sedo had read him better than most. Amol didn't know why the thought came. Perhaps he did.

On the third day, a pair of Dutch tourists wandered in, all sunburn and confusion, looking for somewhere to kill an hour. The old man grunted and waved them to the far corner. Sedo froze mid-sketch, eyes narrow, every muscle coiled. Amol felt it too, that sharp, electric jolt of danger, but the couple ordered beers, took a photo and left before the second round.

After that, Sedo spoke for the first time in hours. 'I shouldn't be here.'

'Then why come?' Amol queried.

Sedo lit another cigarette, hand trembling just enough for Amol to notice. 'Because this is the kind of place they forget exists. No cameras. No phones. No witnesses.'

He wasn't wrong. Even the flies seemed too bored to care about what was happening in the corner. By the fourth day, the papers between them were thick, still more diagrams, dense with looping wires, numbers that meant nothing to Amol but everything to someone who knew.

Sedo finished a drawing, tapped the page with his pencil and finally looked at Amol like seeing him for the first time.

'What's this?' Amol asked, voice deliberately low.

Sedo didn't look up. 'Proof,' he rasped. 'For your people. They'll understand. You, you're not supposed to.'

Amol blinked. 'My people? You think I work for someone?'

The ghost of a smile passed Sedo's face. 'I know you do.'

It wasn't the first time someone had accused him of working for intelligence. In some places, being a reporter and being a spy were the same thing. Sometimes, Amol wondered if they were wrong. His newspaper was rumoured to take money from strange places.

One proprietor had sucked up money from African dictators with improbable sounding names. And then there were the editors, like the one who befriended Kim Philby and another who served in the Special Air Service during the Second World War. They were the ones with pasts no one talked about.

But this time, the accusation landed differently, a sharp pebble in his gut.

In the dead hours between meetings, Amol walked the island, past the tourist beaches, up into the dry hills where the only sound was the wind through brittle grass. He could feel it, the story shifting under his feet. This wasn't journalism anymore. This was something older, colder.

—

That night, unable to sleep, he made a call – a fixer he trusted in Athens. A guy who owed him from the refugee route.

'Sedo Hazan,' Amol said when the man picked up. 'You ever hear that name?'

The silence was immediate. Then, careful. 'Sedo the Kurd? Bomb-maker?'

'You know him?'

A pause. 'Yeah. PKK, back in the day. Heavy guy, married with one son. Had a reputation for building the kind of bombs that don't leave anyone to tell the story.'

Amol felt his throat tighten. 'He says he worked with the Germans. The Athens hit.'

Another pause, longer this time.

'The Americans still talk about that. The US Defence Attaché – 1989. His car went up outside the embassy. German Red Army Faction took credit. But word was they had help.'

'From who?'

'Locals. Kurds, Palestinians, anyone who could get their hands dirty. Germans were good at ideology but shit at logistics. They needed Sedo's people.'

Amol leaned against the crumbling stone wall of the pension, staring out at the sea. 'Tell me about the Red Army Faction.'

The fixer exhaled. 'The RAF … Christ. They were real-deal terrorists. Started in the '70s. Anti-capitalist, anti-imperialist. Blew up banks, killed judges, businessmen, US military. Called themselves urban guerrillas. But by the late '80s, they were on their last legs. No safe houses, no money, everyone hunted. So they cut deals with the Stasi, Syrians, Kurds, anyone who'd help.'

'And they hit the Defence Attaché in Athens?'

'Yeah. Big one. Car bomb. Clean hit. The Germans couldn't have pulled it off alone. Too far from home. That's why people think Sedo was involved. Then he vanished.'

Amol swallowed hard. He wasn't just sitting on a story. He was sitting on a piece of Cold War shrapnel that hadn't stopped killing yet.

By the fourth day, it was unbearable. Sedo barely spoke now. Just smoked and stared, the sketches piled high between them like a funeral offering. That morning, he came empty-handed. No drawings. Just a cigarette, burning down to the filter.

'I gave you enough,' he said, his voice flat. 'Now you tell them.'

'Tell who?'

'Your people.' He smiled thinly. 'You know who.'

Amol shook his head. 'Sedo, I'm a reporter –'

'You're a messenger,' Sedo snapped. 'I want asylum. I want a pension. Otherwise, you'll never see me again.'

Amol stared at him. 'Why not go to the Americans? They'd pay.'

Sedo laughed – a short, bitter sound. 'Americans? They kill first. You British – you think. That's why.'

When it was over, Sedo stood up, nodded once and walked away. He did not say goodbye. Amol watched him go, past the taverna, down towards the square where fishermen were mending nets under the last of the daylight.

Amol wanted to argue with himself, but the words caught in his throat. Because deep down, he knew Sedo was right. That night, Amol stood on the beach, waves hissing at his feet. The sketches weighed heavy in his bag – evidence or a death sentence. Maybe both.

Amol often wondered how much trust he could afford – to his sources, to his editors, even to himself. The line between ally and enemy blurred until it was almost invisible.

He called London. Sean Gallagher answered on the second ring, sounding bright, half-drunk. 'Batty! Still living the dream?'

Amol didn't bother with pleasantries. 'He's real, Sean. It's him. Sedo Hazan. And he's got drawings – bomb schematics, timers. He's talking about the Athens hit. The Defence Attaché.'

The silence was immediate. When Sean spoke again, the charm was gone. 'Where are you now?'

'Naxos.'

'Good. Listen carefully – first ferry to Athens, then fly home. Bring everything. Notes, sketches, recordings. Don't talk to anyone. Don't file.'

'What about Sedo?'

'Forget him for now. There's a team here who needs to see what you've got.'

Amol's stomach twisted. 'Spooks?'

Sean didn't answer. Which was answer enough. 'You're in deep, mate,' Sean said finally. 'Come home.'

The line went dead. Amol stood there, staring out at the black water, the salt wind cold on his face.

He'd spent years chasing stories no one cared about – Yazidi graves in Iraq, chemical weapons in Syria, blood money on London's streets. But this was different. This was not a story you walked away from.

Tomorrow, he'd leave Naxos. But the papers in his bag – the secrets sketched in Sedo's careful hand – they belonged to him now. And there was no going back.

From the ferry port in Athens, he took the long route back to his hotel, walking past the metro station at Piraeus, ignoring the waiting taxis and choosing instead to let the city unfold slowly. It was late afternoon and the heat clung to the pavements like spilled resin. The streets smelled of diesel, overripe fruit and sea-salt still trapped in his collar.

Athens was buzzing, indifferent. Mopeds zipped through red lights. Waiters set out tables with casual authority. A man on a plastic stool played a battered bouzouki near Monastiraki, the strings too sharp but the tune oddly familiar. Life, unbothered.

Amol walked with no urgency, trying to make sense of the conversation he'd just left behind. Sedo's voice still echoed in his mind – flat, unhurried, chilling in its precision. The bomb diagrams, the German link, the American attaché in Athens. The weight of what he now carried pressed against his ribs like an invisible briefcase. He hadn't written anything down. He hadn't needed to.

Sean's voice had been brief on the phone: 'Come back to London. We'll talk when you're in.' That was it. No fanfare, no clues. Just that clipped tone of his, professional with a hint of something else underneath. Anticipation? Worry? Amol couldn't tell.

He passed through Syntagma, where the pigeons never moved fast and the soldiers moved too slowly. The air was beginning to cool. He stopped at a kiosk and bought a bottle of water, nodding thanks to the woman inside who didn't look up from her radio.

He found himself thinking back to his first month on staff at the paper – long before the foreign postings, before Beirut and Baghdad and bylines that got copied into government files. The paper had hired a retired BBC man to run a 'field safety and messaging' workshop. Mostly, it was puffed-up nonsense – how to keep your flak jacket zipped and your copy clean.

But there was one moment he never forgot.

The man had said, 'When it gets bad – when the facts are ugly – just smile and keep the camera rolling.'

Everyone had laughed. Except Amol. He had asked quietly, 'What if smiling becomes part of the lie?'

The man hadn't answered. Just raised an eyebrow and moved on.

It had stayed with him. That, and the sense that journalism had shifted – had become less about revelation and more about performance. He had always resisted that drift. Until now, perhaps.

He passed a row of shuttered antique shops, each window gathering dust and stories no one wanted to buy. His thoughts drifted to Oxford, to Merton cloisters in spring. Tutorials that meandered into arguments. He remembered a note one of his tutors had scribbled in the margin of an essay on imperial narratives: 'You're too honest to survive this profession. Or not dishonest enough.'

Back then, he'd thought it was a compliment. Now, he wasn't so sure.

The light was fading. Somewhere behind him, the Acropolis glowed amber against the purpling sky. For a moment, he could almost hear Delhi – the clink of ice in a glass on the veranda at Golf Links, the low thrum of adult voices speaking carefully around truths that were never quite said.

His Indian grandfather tapping at the Remington, pausing only to sip whisky or adjust the phrasing of a line. Ministers, diplomats, former intelligence men – they all passed through that house. Nobody ever used the word 'spy', but the word hovered in the air like woodsmoke.

He kept walking.

He didn't know yet what Sean had arranged. Didn't know who else had read the transcript or seen the sketches. Didn't know, most of all, what they would now ask of him.

Back at the hotel, his suitcase was packed. Passport zipped into the outer pocket. The ferry from Naxos felt a lifetime ago. In the morning, he'd fly to London. See what awaited. For now, all he could do was wait with it – this story, this secret, this sense that the world had shifted slightly on its axis. And that he was already inside something he couldn't quite name.

2

London

Days later, he was back in London; Heathrow was soaked in drizzle, the Aegean sun already fading from his skin. The Aegean sun felt far behind him now. Naxos reduced to tape hiss, sand in a pocket and the scent of sweat sealed into his clothes.

Amol moved through the terminal like a ghost – no questions, no stops, the bag heavy in his grip. The black cab took him north. Streets blurred past in grey, familiar and foreign all at once. By the time he unlocked the door to his Islington flat, his hands were trembling.

The hallway light in his Islington flat flickered once before catching. He stepped over a pile of free newspapers no one had claimed. Inside, everything was quiet, the kind of quiet that doesn't welcome, just confirms. The sketches – Sedo's careful, damning diagrams – sat on the kitchen table like a live wire. He didn't sleep.

Two weeks of unopened post lay on his doorstep. A single yoghurt in the fridge. He left the suitcase zipped by the door and stood a moment in the dark, listening for something that wasn't there.

Sean's voice was terse when he called the next morning. 'You need to come. Now.'

'Where?'

'Holiday Inn. Farringdon Road. You'll see why.'

The Holiday Inn off Farringdon Road was designed to be forgettable – beige walls, scuffed carpet, the faint smell of old coffee and furniture polish. It could've been a job interview, a seminar. Anything but this.

They were already there, four of them, sitting evenly spaced on one side of the long table. Three men, one woman. All unremarkable. The sort of faces you forget even as you're looking at them.

Two of the men wore glasses with thin metal frames. One had lenses so smudged, it was hard to tell if he could see through them. The third, ruddy-faced with thinning hair, wore a brown tie so plain it might've come with the suit. A supermarket sandwich, egg and cress, sat unopened in front of him, curling at the edges. He never touched it.

The woman was neat, maybe mid-40s. Grey blazer, pale blue blouse. No makeup except for a faint smear of lipstick, as if she'd applied it in a moving car. A biro was clipped to her lapel, its cap chewed nearly to shreds. On her wrist, a battered Casio watch with a cracked plastic strap. The sort of thing bought at an airport or a service station.

Not one of them looked like they belonged to anything as grand as 'intelligence'. They looked like council workers, civil servants, the people who handle paperwork no one reads. There were no introductions. No names. Just a nod towards the chairs opposite them.

Amol sat, feeling the weight of Sedo's sketches in his bag. Sean settled beside him, tight jawed. The woman spoke first. Her voice was polite, pleasant, the tone of someone chairing a dull meeting. 'Thanks for coming.'

It was a form of greeting with no follow up small talk. No wasted words.

The papers were passed across. The four bent their heads, flipping pages, barely making a sound. Fingers – stubby, pale, stained faintly with biro ink – traced Sedo's lines.

Diagrams of bombs, fuses, the ugly mechanics of it all.

'Mercury tilt switches,' one of the men muttered, not to anyone in particular. 'Classic.'

Then there was a whispered aside with Sean, one that went on forever as Sean's hands started to tremble ever so slightly. 'Jesus Christ. You know what you've got here, Amol? This isn't just blueprints, it's a prototype for something new. The PKK's been working on a shaped charge variant, but this …' he jabbed at the cross-section Sedo had drawn, 'this is battlefield-ready.'

There was a long pause.

'They're calling it the "Purple Swan" – early chatter from the Germans. Because once it's out there, nothing will be the same. Thousands dead, convoys, embassies, goddamn shopping malls. These fuckers sell this to anyone, and it's game over.'

Amol felt his throat dry up. 'You're serious?'

'Dead serious. This, this could be the Irish Republican Army's wet dream if it crosses the Channel. Or the Palestinians'. Or the Chechens'. The Yanks will lose their minds over this.'

The celebratory mood continued, Sean whooping and spinning once in the centre of the room. 'Jesus fucking Christ, we've done it. Do you know what this means, Amol?'

Amol blinked. 'We publish?'

Sean laughed, breathless. 'No, you idiot, it means our credibility with the Yanks just trebled in value. Tripled, mate. We're in the big leagues now. Langley will be crawling up our arses for this.'

He did a ridiculous little jig – arms flailing, tie slipping. 'I swear to God, there's a gong in this for you. Fuck it, for both of us. We're golden, mate. We've just moved the needle. We should both fly back to Naxos, thank Sedo in person.'

Later, once the immediate excitement subsided, one of the prim looking four visitors asked something softly, almost conversationally, about the journey. Not about the politics or the danger. Just … the ferry crossing, how rough the sea was. How long Amol stayed in Naxos. What kind of tourists were around.

'Couple of Germans?' the ruddy man asked. 'Scandinavians?'

Amol blinked. 'I … yeah. Some.'

They nodded, satisfied. Notes made, mentally if not on paper.

It was surreal, this cold bureaucracy of death and exile conducted like a housing benefits review. Finally, the woman set her hands flat on the table. 'It's good work,' she said lightly. 'It's real.'

Amol let out the breath he hadn't known he was holding. 'What happens now?'

She exchanged a glance with the man beside her, then looked back at Amol. 'We're going to ask something of you.'

Amol waited.

She continued, voice steady. 'We need you to call him. Sedo.'

Amol stared. 'Me?'

'He won't trust us. He might trust you. We want him to go to the British Embassy in Athens. There's someone there, someone who knows he's coming. If he walks in, he'll be safe. We guarantee it.'

She leaned forward slightly. 'But it has to be you. He won't trust us. He'll trust you.'

Amol's mouth felt dry. 'And if he doesn't go?'

Her shoulders lifted, a small, almost apologetic shrug. 'Then … there's nothing more we can do.'

Sean made a sound, a protest half-formed, but the woman cut him off with a look.

'No threats,' she added. 'We're offering the safest road left. It's up to him if he takes it.'

Sean shifted beside him. 'You're not threatening him?'

'No. Just … offering the only road left.' She turned back to Amol. 'You've got the number. Call him. Tell him to be there by tomorrow night. After that … we can't help.'

'And the story?' Amol asked quietly.

'One week.' Her eyes held his. 'You sit on it for seven days. After that, it's yours. No interference, no edits.'

The room was silent but for the hum of cheap fluorescent lights.

Amol nodded slowly. 'I'll call him.'

Sean gave a tight smile, the first real expression he'd shown all morning. 'I think Amol's done really well,' he said, voice light but now carrying a pointed edge. 'Deserves a gong, really. Something like a CBE, you know, the Commander of the Order of the British Empire?'

The woman didn't laugh. Just gathered the papers into a neat stack. 'We'll know if he goes.'

No goodbyes. No handshakes. They left as quickly as they'd come – no names, no cards exchanged, leaving only the weight of the task behind.

As they left, Sean let out a low breath. 'They look like they run a bloody parish council.'

And maybe that was the genius. No uniforms, no orders barked. Just biro pens, supermarket sandwiches and the power to reshape lives with a nod.

Amol said nothing. The untouched sandwich, the chewed pen, the battered Casio – they were still sitting there in his mind, more frightening than a gun on the table. Because that was the point, wasn't it? Power that didn't need to prove itself.

Somehow, calling Sedo felt heavier than carrying those sketches across the sea.

—

The following morning, Amol stood in the newsroom, staring at his desk phone. The clatter of keyboards, phones ringing, the hum of the office, all of it felt distant. Sean was nearby, pretending to skim a paper, watching without really watching.

The meeting at the Holiday Inn had been clear, polite, terrifying in its calm. No names. No threats. Just the facts laid out like cold stones.

'You'll call him.' The voice dropped, cold and clipped, leaving space for the threat to settle. 'From here. We'll be listening.'

The receiver felt heavier in Amol's hand. The room seemed to shrink, the hum of fluorescent lights suddenly oppressive.

This wasn't journalism. This was operational delivery. Not quite an agent, not quite a journalist. But close enough now that he could feel the cold breath of it on his neck.

The number was scrawled on a scrap of paper in Amol's notebook, Sedo's Greek number, the only way back into the story now. He hesitated. One ring and the line would tighten. He could still walk away, claim neutrality, burn the notes. But the voice in his head – maybe Sean's, maybe his own – said: *Then what?*

Amol took a breath and dialled. It rang twice.

'Yes?' The voice was flat, wary.

'It's me … You all right?' Amol's mouth felt full of ash. He lowered his voice, glancing sideways, but no one was looking.

Except Sean, always Sean, pretending to skim the paper, not missing a word.

He repeated. 'You all right?'

A pause. 'No. You shouldn't be calling.'

Amol shut his eyes. *I know. God, I know.*

'I need to see you.' Amol swallowed. 'Listen carefully. There's a way out. But you need to move. Today.'

Silence. Then: 'Who told you that?'

Amol's pulse thumped in his neck. 'Doesn't matter. You trust me, yeah?'

Another pause. Long enough that Amol imagined the whole thing falling apart – the sketches, the Embassy, the careful lines drawn by people who'd never have to make a call like this. Then, faintly: rustling. Whispered words. A different voice came on the line, a woman's this time. Soft, accented.

'Mr Batty? This is Zerin. I'm his wife.'

Amol blinked. 'I didn't know you were – '

'He didn't want to involve me. But I'm already involved. We both are.'

Her voice carried weight, even in its calmness. 'I told him to listen to you. If there's a door open, even a small one … he has to walk through it. For our son. He's only six.'

Amol's throat tightened. 'If he goes to the British Embassy in Athens, they'll take him in. He must go tonight.'

'And if it's a trap?' she asked softly.

'Then I've damned him,' Amol said. 'But it's the only option I have to offer.'

Another pause. Breathing. Then: 'Tell him to go. I'll make sure he does.'

He hated the weight of what he was doing, the way persuasion blurred into instruction. He hadn't offered safety. He'd delivered a message, like a courier in a war he never agreed to fight. Amol forced his voice steady. 'Go to the British Embassy. Athens. Strefi Hill – you know it?'

A dry laugh. 'I know it.'

'They're expecting you. Walk in. No one follows. No games. Just you.'

'And what happens then?' Sedo's voice cracked, a thread of something close to fear.

'You get what you asked for. Asylum. A way out.' Amol's voice barely held. *I'm lying. I don't know what happens. I'm just repeating what they told me like a good little messenger boy.* 'But it's now or never, Sedo.'

On the other end, nothing but breathing. Finally, Sedo spoke – soft, bitter. 'You sold me.'

In his mind, the offer – 'walk into the British embassy' – sounded like surrender. After all, the British worked with the Americans, the same people who funded the Turkish military. In his mind, he heard himself say, 'No one wants an old ghost like me talking.'

But what were his options? He was desperate and the power balance had shifted. What else could he do? Get protection from publicity? Throw himself at the mercy of Amnesty International? What good would that do? He wanted to scream out to the reporter with whom he'd sat in Naxos for four days.

'I asked you to help me, not deliver me. You went to your people. I should've known.'

From London, Amol did his best to reassure. 'No. I didn't sell you. Of course not. I'm telling you, this is the only door left open.'

A beat. Then, in a voice Amol barely recognized: 'All right.'

The line went dead. Amol stared at the phone. Across the room, Sean gave a small nod. His face unreadable, expressionless, even cold.

The story wasn't Amol's anymore. Not really. And Sean? He hadn't even smiled. No congratulations, no backslap. Just that nod – the kind you give when a dog finally sits. Whatever warmth had existed between them had been filed away, labelled and passed up the chain.

3

The Thames Gambit

A week passed in uneasy silence.

The story had been about Sedo Hazan, Kurdish bomb-maker, once the PKK's most trusted ghost. A man who'd wired explosives for a cause he no longer believed in.

By the time Amol found him, Sedo was done – tired, hollowed out, carrying the weight of every life his devices had claimed. He didn't ask for forgiveness. What he wanted was a way out. A deal – names, operations, the bomb-making secrets that haunted Europe's cities – in exchange for exile and a pension somewhere no one would find him.

That was the story Amol wrote – a man, too late, trying to change his life. It ran three columns on page five. The editor teased it on the front. Amol thought, briefly, it might spark something. But then … silence.

No angry phone calls. No denials. No visits from Kurdish heavies. Just the newsroom hum, London rolling on like none of it mattered.

It felt wrong. A story like that should have made waves. Instead, it folded neatly into yesterday's news. Sean didn't call. No surprise visits. Just absence, louder than a shout.

Until today.

Amol was killing time in a Fleet Street café when the wall-mounted payphone rang, sharp, urgent. He hadn't heard one ring in years. That alone made it feel like a threat.

The waitress barely looked up. 'That'll be for you, love. No one else here.'

He stared, throat dry, then answered.

'Amol?' Sean's voice, smooth, almost playful. 'Time to stretch your legs.'

'Where?'

'South Bank. Noon Dress warm.'

'Who's meeting me?'

'Peter Mone. Says he's a spook. Don't ask questions on the line.'

'Why now?'

'Because you're wondering why no one's come calling about your story,' Sean said. 'The people who care about Sedo Hazan don't write letters to the editor.'

'You're setting me up.'

'I'm giving you the real story. You earned it.' Click.

By the river, the air tasted of damp stone and coal smoke. The South Bank was deserted, cold, grey, indifferent. Sean was already there, leaning on the embankment, scarf loose. He saw Amol, gave a thin smile.

'Didn't sleep, did you?'

'What is this?' Amol muttered.

'Closure. Or the start of something worse.'

Sean jerked his chin. 'Come on. They don't like to wait.'

A hundred yards down, a man waited. He was short, bald, fat. Skin like milk. He cradled a battered paperback of *The Secret Agent*. Behind him loomed a minder; massive, immovable. He said nothing, did nothing, just stood protectively behind Mone like a giant tree or a block of ice.

Amol slowed. He recognized this kind of staging – the literary flourish, the brute in the wings. It was theatre, but not the kind with applause. Just cues, silence and things already decided.

'Peter Mone,' Sean said quietly. 'Let me do the talking.' Mone turned as they approached, sharp eyes taking Amol in.

'This the writer?'

Sean nodded. 'Amol, meet Peter Mone.'

Mone didn't offer a hand. Just stared. 'You wrote something dangerous, Mr Batty.'

'I wrote what I was told,' Amol said carefully. 'I didn't invent him. Sedo came to me.'

Mone sniffed. 'And you believed him?'

'I wrote what I saw. And what I was told.' The phrase tasted wrong in his mouth.

'Told by whom?'

Sean cut in smoothly. 'He's one of our best reporters, Peter. Deserves a bloody gong for that story. No one else would've landed it, no one else had the balls to sit down with a ghost like Hazan.'

Mone grunted. 'One story doesn't make him clever.'

Sean pressed. 'He didn't stumble into this. He earned it. Tight copy. Clean. Not a word wasted.' Then, glancing at Amol, he said 'You are good. Don't let the silence fool you.'

Mone nodded once, almost amused, and gestured to one of the two adjoining benches. 'Sit.'

Somehow, it was dry, the only patch spared by the mist.

Mone and Sean took the other bench. The minder stood like a shadow – solid, unblinking. Amol hovered at the edge, the cold biting through his coat.

The physical differences between the two men on the second bench were stark. Sean – slim, almost translucent with his pale skin, straw-blond hair and freckled face – caught the eye without trying. Were it not for his bitten-down fingernails, raw little crescents of anxiety, he might have passed for a fashion icon, all sharp cheekbones and tailored shirts. At thirty-eight, he still carried the careless elegance of youth. Beside him, Mone did not shrink. Pudgy, bald, sweating through his cheap Marks & Spencer suit, Mone sat like a man entirely at ease in his own bulk – indifferent, almost defiant. He dragged his weight around like it was someone else's problem.

Amol felt the flicker of something sour in his throat – not quite envy, but near enough. Sean played the part, all angles and charm, while Mone seemed to know he didn't have to. In the shadows of the game, appearances mattered, but the trick was knowing when they didn't. And Sean, Amol thought, had always known how to play the surface, even if the cracks showed underneath. Most of what followed between Mone and Sean was low, private – words lost to the river wind. But Amol caught flashes. Talk of whisky, bad pubs, dodgy weekends in distant places, Sean laughing, a sound Amol hadn't heard in weeks.

It wasn't the first time Amol had sat across from men who wanted something dressed as admiration. But back then, the stakes were theoretical, wrapped in footnotes and redbrick charm.

'I was a boy, Mone. Didn't know a Provo from a priest. They sent me to Amsterdam – said file copy, shake hands and make sure the right names reached the right ears.'

Mone chuckled. 'You did it well. Raised a glass with killers, then phoned it all home.'

Sean shrugged. 'Wasn't the worst job.'

Mone's smile faded. 'But this one is. You know why I called you.'

Sean nodded. 'Because you want him.'

Mone's eyes flicked to Amol. 'Not yet.'

The conversation drifted with names Amol didn't recognize, cities he'd only read about. Hamburg. Athens. Cold War stories no one ever printed. Sean listening, nodding, occasionally laughing.

Mone leaned back, watching the river, then almost lazily added, 'You've been useful – years now. Quiet work. Never went loud. Came from Cork stock, didn't you, Sean?'

Sean grinned. 'County Cork. My grandfather raised cattle. I raised hell.'

Mone gave a loud snort. 'You had it sweet in Amsterdam,' he said. 'A little shop for the missus near the Prinsengracht – tea towels and Delft tat, wasn't it? And that boat of yours, moored like a painting on the Amstel. You, with your Genever and binoculars, watching the world go by. Libyan shipments slipping through Rotterdam, Czechoslovak rifles wrapped in tarps. All while stringing for that Dublin paper, and the *Herald Tribune*, wasn't it? Plus, those TV documentaries you did – the well-paid ones. Nice little earners.'

Sean gave a dry laugh. 'If only they knew.'

Mone lowered his voice, just a notch. 'You were perfect. Boring enough to blend in. Foreign enough to vanish.'

Sean didn't rise to it. 'My wife wanted somewhere to root herself. I gave her a shop. The boat was mine. Simple pleasures.'

Mone nodded, approving. 'Always good to park money where it floats.'

He glanced up the river, then back at Amol. 'The Foreign Office suits hate us, you know. Call us cowboys with too much budget and not enough restraint. They sip claret in Pall Mall and pretend they're running the empire. But when the bombs go off, they're always the first to ask for our help.'

Amol shifted in his seat but said nothing. Maybe it was just a joke, a journalist's joke. Or maybe not. Then, finally, as if remembering him, Mone turned. 'You – Batty. You've got a foot in two worlds, don't you? English, Indian. That's rare.'

'My mother was from Delhi.'

Mone nodded. 'Always admired that richness. The language, the food. I'm not a linguist like you, don't speak Hindi, Urdu, Arabic, Persian … not a bloody word. But I love the films, the singing, the dancing. Those Bollywood plots … beautiful in their simplicity. Good, evil, love wins in the end. Whole different world, that.'

Mone smiled faintly. 'A shame it's all make-believe.'

Mone's gaze held him a beat longer. 'If they'd spotted you at Oxford, they'd have snapped you up. Sent you to MECAS – Middle East Centre for Arab Studies – out in Lebanon. Boost your Arabic.'

Amol shook his head. 'I'm fluent. Arabic, Farsi, Hindi, Urdu too, though they don't teach those at MECAS.'

Mone's smile twitched. 'Pity. Would've made you useful. Maybe you still are.'

The wind bit harder. Somewhere upriver, a barge sounded, low and mournful. Mone stood, tucking *The Secret Agent* under his arm. 'We follow your copy, Batty. Clean stuff. You know where to stop, that's rare.'

Sean stayed sitting, watching him go. The minder followed, silent as death. Amol turned to him and said, 'What does he want?'

Sean's smile was thin. 'He wants to know if you're useful. The next time he calls, it won't be to talk about Bollywood.' Then, almost lightly, he added, 'You handed them the Purple Swan,' Sean added, almost lightly. 'That doesn't just buy goodwill. It buys leverage. And memory. Trust me, they won't forget you.'

'I'm not working for him.'

Sean shrugged. 'That's what you think. But you stirred the river, Amol. Now you wait … see what floats to the surface.'

He stood, pulled his coat tight and walked off, boots echoing on the wet stone.

Amol stayed a moment longer, staring at the grey water – endless, uncaring. But even as he watched, something gnawed at him; not fear, exactly, but distaste. There was something crude about the whole encounter.

The way Sean and Mone spoke – all implication, dangling carrots, testing his worth like a transaction. It wasn't what he'd been trained for. Foreign correspondents dealt with all sorts – warlords, diplomats, criminals – but always with distance, that careful detachment drilled into him: Keep the line clear. Stay above it. Never let your judgement warp.

This … this was different. Sean and Mone – backroom boys from provincial universities and perhaps even more provincial polytechnics – didn't understand the difference, never moved in circles where ideas mattered more than outcomes. They rose through back doors and service lifts, learning power not as tradition but as transaction.

They didn't read Tacitus or Clausewitz. They read people. They promised favours, called in debts, moved pawns and took credit.

In a different world, a later one, they might have been early godfathers of Trump, instinctive salesmen of half-truths, allergic to complexity, always more comfortable with the con than the confession.

What they were dangling was a crude, transactional give and take of intelligence gathering – far removed from an elegant, high-stakes world of carefully cultivated relationships. This was the murky underbelly of deals struck in grey, rain-slicked corners. A far cry from the world Amol had known at Oxford.

His mind flashed back to Merton College. Dinner in hall, candles flickering, silver gleaming. That night, his first formal invite, he sat next to his old tutor, Sir Michael Howard, the great military historian.

Ever gracious, Howard was his usual wry self, the embodiment of an older, subtler England. 'Matters not if you win or lose,' Howard had told him, quoting the old cliché, 'but how you play the game.'

Words that lodged deep.

Further down the same high table sat Professor Tolkien – old now, frail but sharp-eyed, with that half-smile of a man who'd dreamt whole worlds into being. He'd beckoned Amol down the table after the second course, curious about the Indian boy with the Oxford vowels.

They spoke not of hobbits or elves, but of language, myth and war. 'The real battlefield,' Tolkien said softly, 'is always the soul. Men write their wars in blood and fire, but the truest wars are quieter, fought in the choices we make, the things we cling to when the world turns dark.'

He sipped his claret and regarded Amol with that bright, piercing gaze. 'You know that already, I think. Men like us, born between worlds, we carry stories whether we choose to or not.

Be careful which ones you tell … and which ones you let others write for you.'

That line stayed with him, even now. Was he still the teller of stories, or had he become someone else's footnote?

Merton had always attracted a particular kind of student. Not just for the tutors or the library or the cloisters – but because, unlike most other colleges, it served free wine at dinner for undergraduates. The low murmur of voices, the clink of glasses and the flicker of candlelight lent the hall a warm glow, masking the weight of expectations hanging in the air. A small indulgence, perhaps, but a telling one. It hinted at old money, quiet confidence and the belief that young minds deserved civilized vices.

Benazir Bhutto was there too, luminous as ever, wrapped in silks the colour of dusk, her laughter ringing clear through the candlelit hall. Amol remembered the way the soft light caught her eyes, how her presence seemed to fill the room despite her quiet poise.

They'd bonded early, drawn together by dual identities and a shared instinct for political theatre. She drank chilled white wine, always poured through the spout of a lovely porcelain teapot, a small act of rebellion disguised as decorum.

It was her way of shielding a private pleasure behind the appearance of piety, protecting her reputation as a Muslim woman respectful of Islamic law. 'Appearances,' she once whispered, eyes glinting, 'are the last defence.' Amol felt a quiet chill, realizing how much lay beneath those words – the careful balancing act between truth and survival, identity and expectation. From that night, they were lifelong friends.

Howard and Tolkien, they represented a world where academics held their integrity like a shield, fiercely independent from the machinations of the government. Their minds were tools for understanding the complexities of history, war and culture – tools used not for political gain, but for education and the deepening of knowledge. They were above it all, immune to the subtle pressures of the Foreign Office or the whispering corridors of Whitehall.

But Oxford had its other kind of professor. The kind who, with one foot in the lecture halls and the other in the shadowy world of intelligence, earned stipends not from teaching but from quietly feeding talent into the hands of the spooks. These were the men who recruited students like hungry fishers casting their nets in the eager waters of academia. The ones who had either failed or never quite made it in the more refined corridors of the Foreign Office, but found a welcome in the world of MI6 or the Home Office. Among the students, they were known by a cruelly affectionate nickname:

FIFOTS. Failed in the Foreign Office, Try the Spooks.

Amol had always regarded them with a kind of cold amusement – these men who could never quite match the elegance of the truly great professors like Howard and Tolkien, who had walked the world of ideas and philosophy with their heads held high.

The FIFOTS were different – more pragmatic, willing to bend or break in the service of power. They taught their students not about the beauty of the world or the complexity of human understanding, but about how to manoeuvre in the shadows, how to play the game.

When Amol had started at Oxford, he had been drawn to the likes of Howard, Tolkien and others who saw the world as a place to be understood, not manipulated. They weren't like the FIFOTS – those had a certain crudeness about them, a transactional edge that seemed almost too easy. No, Howard and Tolkien didn't need a stipend to be influential – they were simply enough in themselves. But over time, he had grown to notice the quiet whispers, the way some of the older fellows had their ties with men in dark suits and the occasional call to serve 'national interests'.

Mone and Sean, hinting at another universe, were closer to the domain of the FIFOTS. They didn't see the world as a place of stories to be told, but as a playground where the rules were made by those who controlled the flow of information.

Amol had always seen Oxford as an ivory tower – idealistic and removed from these gritty realities – but now, even the ivory tower felt like a dream. He drifted through the city, lost in the late afternoon haze, until Islington rose up around him, red-bricked, familiar. His flat waited – small, tidy, silent. The sort of place no one waited up.

Later, he changed his jacket, shirt and walked to Frederick's on Camden Passage. Treated himself. A quiet table. A glass of red. The food was good, rich, comforting, but he barely tasted it. All he could see was Mone's pale face, the giant minder looming like ice, Sean's easy grin covering something harder underneath. It wasn't a threat. Not yet. But it wasn't friendship either.

Amol sipped his wine, staring at his reflection in the restaurant's window – a man caught somewhere in between. Outside, couples laughed. Waiters poured drinks. London carried on.

The story wasn't over. But whose version it became, that was no longer his to decide.

4

The Soft Kill

Amol had Mondays off. A small mercy in a job that otherwise owned his time. He never used to dread them. Mondays were for sleeping late, maybe a walk through Highbury Fields or sitting by the window of a café on Upper Street with the paper, pretending there was a life outside deadlines.

It had been a month since Naxos. The story had gone quiet, but Mone hadn't. So, when Mone – if that was even his real name – rang again suggesting another lunch, Amol hesitated.

'I don't know,' he muttered to Sean later. 'What does he actually want?'

Sean barely looked up from his desk. 'He might have some useful tips,' he said. 'You might get a few new ideas. And anyway, you won't be paying.'

'He just wants to say thank you,' Sean added, eyes back on his copy. 'You gave him the bomb-maker.'

Amol said nothing. He hated that phrase. Like Sedo was a wrapped gift, delivered, opened.

Then, more softly, Sean said, 'You've impressed Peter, you know. He really likes you. Says you're different from the rest of the crowd. Most of them would sell their souls and their mothers for a byline. But you? You're solid, you do your research. Makes you dangerous, if you ask me.'

And just like that, it started.

Always the same side of the Thames – South bank, downstream of Westminster – never too close to Vauxhall Cross, but always within sight of that angular glass fortress.

'You ever think about the view from up there?' Mone asked once, nodding towards the building's jagged silhouette. 'See the world from that angle long enough, it starts looking smaller.'

Amol grunted. He didn't like being reminded how close he was sitting to the flame. They ate their way through a rota of riverside pubs. The Morpeth Arms with its soot-dark Victorian brickwork and that upstairs Spy Room, once used to watch the Russians from across the river. Doggett's Coat and Badge by Blackfriars Bridge, all polished brass and worn pub carpet. The Anchor Bankside, where Shakespeare's Globe gleamed over the river and tourists nursed pints they didn't really want.

It was always the same script – weather, football, soft insinuations. But beneath it all lay Sedo's sketches, now digitized, decrypted, passed hand to hand through the corridors of Vauxhall. Mone never said his name. He didn't need to.

Some weeks they ended up near the Tate Modern, the power station hulking behind them, or close to Gabriel's Wharf where the street artists sketched caricatures of bored children.

The places were always Mone's choice. Once, and only once for no apparent reason, they met in a café close to the British Museum in Bloomsbury.

The minder came too – big, heavy, unspeaking. He'd sit a table away, nursing a lime and soda, eyes fixed somewhere in the middle distance. Close enough to hear. Far enough to be ignored.

Mone played the long game. Never pushed, never sold it too hard. Some days, he spent half the lunch moaning about London traffic, the price of pints or the misery of his daily commute from some anonymous suburb. 'Trains are knackered,' he muttered once over bangers and mash. 'Takes me bloody forever to get in. But they don't like us living in town. Too easy to get comfortable, start feeling like civilians.'

Amol listened, mostly. Occasionally he'd push back. 'Why are you so interested in me? There's no shortage of hacks sniffing around looking for a leg up.'

Mone shrugged, wiping gravy off his chin. 'Plenty of them, sure. But most of 'em? Cowards. Or too dumb to know the difference. You've handed us more than most officers do in five years. That Kurd – he's like a bloody Rosetta Stone. Everyone wants a look. You've been abroad, you know how it works. You've looked the worst of it in the eye and kept your pen moving. That counts.'

Amol flinched. They'd turned Sedo into a briefing slide. He wondered if Zerin and the boy were safe. If the embassy offer had held. If anyone kept their word.

The routine lasted three months. Mondays, always Mondays. Amol came to dread the call, usually mid-morning when he was still deciding whether to brave the damp Islington streets or crawl back under the covers.

'Alright, Amol. Thought we'd try the Anchor today. Decent fish pie. Be there at one?'

Mone was always cheerful. Pubs always grim. Weather, invariably grey.

Sean joined once or twice, grinning his way through a pint. 'Honestly, mate, Peter thinks you're the real deal. Not like half the tossers on this floor writing second-hand analysis off the wires.'

Amol felt it, bone-deep. This wasn't friendly. This was a siege.

Over time, Mone peeled back parts of his life like it was nothing. Born in Hull, local polytechnic. Flogged brushes door-to-door straight out of school.

'Good training, actually,' he mused over a pie and mash at The Windmill in Lambeth. 'Teaches you to read a face fast. The ones that take you at face value. There's that moment, right? Then the others who're about to slam the door. You learn to spot the soft ones. Work the angle.'

The police came later. Beat copper, CID, Special Branch. 'I got lucky, ended up on the right desks,' he'd say. 'Saw the right cases. Belfast mostly. London too, when it mattered.'

He never named the mentor who steered him towards the Service. He made that leap sound accidental. Amol didn't believe him.

Some weeks they talked about nothing. Tube strikes. Football.

Mone was a Hull City fan – called them 'the Bloody Tigers' – grumbling about relegation over a pint of bitter at The Doggett's. 'Sheffield, Wednesday next week. Away. We'll lose, mark my words. Only a bloody fool stays loyal to Hull City.'

Another Monday, they were at The Ship, near Southwark. A Thames barge chugged past the window, fat gulls riding the wake. Mone let Amol talk too, asking about his years abroad – Cairo, Beirut, Jerusalem.

'Always wanted to see Cairo,' Mone mused. 'Bet it's all noise and diesel and the smell of hot bread.'

Amol shrugged.

'Tell me about Beirut,' he said one grey afternoon at The Ship near Southwark. 'That was in the eighties, wasn't it? When the Israelis first went in. Must've been chaos.'

'It was,' Amol admitted. 'That war stank of diesel and blood. You felt like you were breathing history, except none of it would last.'

Mone nodded, pleased. 'See, that's the difference. Half the kids in this office? Never left Zone 2. You … you've smelled the real thing.'

'I miss it sometimes,' Amol said, surprising even himself. 'You feel alive out there. Here … its all layers of noise pretending to be news.'

Mone nodded like he understood. 'Layers is right. London's nothing but layers of secrets built on top of each other. You know where to peel, you find the good bits.'

Weeks blurred. Mone, steady, methodical, applying the same quiet pressure every time. For nearly three months their Monday ritual had continued, a slow dance of questions and flattery.

One Monday, upstairs at The Rose, Mone surprised Amol.

'Got a daughter,' he said, staring out at the river. 'City University. Law student. Reckons she's gonna change the world.'

Amol blinked. 'Does she know what you do?'

Mone gave a dry laugh. 'Thinks I'm a bastard. Probably right. She says the Service's just a bunch of old men protecting the status quo.' He shrugged. 'Maybe it is. Doesn't stop me wanting her to finish that bloody degree.'

'What about her mum?'

'Gone. Years now. Couldn't live with the half-truths. Or maybe just couldn't live with me.' He drained his pint. 'This job … it hollows you out, if you let it. Family keeps you honest, even when they hate you for it.'

For a moment, Amol felt something close to sympathy. But it passed.

Then, one day, the mask slipped.

It was a wet September Monday. That low, heavy sky London does best – like the clouds might just fall and crush the city. They met at the Morpeth again, upstairs, near the cold fireplace. Mone picked at his shepherd's pie, then wiped his mouth, leaned in and said it almost casually: 'I should tell you my real name.'

Amol stiffened.

'It's Peter Dexter. I run a department called Operational Intelligence. My job's simple – cultivate useful people. People like you.'

Amol's heart skipped. A cold knot tightened in his stomach, the casual weight of Dexter's words suddenly heavy and sharp. The friendly mask dropped, revealing something far more real and far more dangerous. He swallowed hard, tasting dust. Not a threat. Not a pitch. Just fact. For weeks, Peter Mone had seemed a jovial, pudgy spook with a minder and a taste for pub pies. Now the mask was gone. Peter Dexter – the man underneath.

'I've got two nationals on the list,' Dexter continued. 'And that famous magazine everyone claims they don't read but secretly do. You're not the only one I talk to. But you?

You've got the head for this.'

He let the words settle, heavy as fog.

'Look,' he added, softer. 'I'm not recruiting you. Yet. Recruitments are for people who need a handler. This? This is cultivation. You'd know if you were being run. You're not – yet.'

Not yet. But the leash was already visible – not on his neck, but coiled neatly on the table, waiting.

Amol remembered reading somewhere that Secret Intelligence Service (SIS) officers were quietly retired at fifty-five. Watching Dexter now, all control and charm, but with an urgency just beneath the surface, he wondered if the clock was already ticking. Maybe that's why the courtesies were dropping. Maybe this was what men did when they saw the door closing and still had ghosts to tidy up.

Amol exhaled, staring at the dark window, the river outside swallowing the light. 'And if I say no?' he asked.

Dexter smiled thinly. 'You won't. You're too smart for that. Of course you'll manage, regardless. But maybe someone else will take your chair, happens all the time. So, you know how this ends. If you stay close, you stay warm. Or you freeze on the outside, watching the bylines you should've owned go to some chancer who said yes.'

Amol said nothing. But he felt the chill already – not from the river, but from the space between refusal and consequence. He looked down at his plate. Cold chips. A smear of gravy.

'I can help you,' Dexter said gently. 'You want a fellowship? Another foreign posting? Access? I know people. I know where the bodies are buried. All I ask,' he smiled, 'is you stay in touch. Thing is, we don't have to be enemies. You give me the lay of the land, what the hacks are chasing, what's bubbling under. And maybe … when something comes along, I make sure it's you holding the pen.'

He let it hang there. No contract. No promises. Just a suggestion thick with meaning.

'I'm not here to own you,' Dexter finished. 'That's not how it works. This is … alignment. You stay close, we both eat.'

Dexter leaned back, eyes narrowing towards the window and the river beyond, like he could see Vauxhall from there. 'You know, it's not all secrets and champagne behind those bloody windows,' he muttered. 'They cram us in – open plan, same as any insurance office. Cheap strip lights. Half the computers don't work. Place smells of bad coffee and boiled cabbage by three o'clock.'

Amol said nothing. He was thinking of Belfast. Orange Day. He'd been sent to cover the marches – just another assignment, boots on the ground, careful phrasing about sectarian tension. But something shifted in the crowd. A bottle shattered near his feet. Then came the chant, 'Grab the coon!'

He ran – camera swinging, press ID useless – chased down a narrow road by boys drunk on loyalty and lager. He ducked into the back of a Chinese takeaway, chest heaving. The cook looked up from his wok and didn't blink.

'I thought you were one of them,' the man said, handing him a towel like it was just another Tuesday.

Amol had never forgotten that line. Or the fear. Or the realization that in some corners of the kingdom, he was still foreign. Still the other. Dexter could keep his coffee and cabbage. Amol had already passed his own test. He gave a dry smile. 'Doesn't sound very Bond.'

'Christ, Bond'd last five minutes. We've got budget meetings that'd kill a horse. Bloody hell. Had one last month – whole lot of us shuffling out like pensioners on a day trip. Standing on the pavement trying not to look at the cameras.' He scratched his chin. 'Not that the building's easy to hit. Though some poor sod tried once.'

Amol glanced over. 'Tried what?'

'Rocket-propelled grenade,' Dexter said, almost lazily. 'Nineties. Palestinian – one of the factions, doesn't matter which. Pulled up on the bridge, broad daylight, had the launcher out the boot. Thought he was gonna make the evening news by hitting our newly opened HQ.'

'What happened?'

Dexter shrugged. 'Launcher jammed. Cheap Soviet knock-off. By the time he figured it out, the firearms lads were on him. He was arrested on the spot – barely got a chance to run. I watched them pull him out of the car, still clutching the bloody launcher like it might grow legs and run.

'We kept it fairly quiet at the time – hardly made the papers – but among our lot it became one of those whacko legends about how close it could've come. The reality is, the building could've shrugged it off anyway. Whole place is built like a bloody bunker. Cost a fortune.'

Amol gave a low whistle.

Dexter grinned. 'See? Even the terrorists can't get it right these days. But it sticks with you … makes you think about what's real. What's worth betting your life on.'

Amol didn't answer. Not then.

Meanwhile, word came from Athens. Sedo had done it. Walked into the embassy like a man returning a library book. Calm, cool. No fanfare.

Or at least, that's how the report came back. Amol had learnt by now: when spooks said 'no trouble', they meant no witnesses. Just a man walking through the gates of the British embassy in Athens asking to speak to the right people.

'Grinning over a pint at The King's Head in Islington, Sean told Amol later, 'They're debriefing Hazan now. We're in mate. This is the big one.'

But 'we' meant nothing anymore. And 'in' didn't feel like a place Amol wanted to be.

That night, back in his Islington flat, Amol stared out at the wet rooftops and wondered when noise had started sounding like momentum. And whether Dexter was right. Maybe you were either inside or you were nothing at all. Unless you were Sedo – trapped between sides, still carrying the fuse.

5

Krug and Consequences

He should've seen it coming. Of course he had. After weeks of polite conditioning – pints by the river, the charm of Mone, the deadpan confessions of Dexter – there was only one step left. So, when the envelope landed at the reception – stiff, cream-coloured, written in a hand so careful it could've been forged by a monk – Amol didn't flinch.

The Ritz. 1.00 p.m. A friendly lunch.

They never push at first. Just pub lunches, pub talk, the illusion of choice. But this – this was the moment you couldn't ignore. The setting said it all.

Dexter was careful, measured. Even the wording – a friendly lunch – felt calibrated. As if to reassure him. As if to make it clear that nothing binding would happen today, at least not on paper.

Amol had known this moment was coming. The past few weeks had been a slow, careful dance. Peter Mone, or Dexter as he finally called himself, had softened him up with weekly coffees and casual charm, conversations that weren't casual at all. The affability had been theatre. This was always the destination.

—

The doorman at The Ritz barely acknowledged him, a subtle nod of the head, the kind reserved for those who belonged. Or at least those who looked like they might.

He wondered if someone like Sedo would recognize this place. The chandeliers, the Krug, the silence so expensive it didn't need guards. Would they ever bring him here – the man with the calloused hands and blood under his fingernails – or was Amol his stand-in?

Inside, the hush of old money wrapped itself around Amol like an expensive overcoat. The hotel smelled of polished wood, aged leather and the ghost of cigars smoked in better decades. It was a place where the weight of history was measured not in years but in quiet decisions, whispered deals and betrayals masked as polite conversation.

The dining room was a study in controlled opulence. Gold chandeliers, high ceilings, the murmur of voices in multiple languages. A pianist in the corner played something light, unintrusive – the kind of music that filled the gaps between espionage and excess. Amol glanced at the other tables, at the well-dressed men, some alone, some in quiet pairs, speaking in low tones. He wondered how many were like him – journalists, spies or men caught in the grey space in between.

A waiter in a perfectly pressed uniform approached, bowing slightly. 'Sir?'

'Peter Dexter,' Amol said.

A flicker of recognition crossed the man's face, quickly hidden. He gestured smoothly. 'This way.'

Dexter was already seated. He hadn't ordered yet, but there was a bottle of chilled champagne resting in a silver bucket at his side. It was Krug. The best. The kind of bottle you didn't open alone.

The Ritz had its own gravity, thick carpets swallowing footsteps, liveried waiters who moved like stagehands, white gloves cradling silver trays with devotional care. Even the Krug arrived with ceremony: the pop muted, the pour slow, like mass being served. The cutlery gleamed with the weight of centuries. Conversations didn't echo, they hung, suspended, like secrets in a vault. This wasn't just lunch. It was theatre. The kind where no one claps and everyone leaves changed.

Dexter looked up as Amol approached, offering a wide, easy smile. The kind of smile that could be mistaken for warmth. The kind of smile that had probably convinced men to say yes to things they didn't fully understand. 'Ah, Amol,' he said, rising slightly in his seat, offering his hand. 'Right on time.'

His grip was firm but unhurried, the handshake of a man who never needed to rush.

Amol sat, glancing at the champagne. 'Celebrating something?' he asked.

Dexter chuckled. 'Oh, we always celebrate at The Ritz.'

The waiter reappeared, pouring two glasses without asking. Dexter raised his. 'To old friends and new beginnings,' he said.

Amol raised his glass, but in his mind he saw the plastic café in Naxos. Lukewarm water. Sketches curling in the heat. 'To betrayal,' he almost said – but drank instead.

Dexter wasn't the kind of man who wrote things down unless he wanted them to be seen. 'You sold me,' Sedo had said. The words returned now, uninvited. Even here, in the hush of The Ritz, where everything shimmered with politeness, they landed like grit in the champagne.

The bubbles rose and burst, delicate, ephemeral. The champagne was cold, crisp, absurdly smooth. A long way from the raki he'd drunk in smoky bars in the Middle East, trading stories with rebels and smugglers.

Dexter set his glass down and leaned back slightly, regarding Amol with quiet amusement. 'You seem nervous,' he said.

'Should I be?'

Dexter gave a small smile. 'They've been poring over those drawings ever since you got back. Passed around like sacred text – analysts, foreign desks, even the Yanks.'

Amol stared at the bubbles rising in his glass.

'You've seen worse,' Dexter murmured. 'But somehow this feels like enemy ground, doesn't it?'

Amol didn't answer. It wasn't a question that required one.

There was a rhythm to these kinds of meetings, an unspoken structure. Dexter wasn't going to start with business. He was going to ease into it, let Amol relax, give him just enough rope.

So, Amol played along. They spoke lightly at first – about Beirut, about old correspondents they both knew, about stories that never made the front page but should have. Dexter had a way of making it feel like two colleagues catching up, like there was no agenda behind it. But there was always an agenda.

Amol caught Dexter watching him carefully, reading every micro expression, every hesitation. Sizing him up, even now. And then, as the first course arrived – an absurdly delicate plate of scallops arranged like something out of a museum – Dexter leaned in slightly. 'Not many get this lunch, you know,' he said.

Amol kept his expression neutral. 'I assumed as much.'

Dexter smiled. 'You're either in or you're out, Amol. But by now, I suspect you know that.'

Amol held his gaze. The words weren't a threat, not exactly.

But they weren't an invitation either. They were a statement of fact.

He took another sip of champagne, feeling the weight of the moment settle over him. This wasn't just a lunch. It was a marking.

A point in time he would look back on, years from now, and recognize as the moment when something shifted. The moment when the door was left open, just a crack. And the question, unspoken but undeniable, hung between them.

Would he walk through it? The scallops disappeared with minimal conversation – just polite murmurs about the quality of the seafood, the right balance of citrus in the sauce. Dexter wasn't rushing. He let the silence stretch just long enough to remind Amol who controlled the tempo.

Then he leaned back, wiped his mouth delicately and sighed as though shifting into another register. 'You know,' he began, swirling what remained of his champagne, 'I was thinking last night how funny it is … how life moves you towards certain moments without you ever really knowing.'

Amol said nothing. He knew better than to fill silences like that.

Dexter smiled faintly. 'And then you wake up one morning and realize – ah, here it is. The moment. The conversation that changes the shape of things.' He gestured around the room. 'Hence this … this little production. The Ritz. The Krug. All the trappings. I'd say it's well-deserved.'

Amol forced a smile. 'And what exactly have I done to deserve all this?'

'Oh, more than you realize,' Dexter said, his voice soft but certain. 'You've been on our radar for a long time, Amol. Longer than you'd like to think.'

That made Amol blink. How long? He kept his face still, but a tiny part of him flinched at the implication.

'We've watched you,' Dexter continued. 'Like Jesus, we've always been with you.' He grinned at his own blasphemy and caught the flicker of amusement cross Amol's face. 'Not in the religious sense, of course. Though I imagine, at times, it must've felt like providence – how certain doors opened for you, certain conversations went your way, people vouched for you when it mattered.' He leaned in – 'That wasn't luck.'

Amol exhaled slowly, half a laugh. 'So what was it, then? Recruitment?'

'Not quite. Call it … assessment.' Dexter shrugged. 'You're a journalist. You understand – sometimes a source needs to be seasoned before he's useful. Sometimes a man has to be tested, not just once but across the years. Different fires, different storms.'

A waiter appeared, whisking away their plates and placing menus in front of them again. Dexter waved him off. 'Chef's tasting menu, please. And keep the Krug coming.' The man bowed, vanished.

And now, Dexter's eyes locked on Amol. 'Would you like to hear about your tests?'

Amol swallowed. 'Tests?' He hadn't realized he had been taking any. His throat tightened unexpectedly, fingers curling briefly around the edge of the table.

Dexter nodded slowly. 'Six of them. We don't always plan them … life presents the opportunities. But we pay attention. We watch how a man behaves when it matters. Whether he's the sort we can bring inside. Because, let me be blunt, Amol – outsiders don't get this lunch. People like you don't sit here. You're either born into it or you survive long enough in the wild for someone like me to drag you inside.'

Amol's pulse quickened. This was it. The offer. Or something like it.

'The first test,' Dexter began, 'was loyalty. Loyalty to something larger than yourself. We could've picked it up in a hundred ways, but you made it easy. Embassy parties, consular dinners … you showed up. You listened. You paid attention. Never fully drunk, never making a fool of yourself.

And when it counted, you chose your side.'

Dexter continued. 'Second test – risk. Can you function under pressure, where it matters?' He smiled coldly. 'That wasn't hard to observe. You kept going back, didn't you? Jaffna, West Beirut. Even Karachi in '88.'

Amol flinched involuntarily at the memory – dull, dusty streets, the smell of burning rubber, gunfire somewhere too close.

'Plenty of men file dispatches from the bar,' Dexter said. 'But you … you got out of the car. You crossed the street.'

'I didn't see it as a test,' Amol murmured.

'Exactly,' Dexter replied. 'That's what made it matter. Instinct. Either you have it or you don't.'

He topped up Amol's glass, his own still half-full. 'Third test,' he said. 'Courage – but of a different kind. Intellectual courage. The willingness to ask the questions that burn bridges. Johannesburg, wasn't it?'

Amol winced. 'Botha.'

Dexter laughed. 'Yes. You called him a racist. To his face. Told him President Kaunda said so. God, the look on his face.'

'I was younger.'

'You were correct,' Dexter said, shaking his head. 'And you understood the deeper point. Journalism's not just stenography. It's confrontation. You passed.'

They sat in silence as the main course arrived – veal, delicately plated, the kind of dish that belonged to a different century.

Dexter took a bite, chewed, swallowed. 'Fourth test – congeniality. Strange one, that. But in our line of work, the likable man survives. The man who gets invited back. The man who knows when to smile and when to shut up.'

'Tennis,' Dexter added. 'We liked that. You didn't know it, but we watched you. You don't smash the ball. You don't humiliate the weaker player. You play the game the way it should be played – easy, social, always leaving the opponent intact.'

Amol blinked. 'You watched me play tennis?'

'Of course we did,' Dexter said. 'The David Lloyd clubs here in London, the Gezira in Cairo, Jerusalem's Ramada. It's the little things, Amol. Anyone can be brave with a tape recorder. But character … character is revealed when no one's watching.'

The fifth test was unexpected and took Amol completely by surprise. Dexter almost blurted it out. 'You have compassion, even for someone so hardened by his life experiences. We know the full story of how you cradled the head of your dying colleague in Sudan. How you wept without stopping, how you lied to his parents about the manner of his death – all of it to spare them more agony about the way their son departed.'

The last test came with a different tone – softer, even more respectful. 'And finally … technical competence. The world's complicated now. We don't need poets. We need men who understand nuclear weapons, satellite grids, chemical agents. Men who don't flinch at the math.'

Dexter smiled. 'Your doctoral research. Third World proliferation. We read it.'

Amol's throat went dry. 'You read my DPhil thesis?'

'Twice,' Dexter said. 'And footnoted it, too. You're the rare kind, Amol. A field man who can also read a reactor diagram.'

Dexter leaned in slightly, the rim of his glass resting against his lip. 'It's a pity you're Hindu. And uncircumcised. If not, you'd be the perfect cover for a Muslim operative – SIS – trained, fluent, invisible. You could've walked into Tehran or Riyadh, maybe even rising to become a deputy minister one day.' He set the glass down with a soft clink. 'That's the sort of thing we dream about. Assets who already belong.'

The weight of the moment settled between them. Dexter pushed his plate aside, resting his elbows on the table. 'You passed years ago. We've just been waiting for you to realize it.'

Amol looked at him – *really* looked. The puffed cheeks, the satisfied grin, the practiced lines. It struck him then – not for the first time, but sharper now – that Peter Dexter wasn't a handler, wasn't a civil servant, wasn't even a spymaster. He was a predator.

'You know what you remind me of?' Amol said softly. 'A boarding school prefect. The kind who used to wallop the younger boys and call it character-building.'

Dexter didn't flinch. He even chuckled, slow and low. 'Well, your school prefect walloped your backside and didn't pay you a penny. We're offering to wallop you – and pay handsomely for the privilege.'

The bubbles in the Krug suddenly felt bitter.

'That's your sell?' Amol said, voice low. 'Pain, dressed up as patronage?'

Dexter didn't blink. 'Call it what you like. But if you walk away, don't pretend you weren't offered something better than most. You're inside the circle now – if you want to be.'

Amol studied him, then leaned back. 'Tell me something,' he said. 'I know I asked before, but its worth repeating. Why me? Why not someone from inside? A soldier. A diplomat. One of your own.'

Dexter exhaled through his nose like a man amused. 'Because even the good ones screw up. Remember what happened with that Libyan fiasco? Blair's people thought they could manage Gaddafi – ended up handing over his enemies. The bastards survived. Sued. Won. Ugly business.'

He topped up Amol's glass, uninvited. 'That's what happens when you trust your own. They're overconfident. You … you're careful. Careful's useful.'

He swirled his champagne and added, almost as an afterthought, 'Mind you, we do look after our own. Even after the worst happens. You remember The Iranian-born reporter hanged by Saddam's regime?'

Amol nodded.

'He wasn't one of ours,' Dexter continued, 'but he was close. Too close. The Foreign Office moved heaven and earth. British passports for his parents – new names, new lives. Took three months.' He chuckled. 'They called them Mr and Mrs Dennis Thatcher. No one batted an eyelid at Heathrow.'

Amol stared at him. The gall of it. The grim efficiency. The grotesque wit.

He remembered the rumours – a reporter caught at the airport with a soil sample taken from a burnt-out weapons site. They were testing for boron, to see if Saddam's people had used it to contain a radioactive leak. No regular hack carried that kind of sample unless someone gave him instructions. It hit him, sudden and sour: that was the game. Soil in one bag, sketches in another. Different wars. Same fate.

'That's what it means to be inside,' Dexter said, gently.

'Even when we lose someone, we protect the people they love. It's not just champagne and parties. It's insurance.' His voice dropped. 'Few men get this conversation. Fewer still get the pension, the protection, the … future we offer. We've been following you closely because you're one of us. You just didn't know it yet.'

Amol stared at him. 'And if I've already made up my mind?'

Dexter smiled, unfazed. 'Then you'll finish your meal, enjoy the Krug and we'll never speak of it again. But you won't say no, Amol. Because you're tired. Tired of being on the outside, guessing. We're offering you certainty. A place at the table.' He gestured around. '*This* table.'

And just like that, the hook was set.

The waiter returned, refilling their glasses with a practiced pour, the gold of the Krug catching the light. The dining room had filled around them – power lunches, quiet murmurs, the scrape of silver on porcelain – but in Amol's mind, they were suspended in their own orbit now.

Dexter sat back, watching him with that slight, almost fatherly smile. He toyed with the stem of his glass, swirling the champagne as if waiting for the precise moment to speak again.

'You know why I brought you here, Amol?' Dexter asked softly.

Amol gave a dry chuckle, trying to ease the coil of tension in his chest. 'The scallops? The veal? The Krug?'

Dexter smirked. 'All part of it. But no.'

He let the pause stretch. 'It's because this place – this room – matters. Not just for the food. For what it represents.'

Amol waited. He knew the performance when he saw it, but that didn't make it any less compelling.

'This is where the Service holds its annual gathering,' Dexter said at last. 'New Year's Eve. 31 December. Right here. Always here.'

His eyes gleamed as he leaned in conspiratorially. 'And the Krug flows all night. Bottles of it. A sea of it.' He gave a low laugh. 'The running joke is, the more we drink, the better it is for us. Because it's all added to next year's budget.'

Amol snorted. 'Creative accounting.'

'Exactly,' Dexter grinned. 'We're nothing if not pragmatic. You should come. It'll amuse you. Show you the real players.'

There was a beat of silence, then Dexter's tone shifted again – more serious now, the warmth lingering only at the edges. 'But it's not just the champagne, Amol. It's the principle. This,' he gestured around them, 'is home ground. Our ground. No journalists allowed, no cameras, no leaks. Just the people who matter. The people who know what really happens when the headlines stop printing.'

Amol studied him, the weight of it all sinking in. This wasn't flattery. It was a proposition dressed in history, soaked in Krug and clubland rituals. 'And you brought me here … why?' he asked finally, his voice even.

Dexter didn't miss a beat. 'Because I'm offering you the rarest thing we have. A seat. Next time, you don't just write about us, Amol.' He paused. 'You are us.'

The words hung there. Impossible to misinterpret.

Dexter went on, almost gently now. 'Outsiders don't get this chance. Hell, most of the insiders spend a career trying to claw their way to that table on the 31st. But you … you've earned it already. Not because of birth. But because you passed every test we could throw at you – and survived.'

He sat back, letting the statement breathe. 'And the truth is, there aren't many left like you. People who understand risk and restraint in the same breath. People who know when to ask the unaskable question … and when to keep their mouth shut.'

Dexter drained his glass, motioning lazily for another refill. 'You've lived on the margins for long enough, Amol. Margins of newspapers. Margins of conflicts. Margins of power.'

A long pause. 'It's time to choose the centre.'

Amol stayed silent, staring down at his glass. He felt the pull – dangerous, inevitable – as if the decision had been made long before either of them sat down.

Dexter's voice softened to almost a whisper. 'To this conversation. To this … magic moment.'

He smiled. 'And that's what this is, Amol. A magic moment.

One you only see once, if you're lucky.'

Amol looked up finally, meeting Dexter's gaze. 'And after this?'

Dexter shrugged lightly. 'After this, we finish the champagne. You think about it. Maybe I see you again in January. Maybe I don't.' He smiled. 'But I will.'

The waiter arrived with dessert – something delicate, French, forgettable. Neither man touched it.

Instead, Dexter reached into his jacket and pulled out a small card. Cream, thick stock, no writing but a single number embossed in gold. He slid it across the table. 'When you're ready, call that. Only once.'

Amol stared at the card, then back at Dexter. 'And what do I say?'

Dexter smiled thinly. 'You won't need to say anything. Just let it ring once. We'll know.'

Then he stood, smoothing his jacket, adjusting his cufflinks with casual precision. 'Enjoy the rest of your day, Amol. And remember,' he glanced back, eyes gleaming, 'it's already been written, this moment. Everything after this … is just detail.'

With that, Dexter walked away, leaving Amol alone in the mirrored room, the gold-rimmed glasses catching the winter light.

The world outside moved on, oblivious.

Inside, the offer hung in the air, heavier than the chandeliers above.

—

Amol walked down Piccadilly in the brittle afternoon light, the pale sky washed clean by a night of rain. The card in his pocket felt heavier than it should, as if it carried its own gravity. He'd left The Ritz without looking back. Dexter hadn't expected him to. That was part of the design – deliver the pitch, leave the mark to wander, stew, imagine.

The streets buzzed with people, oblivious to the choices men like Dexter made over lunches like that.

By the time he reached Green Park, Amol had lit a cigarette, hands trembling just enough to notice. The rush of nicotine steadied him.

Magic moment. Dexter's words looped back. *It's already been written. Everything after this is just detail.* What did that mean, exactly? That the deal was done, even if Amol didn't know it yet? That they'd been circling him for years – Sean, the paper, the favours, the 'accidental' scoops – and all of it had led to today?

He sat heavily on a bench, watching the slow drift of clouds. Somewhere in the distance, a plane carved a white line through the sky.

He'd always assumed, foolishly maybe, that he could keep control. Stay close enough to power to witness it, never close enough to burn. But the line was gone now. Crossed.

Amol reached into his pocket and pulled out the card. Cream stock, gold number. Beautiful in its simplicity. A door, waiting to be opened. He stared at it, thinking of the years he'd spent filing copy from war zones, chasing the next story, the next hit of adrenaline – Beirut, Grozny, the camps on the Afghan border. He'd bled for the byline. He'd believed it mattered.

And now? Now, the men who really ran things had shown him their face. Not the government, not the editors – but the people in rooms like The Ritz, over Krug and veal, laughing about budget tricks and civil service pensions. They weren't offering him a job. They were offering him a place.

He laughed bitterly. 'Christ,' he muttered, to no one. 'And here I thought I was the clever one.'

A woman walking her dog glanced over. Amol smiled weakly, waving the moment away. He crushed the cigarette out, slipped the card back into his pocket and stood.

Decision time could wait. For now, he just needed to walk. The city unfolded around him, indifferent. London had that talent – swallowing men whole, making their private agonies look small against its endless, heaving sprawl.

Amol kept walking, head down, past the stone facades of clubs he'd never belong to, past windows full of Savile Row suits and leather-bound books.

Tested. The word made him flinch.

He crossed St James's, drifting aimlessly, ending up outside the Athenaeum. A line of black cars idled nearby, their chauffeurs waiting patiently. Somewhere in there, Amol imagined another meeting like his was underway. Another man being offered the key to a door he didn't know existed until it swung open in his face. The air smelled of old money, polished wood and dying roses. A London smell. Permanent.

Amol lit another cigarette. Two in half an hour – he hadn't done that since Beirut. He should have felt flattered. Instead, there was a tightness in his chest, a rising anger he couldn't quite place. Not at Dexter. Not even at Sean. At himself, maybe – for not seeing it sooner.

You're tired, Amol. Dexter's voice, maddeningly calm. *We're offering you certainty. A place at the table.* Certainty. God, what a word. What a trap.

For years, he'd convinced himself that journalism was about bearing witness. Standing apart. Watching the game but never playing it. Now he saw how childish that had been. There was no neutral ground. You were either in, or you were nothing. He stubbed out the cigarette and moved on, crossing into Mayfair.

The shops thinned. The buildings grew heavier, quieter, their windows dark like watching eyes. The afternoon light was thinning. Shadows grew longer. He thought of his parents, his mother's father back in Delhi – sleeves rolled, reading aloud from the newspaper he edited, declaiming foreign dispatches like scripture. 'It's a noble trade, Amol. Hard men telling hard truths.'

What would the old man say now? That it was all bullshit? That the men writing those dispatches had already chosen their side, whether they knew it or not? Amol's mouth twisted. Maybe his grandfather had always known.

He found himself outside a pub – one of those old places, all wood and brass and stained glass. Without thinking, he ducked inside.

The warmth hit him first, then the smell – stale ale, wet coats, the low hum of men pretending not to listen to one another. He ordered a whisky. No ice.

At the corner table, Amol sat, staring into the glass as if the answer might float up from the amber depths. Was this what it felt like to be recruited? Not flattered, not seduced – but … cornered? Made to see the world too clearly, all at once?

The offer wasn't really an offer. It was a reveal. This is how it works. This is who we are. This is who you've been serving all along. A man didn't walk away from that. Not really.

Even if he said no, the knowledge would remain. The circle would remain. And somewhere, in some file, there'd be a tick by his name. Offered. Declined.

But still in play.

The whisky burned going down. Amol relished the pain of it.

Outside, the sky darkened. London folded in on itself. He thought of Sedo – how terrified the man had been, how easily Amol had swallowed the story, chased it. How useful he'd been.

You don't smash the ball. You play the game the way it should be played … Amol laughed under his breath. 'Fuck me. Even tennis was a test.'

He finished the whisky in a gulp, set the glass down too hard and sat back.

There was no way back. Not really. The card in his pocket seemed to pulse. Heavy. He didn't take it out again.

For now, he just sat, watching the city close in, the game moving on without him – for a little while longer.

The next summons came in the form of an embossed card slipped through Amol's letterbox – no name, no number. Just the date, the time and the place. The Ritz. Private Dining Room. Same as last time.

This time, Amol didn't hesitate. He shaved, ironed a shirt, polished his shoes. He could already feel the shift: somewhere in his mind, he was rehearsing a part.

The doorman barely glanced at him. Upstairs, Dexter was already waiting. Same room. Same view over Green Park. A bottle of Krug chilling in a silver bucket, condensation beading slowly down its neck.

Dexter stood as Amol entered. No handshake this time – just a nod, as if they'd known each other years. 'You came.'

Amol shrugged off his coat, took his time. 'Didn't say I wouldn't.'

Dexter smiled faintly. 'There's a point in every courtship, Amol, where both parties know where this is going. You're here because you've already decided to hear it. Shall we sit?'

They did.

Dexter poured, careful, measured. The Krug was cold, sharp on Amol's tongue. A silent toast to inevitability.

'You're wondering what happens next,' Dexter said. 'What the offer really is. What it means.'

Amol didn't answer.

'You'll still be a journalist. We want you exactly where you are. Writing what you write. Moving as you move. But you'll have … Guidance. Access. Protection.' Dexter leaned forward. 'And a pension, by the way. A real one. Civil service. Not many of your kind get that.'

'My kind?'

'Outsiders. Wanderers. Useful men, but not the sort who retire well.'

Amol snorted. 'You make it sound like charity.'

'No,' Dexter said. 'It's business. You've passed every test, Amol. Over years, not months. Loyalty. Risk. Curiosity. Charm. You play the game without needing the rules spelled out. That's rare.'

He topped up Amol's glass.

'We're not buying you, if that's what worries you. You've already been ours, in your way. Embedded without knowing it. But now, it's time to stop guessing which way the wind blows.'

Silence stretched between them. Amol still said nothing. Dexter stood. 'Take your time. But not too much. The world's moving fast. Lines hardening. You'll want to be on the right side when it breaks.'

He left the card on the table, along with the bill – unsigned. Amol sat there long after Dexter was gone, finishing the champagne alone.

Amol touched his napkin, folding it without thought. He remembered how Sedo's hands moved – careful, quiet, precise – drawing wires like a prayer. They'd said he'd be safe. Dexter had said nothing.

The city glittered outside, uncaring. The game, it seemed, was already being played.

Later, as he stood still in the cold air, he wondered what it was he'd just been offered. And why Dexter had seemed so sure he'd say yes.

On another day, Dexter suggested they meet somewhere else, somewhere he deemed 'even more civilized'.

Amol followed him through the Peers' Entrance of the House of Lords, past reception staff immaculately dressed in white morning coats. No one asked for ID. No security checks. Just a nod and then a hush, like stepping into a cathedral that had forgotten it was also a stage set.

'It's been de rigueur attire like that since Prince Albert died,' Dexter murmured, offering no further explanation.

They sat in the tea room, where the silver teapots bore the crest of Victoria's reign and the sponge cake was served with absurd precision. Amol said nothing. The message was clear: Dexter moved through worlds where velvet ropes didn't apply. He belonged – had always belonged. And now he was offering Amol a taste. A place at the table, if only he would stop asking questions and start following instructions.

That night, Amol couldn't sleep. The Krug still lingered in his bloodstream, sweet and oily. He'd expected a seduction; he hadn't expected the flattery to feel so clinical. Six tests passed, Dexter had said. Like a performance review.

The call came at 1.12 a.m.

Not his phone. His door. Amol's heart skipped. His skin prickled with sudden alertness, the room seeming colder all at once. A young man in a navy peacoat stood on the landing. The cut of the coat and the dullness of his shoes screamed officialdom.

'Mr Batty,' he said. 'There's been a situation. You're requested at Vauxhall. Immediate clearance has been given.'

Requested. Not ordered. Not invited. Amol rubbed his eyes, grabbed his coat. Twenty minutes later he was in a glass-walled room facing Peter Dexter again – tie off, shirt unbuttoned at the collar.

The room smelt of stale takeaway and chlorine. Dexter didn't waste time. 'We believe there's a planned strike on London. The signals are faint, but familiar. Gas canisters, transport nodes, recycled timers. The signature matches cells we know operated with PKK support in Germany.'

'You're saying this is Sedo's old crew.'

'Or someone trained by them. We're watching Frankfurt and north London, but the intelligence is incomplete.'

Amol sat very still. This wasn't just another story to chase – it was a nightmare that could explode in the heart of his city, and he alone held a thread that might unravel it. A creeping chill tightened his nerves.

'We need to talk to him,' Dexter said quietly. 'You're the only one he'll talk to.'

'Why now?'

'Because we've intercepted fragments of a plan – and because you saw his face. You know he wasn't done. You know he wanted something.'

'He wanted asylum and a pension.'

'And credibility. That only comes if we prevent something before it happens. Not after.'

'Where is he?'

'Skopje. UN refugee agency flat, supervised by the Macedonians. We're not officially welcome.'

Amol rubbed his hands together slowly.

'You won't be paid. This is not an assignment. You'll be listed as visiting a source. But we'll cover the ticket and we'll provide a translator if needed.'

'Why me?'

Dexter's eyes sharpened. 'Because he gave you the map.

Because he sketched those bomb parts on your hotel notepad. Because something about you made him think you weren't a puppet. Use that.'

'And if I refuse?'

'Then we all lose the chance to stop this. And if something happens next week – at Victoria Station, on a rush-hour train – how will you sleep, knowing you could've done something?'

The room was silent.

'You don't owe us anything,' Dexter said, almost kindly. 'But you do owe the story. And he's still the story.'

Amol looked at the map again. London. The red circle around Victoria Station. A blurred CCTV still of a man with a duffel bag.

'What if I go and he tells me nothing?'

'Then at least we tried. Then you can go back to your editor and say you did your job.'

'And if he does tell me something?'

Dexter smiled faintly. 'Then we do ours.'

A long pause. Then Dexter stood, signalling the meeting was over. 'We've booked you on the 9.40 to Thessaloniki. Someone will meet you airside. You won't need to check in.'

'You assumed I'd say yes.'

'No,' Dexter said. 'I assumed you'd want to sleep tonight.'

He handed Amol a folder. Thin. Just a photo of Sedo outside a bakery, a sheet of bullet points and a one-way ticket. 'Call it professional curiosity,' he added. 'Or call it insurance.'

The glass door opened with a hiss. A young woman with a clipboard was waiting outside.

Amol's eyes flicked to the woman, noting her calm, unreadable expression. A flicker of suspicion tightened his chest. Was she just an escort, or part of the quiet eyes always watching? The sense of being a pawn in a game he barely understood pressed down like a weight.

'Try not to look too serious,' Dexter said. 'You're just a journalist chasing a follow-up. That's all anyone needs to know.'

6

Doubt

'Some hesitations mark a soul's border.' – Anonymous.

Amol didn't think of it as hesitation at the time. Not exactly. More like drag, the pull of memory or gravity, or something close to fear. He hadn't meant to go. It had been three weeks since The Ritz. No follow-up.

But as the plane dipped over the brittle hills and the straight lines of Yugoslav-era flats – all concrete lines and post-War silence – crossing the invisible threshold between Thessaloniki and Skopje, Amol realized he had said yes.

The moment had passed so quietly: a glass door opening, a folder handed over, the hum of Dexter's voice saying, 'Call it professional curiosity.'

Sedo had opened the door wearing two jumpers and a scarf. His eyes, sharp despite the shadows beneath them, flickered briefly with something unreadable – a mixture of exhaustion and a latent, dangerous edge. The faint scent of sweat and old gunpowder clung to his clothes, a reminder that the man hadn't fully escaped his past.

The flat was cold, dim, the curtains closed though it was midday. A single electric heater glowed in the corner.

'You came,' Sedo said, with something between surprise and resignation.

'They said you might talk to me.' Amol felt a flicker of unease. The silence between them thickened like fog, pressing against his ribs.

'Only you,' he said, leading Amol in. 'You're not them. Not yet.'

There was no coffee, just tap water in cloudy glasses. On the table sat a half-smoked cigarette in an ashtray that looked older than the country it sat in.

'They know,' Sedo said. 'About the gas. About the boy in Frankfurt.'

'Then why do they need you?'

'Because they don't know when. Or where. And I do. But not everything. Just threads.'

He scribbled a name on a torn bit of envelope – *Halil.* Underlined it once.

'I gave them enough,' he said. 'More than enough. But they didn't protect me. They just moved me. Like I was furniture. They said Macedonia was safe.'

'It's not?'

'Nothing is safe when you're Kurdish and quiet.'

He leaned back, bones creaking under his layers. Amol could see the outline of the man he had interviewed in Naxos – the chemist, the defector, the one with blood and bomb powder under his fingernails. But this Sedo was fainter, smudged, like a figure disappearing from an old photograph.

'Why are you still helping them?' Amol asked.

'I'm not helping them,' Sedo said. 'I'm helping you.'

Amol didn't know what to say to that.

They spoke for under twenty minutes. Names. A partial phone number. A phrase: 'After the fast breaks.'

'I heard it in Berlin. Just once.'

'Ramadan's over,' Amol said.

'Then they're late. Or waiting.'

When Amol left, Sedo didn't shake his hand. He simply turned back inside and closed the door with a soft, padded thud.

Now, lying awake in Islington, Amol remembered that sound more than anything. It was like something being sealed shut. He got up and made tea. The milk was off. He drank it black and bitter, and let the doubt settle back in.

The sharp bitterness burned down his throat, matching the knot tightening in his stomach. The cold London dawn gave way to older heat – not just memory, but a place with its own gravity. Delhi was never far away. It waited behind the steam of tea, in the echoes of doors closing softly.

Was this what his grandfather had meant when he said journalists walk the edge of things? 'Never become the story,' the old man had warned, one night in Delhi, as the ceiling fan clicked overhead and the air smelt of sandalwood and whisky.

Amol had been twelve. Small enough to be overlooked at parties, but old enough to understand that the quietest men in the room were often the most dangerous. Sitting in a wicker chair with his feet dangling, listening to a garden party unfold just outside – diplomats laughing, glasses clinking, the rustle of cotton saris and rustling Nehru jackets.

'They'll all try to pull you in,' his grandfather had said. 'The diplomats, the spies, the rebels. Each with their own little truths.'

Years later, Sedo would echo the same warning, though he wore it like a scar. 'You're not them,' he had told Amol. 'Not yet.'

The phrase had stuck – not just for its truth, but for its timing. A confession delivered too late, from a man already cornered.

'How do I know whom to trust?'

'You don't. But you'll know when you're being lied to.

That's the best you'll get.'

The best he'd get. And yet here he was, years later, flying to Skopje on a one-way ticket handed to him by a man with access to satellite footage of Victoria Station. Dexter hadn't asked for anything in return. Not yet. That was what made it worse.

The story, if it was one, had no shape. No ending. No body count. Just whispers and a note in Sedo's handwriting now sitting in a manila folder in someone's drawer at Vauxhall. And yet, Amol knew – even as he sipped the last of his bitter tea – that something had shifted.

The next time Dexter asked for something, it would be harder to say no. The doubt wasn't whether they were using him; that much was clear. The doubt was whether, deep down, he had already agreed. His grandfather in Delhi would have known what this was – would have seen it for what it was, named it with an arched eyebrow and an extra measure of whisky.

'They always come for the in-betweeners,' he had once said.

'What do you mean?' young Amol had asked, cross-legged on the floor beside his Remington typewriter.

'Half this, half that. One foot in, one foot out. The ones who blend in at the embassy and in the old city lanes. You, me, your mother.'

It had taken Amol years to understand what that meant. His mother, Asha, had grown up in the same Golf Links house with mango trees in the garden and a string of cousins sleeping on mattresses in the TV room. Before she met his father. Before she moved to Oxford. Before her silence and bookshelves and trimmed vowels, Asha had been something else.

She worked at the American Library in Delhi, helping visiting scholars find old books no one else could track down – always careful, always polite, always prepared to vanish into the background. She never raised her voice, but she never gave way either. Not to diplomats, not to landlords, not even to her father.

Amol remembered once, aged sixteen, watching her gently but firmly correct the British High Commissioner at a garden party. He had misquoted a verse from Ghalib. She smiled and recited the original under her breath, just loud enough for him to hear. He nodded and walked away a little less certain of himself.

His father was quieter still – an Oxford man with tweed jackets that smelled of pipe smoke and old books, who rarely left the college except to teach or to walk along the river.

David Batty, an Englishman to his bones, never shouted, never fussed, never indulged the dramas of the newsroom when Amol began writing from abroad. When Amol had sent him a clipping from Beirut – his first byline under fire – David replied with a one-line postcard: 'Write what matters. Ignore the noise.'

That was all. No celebration, no critique. Just principle.

And now, here he was, walking the same line both of them had warned him about: not spy, not soldier, not traitor – but not entirely clean either.

The Skopje trip had left a trace. Not in his passport; he'd flown under a different name. Not in his notes; he'd left the scribbles behind. But in him. In the pause before each sentence, he now wrote. In the new awareness of who might be reading. In the fact that he had told no one. Not even Sean. Especially not Sean. He hadn't even written it down. The name Sedo was whispered still, but Amol was starting to hear it differently – not as a source, but as a reckoning.

In Naxos, Sedo had spoken of bridges and bombs, of dreaming one and delivering the other. At the time, Amol had thought it rhetoric. Now he understood: it wasn't a metaphor, it was a diagnosis.

He rinsed his cup and stood at the kitchen window. The street below was quiet, rain softening the outlines of cars and paving stones. A fox darted between two wheelie bins and paused, looking up as if it could see him.

Amol watched the fox's sharp eyes, thinking how survival often meant staying hidden – moving quietly, trusting no one fully, not even those closest. In a world of shadows, instincts mattered more than promises.

He had inherited his mother's stillness, his father's suspicion of noise and his grandfather's talent for walking into rooms where nobody trusted each other and everyone wanted something. What he hadn't inherited – what he now felt slipping away – was certainty.

The kind of certainty he used to feel when filing a story that could crack open a ministry, expose a lie or unseat a man who thought himself untouchable. That certainty was gone.

In its place: doubt.

Soft at first. Then heavier. Like a coat you hadn't meant to put on but now found yourself wearing everywhere – even in rooms that smelled like home.

7

Inheritance

The scent of jasmine caught him off guard. It drifted through the streets of Zamalek as Amol walked home alone from another reception where everyone had been too friendly, too knowing.

Not his first foreign posting and years before everything turned. But tonight, Cairo had triggered something older.

A curated kind. Where the smiles were soft and the silences heavy. Tonight, someone had leaned in close and said, 'You carry yourself like someone who's been taught to listen.'

That one line cracked something open. Not Cairo as it was. Not the Service or the masks. But Delhi. The old house. The quiet. The voices behind closed doors.

Amol was twelve when he began spending his summers in Delhi. His parents were teaching in China and the white house in Golf Links became his sanctuary and his schooling. His grandfather, Amol Senior, a man of unshakeable calm, had long retired from formal journalism but still held court each evening in his shaded veranda, a glass of Darjeeling in hand and his Remington never far from reach.

The Golf Links house was more than a residence. It was a listening post. Politicians, diplomats, civil servants and foreign correspondents came and went like migratory birds.

Sometimes they arrived with little fanfare: B.M. Kaul, the army general whose fall from grace after the 1962 war still clung to his slippers; Ashoke Sen, India's law minister, who joked in Sanskrit and rewrote Cabinet minutes in ink; R.N. Kao, founder of India's foreign intelligence agency, RAW (Research and Analysis Wing), who always arrived with his Alsatians and once whispered something in Amol Senior's ear that ended the evening early; and, once, Indira Gandhi herself – not yet prime minister, but already taut and watchful – daughter of Nehru, India's first prime minister.

She was accompanied by her aunt, Vijayalakshmi Pandit – Nehru's sister, India's first woman cabinet minister and former president of the UN – who wore her disdain like perfume. Shuk, Amol's grandmother, served tea without comment but switched from Darjeeling to Assam – stronger leaves for sharper tongues. The drawing room hummed with elliptical sentences. Every sentence seemed to contain a second clause left unspoken.

Morning callers were mostly ignored by Amol Senior, hunched over his typewriter, trying to make sense of Indian politics before relaying his published findings to bands of loyal followers. The true magic started in the evenings when the guests clamoured for his stories behind the stories, his gossip, his unerring sense of where power was shifting.

But most of all, they came for the spies.

Amol learnt early to remain still, to observe. He'd sit behind the curtain or crouched on the stairs, feeling the rough wood between his palms, absorbing voices that floated like incense through the afternoon heat. He rarely understood everything, but he recognized tension, flirtation, the sudden change of pace when something mattered.

Keir was among the earliest visitors that summer. Douglas Keir – urbane, unhurried, elegant to the point of parody. Officially the head of the British Council, but his long lunches with Indian editors and his habit of arriving with annotated books gave away more than he admitted. He handed Amol a slim volume of Orwell's essays, wrapped in brown paper.

His wife, Elizabeth, sometimes sent handwritten notes on thick cream paper – always gracious, always slightly apologetic for her husband's lateness. Amol never met her, but Shuk once remarked, 'She knows when to step back. That's power of a different sort.'

Tucked underneath was another book, older and heavier – Conrad's *The Secret Agent*. 'A bit dark for your age,' Keir said, 'but useful. Everyone in our trade ends up quoting Conrad eventually. Even the ones who pretend not to read. The best way to understand empire is to read the men who could never quite forgive themselves for building it.'

At dinner that night, Keir spoke about diplomacy as theatre. 'You play to the balcony,' he said, 'but you negotiate in the wings.'

Amol's grandfather sipped his tea. 'The trouble is knowing who wrote the script.'

Keir nodded approvingly. 'And who's improvising.'

There was warmth in his tone, but something in the way he said it stayed with Amol. Years later, he would hear that same softness laced with steel in Dexter's voice – the kind of man who never needed to raise his volume, because the message had already been rehearsed. Dexter would even carry his own dog-eared copy of *The Secret Agent*, quoting from it carelessly over lunch, as though Conrad had been writing memos for Vauxhall Cross. For some in the Service, Amol would come to realize, the book wasn't literature. It was lanyard and mask, a crude badge of honour.

That night, Amol wrote a private note about masks and mirrors. His grandfather read it the next morning, said nothing, but placed it inside the Remington case – the family equivalent of publication. He folded the note carefully, a shadow passing over his face – part reverence, part unease.

Jack Curran arrived like a different weather system. American, confident, slightly coarse. His jokes cut too close to the bone. 'You've got a spy in the kitchen,' he once quipped. 'I can smell MI5 on the curry leaves.'

He claimed to be cultural attaché, but everyone knew otherwise. He was the kind of man who left his briefcase unlatched but his stories air-tight. One evening, lounging on the veranda with a drink in each hand, he told the story of Air India's Kashmir Princess.

'Plane was rigged to blow. Chou En-lai never boarded. Killed a handful of others. Wrong timing, right message.' He leaned back. 'You don't have to hit the target – just make them change their flight plans.'

Amol's grandfather smiled thinly. 'That's the difference between a journalist and a spy. A journalist hopes the truth lands. A spy just wants the tremor.'

Curran spoke often of his wife, Cathy, who stayed behind in Washington DC. 'She hates the heat,' he joked once, 'but loves my pay cheque.' No one laughed. Shuk rolled her eyes and left the room.

Later that night, clearing glasses, Amol asked, 'Is it true?'

'Maybe. Maybe not,' came the reply. 'But what matters is that Curran wants us to believe he knows. That's his theatre.'

Curran reminded Amol of other Americans who had passed through the house in previous years, like Harry Rositzke, always spinning tales about Eastern Europe; or David Blee, who quoted Persian poets while casually suggesting someone might disappear.

They were polished storytellers who blurred lines between intelligence and seduction.

Years later, in Cairo, that same cultivated charm – a mixture of literary flair and concealed menace – would surface again in another young American, one who dressed better, smiled easier and carried danger like a scent. Amol would know the type instantly, even if he didn't yet have a name for it.

Sergey Efimov was subtler. Russian cultural attaché, slight of frame, with delicate fingers and mournful eyes. He arrived with gifts wrapped in newspaper – samizdat poetry, boxes of dried apricots and once, a silk scarf Amol suspected was meant for Shuk.

His wife, Nina, came with him once, dressed in a linen suit the colour of smoke. She said almost nothing, but when she watched Shuk, there was a flicker of mutual recognition – two women fluent in silences. Later, Shuk simply said, 'That one's no fool. She's the kind who wraps poison in poetry.'

He said he was from the city of Lvov, not far from the western frontier – a place where languages overlapped and where borders had shifted so often that the past felt like a line of smoke. Whether it was true or just part of the act, Amol couldn't tell. But the tone – that quiet edge of ambivalence – would return to him later.

Efimov's conversations were always elliptical. He'd quote Pushkin, then ask about India's steel production. He praised Gandhi's asceticism, then lamented the lack of Soviet tractors in Uttar Pradesh. His questions came wrapped in admiration – never accusations, always invitations. He praised restraint as if it were revolutionary.

Amol, young as he was, found it hard to place the man politically, but even harder to forget his phrasing. Years later, he would recognize that same delicate ambiguity in another East European – a man from Tanjug, the Yugoslav news agency, who also smoked too much, dressed too well and asked about danger as though it were a type of wine. Like Efimov, he claimed neutrality but smelled of alignment. Efimov's questions always circled something invisible.

One afternoon, Efimov gifted him a volume of Russian folktales. One story had been underlined in red: 'Even a Dancing Bear Dreams of the Forest.'

His grandfather flipped through the book that evening and quietly tore the page out.

'Why?' Amol asked.

'Because no one gives you folklore without a reason. That's how people claim you – by giving you the stories they want you to tell.'

There were other visitors, a man from the Kenyan High Commission with a gold pen he kept polishing. An Israeli diplomat with a fondness for Tagore – soft-spoken, inquisitive and unexpectedly lyrical.

He was the Bombay-based consul general who made regular trips north to mingle discreetly with the great and the good of the Indian capital. Rumour had it his ancestors were from a remote region of Turkey; that he was a personal friend of

Moshe Dayan; even that he had once headed Mossad – Israel's legendary intelligence agency – and that this quiet posting to India was a pre-retirement reward. In looks, manner and bearing, he uncannily resembled a man who would later become a shadow presence in Amol's adult life.

As a boy, Amol hadn't known who Moshe Dayan was, only that the name drew whispered awe from older guests and provoked a tightening around his grandfather's eyes. Only much later would he understand who Dayan really was – soldier, myth, shadow maker, embodying both the myth and menace of the young Israeli state. If the Consul General truly counted such a man as a friend, it spoke volumes.

Amol remembered the Israeli's watchfulness, the way he never quite relaxed over whisky and kebabs. 'Years later, another man on a Greek island, then again in an obscure restaurant in Beirut, reminded him of the Consul General always hovering near the door – always listening before he spoke.

There was something unnerving about him. Not the content of what he said, but the careful way he said it – like a man whose hands still smelled of the fuse offering peace.

Amol found himself strangely drawn to the diplomat's voice, the stillness in it, the delay between thought and word. It made him uneasy.

He would come to recognize that scent in Sedo too – not the blast, but the preparation. Not the violence, but the shape of it. And when that voice returned in a darker register, years later, the consequences were no longer hypothetical.

Back then, he hadn't understood that civility could be a weapon. Later, he would watch as it was used to sanctify violence, not just by men like Sedo, but by those who made use of him.

'You don't learn anything by shutting people out,' he once told Amol. 'But you must learn which truths come scented, and which come loaded.'

What unsettled Amol most, perhaps, was how familiar the diplomat felt. Not in accent or manner, but in the way he held his doubts close – like a man raised to endure history, not escape it.

Later, when he found himself again between a watchful Israeli and a woman whose voice carried exile like perfume, he would realize how long these shapes had been with him.

It had never been about politics. It was always intimacy and the danger that came with it.

Once, a Lebanese French girl visited with her father, a visiting cultural attaché. She was no older than Amol, but sharper, quicker – with charcoal-dark eyes and the habit of underlining poetry in whatever newspaper was at hand. She asked Amol what language he dreamed in.

'Depends on where I am,' he said.

She smiled. 'I envy that. My mother says exile is when your dreams start changing their accent.'

She recited a line from Gibran before dessert, caught Shuk's eye across the room and kissed her father on the cheek as though it were a goodbye in stages. Her voice had a rhythm Amol couldn't place – part French lycée, part Beirut. She asked questions Amol couldn't answer: about silences in crowded rooms, about whether a country could miss you back. At one point, the Israeli diplomat offered to refill her glass and misquoted Tagore. She corrected him gently but with precision, and Amol remembered how the Israeli's smile didn't quite reach his eyes after that.

She stayed only a day, but Amol remembered her long after the others blurred. Not because of what she said – but because she was the first person who seemed to speak from the inside out.

When Layla entered his life with poetry and flame, he would

think not of romance, but of resonance – and of a girl in a cream shawl who had named exile without bitterness. He would remember, too, how she held her own in a room full of watchers, and how her quiet correction of the Israeli landed harder than any argument.

Amol noticed patterns. Who lingered too long. Who never returned. Who smiled too much. The Golf Links house became his first newspaper, and the guests were his headlines.

Over time the signatures revealed themselves: the too-polished warmth of Keir that Dexter would later deploy; the bluff performance of Curran – all confidence and narrative control – echoed faintly years later in the newsroom manipulations of Sean, whose cruelties came not from force, but from knowing what people needed to hear; the silent calculation of Efimov that would later reappear in another guise – the cool, observing patience Amol would one day recognize again, unnamed at the time, but just as deliberate.

He was learning the front page long before he knew what questions to ask.

He began writing mock articles.

'RUSSIAN DIPLOMAT BRINGS FOLKLORE, EXITS WITH MANGO PICKLE'

'AMERICAN JOKES ABOUT BOMBS, ENJOYS SECOND HELPING'

He even drafted pretend ribbons and subheads, mimicking the papers his grandfather once edited. His grandfather used to say, 'A clean ribbon is more important than clean copy. One cuts through the fog.' When Sean began feeding him stories heavy with adjectives but light on truth, that phrase would return like an admonition.

His grandfather read them all. 'You'll either be very good,' he said, 'or very dangerous.'

He also warned Amol, more than once, never to trust charm too easily. 'The ones who flatter you,' he'd say, 'are the ones most likely to betray you.'

And on a quiet evening, when Amol asked why certain guests kept returning, his grandfather replied, almost too lightly, 'Spies love journalists. They like people who lie for a living – it's easier to believe in your own story when someone else is paid to write it better.'

Shuk would drift in and out of the drawing room. Her presence was like a silk curtain – soft, almost imperceptible, but impossible to ignore. Amol sometimes caught the faint scent of jasmine on her clothes, a reminder of quiet strength.

She was the quiet observer in a house full of watchers, the one person who never needed to speak to command attention. In the evenings, after the guests had gone, she would sometimes sit with Amol and gently ask what he had noticed.

'Not what they said,' she'd whisper, 'but how they sat, how they stirred their tea. That's what matters.'

In these moments, Amol absorbed something deeper than politics, the moral undercurrent beneath every silence. She rarely spoke in the presence of the men, but when she did, people listened. She once told Amol, 'Your grandfather thinks information is power. But love and shame are what people act on.'

She kept the household together. The cook, the gardener, the sweeper – all loyal to her. Amol watched her resolve arguments without raising her voice. She taught him how to slice mangoes, how to read someone's exhaustion in the way they held a spoon. 'You can trust a tired man more than a hungry one,' she told him. 'Tired men have stopped pretending.'

The final summer before university had a different rhythm. The guests came less often. Letters arrived but with fewer stamps. Keir sent a note about retiring early. Efimov's gifts stopped altogether. Curran vanished. Shuk seemed to shrink slightly, as if the weight of holding things together had shifted.

One evening, Amol found his grandfather burning old notes in the garden. He said it was routine. 'No one needs records of a conversation they didn't have.'

On Amol's last Sunday, they walked together in Lodhi Gardens. It was hot and windless. His grandfather carried a newspaper but didn't open it.

'You've listened well,' he said.

Amol looked away.

'There's one last thing,' his grandfather said. 'Power isn't in what they say. It's in what they don't have to explain. Watch for that. And never speak first in a room full of men who make laws or start wars. Let them guess what you already know.'

Amol closed the window. The sounds of Zamalek had receded. He poured himself a second drink and opened a blank notepad.

He remembered the curve of Keir's sentences, the riddle-like warnings from Efimov, Curran's ugly laughter. He remembered how each of them – men with titles and missions, pretences and passports – circled his grandfather like rival suitors around an old king.

He would one day realise that he had grown up not around

power, but within its staging ground. That was the part Dexter could never grasp. Dexter assumed Amol had been seduced into this world, when in fact he had been born into it – the son of teachers, yes, but the grandson of a man whose drawing room had once rivalled any embassy for discretion and reach. The games Dexter played over Krug and oysters were old parlour tricks here, performed decades earlier in cotton kurta and fan-cooled stillness – and the quiet strength of his grandfather.

He had inherited more than memories. He had inherited instincts. The kind that didn't win awards or earn promotions. The kind that saved you.

He picked up his pen and wrote one line: 'Everyone wants something. The question is, what will they give for it?'

Then he underlined it twice.

It wasn't just a memory. It was a briefing he hadn't known he'd attended. And now, years later, the language of that house was returning – fluent, familiar and fatal.

He stood at the window a moment longer, then let the curtain fall. The streets below shimmered with sodium haze, indifferent. But his thoughts were elsewhere. Skopje. Naxos. A man with calloused hands and a mouth full of warnings.

Sedo wasn't haunting him.

He was hunting him like a ghost with a map of the future.

Part II – 1978–1990

Fieldwork and the Shadows

8

Bees and the Honeypot

1978, Cairo

That year was Amol's first Cairo assignment as a foreign correspondent.

Amol didn't know it then, but this was one of the first tests. The kind Dexter would later catalogue in cold, congratulatory tones. Loyalty, risk, questions, charm and technical knowledge. Amol would wonder how the man had known so much about his life in the Middle East. About the water conferences, the phone taps, the birds.

Cairo had felt like chance at the time. A hard-earned posting, not an audition. The kind of test a man he would meet one day might fail – or pass, depending on who was keeping score.

It wasn't just diplomats and spies who got tested. It was those who watched too closely and those who remembered too much.

Perhaps the test had started the moment he stepped off the plane into the stifling Nile air, rented a flat in Zamalek and began reporting from a city where every conversation seemed overheard.

They had been watching him long before Cairo. That was the part that stayed with him. Even in Delhi, long before his first dispatch, there had been glances that lingered too long, compliments that felt rehearsed. He'd chalked it up to curiosity. Later, he understood it was assessment.

The apartment in Zamalek had charm – arched windows, a fan that squealed at high speeds and a cracked balcony overlooking the Nile. Outside, a solitary bee circled a wilting jasmine bush, its persistent buzz slicing through the evening's heavy air, a tiny echo of the city's hidden sweetness and stings. On some evenings, the sunset lit the water gold; on others, it was just diesel fumes and neon.

Amol had arrived in high summer, when Cairo was a furnace and the city's secrets were half-melted on the pavement. The air buzzed with something larger than heat. Anwar Sadat had just returned from his unprecedented visit to Jerusalem, and already the region was murmuring with what might follow – Camp David, recognition, withdrawal, peace.

Amol was one of the few foreign correspondents trusted enough to cover the unfolding negotiations. Between terse communiqués and cryptic embassy briefings, he filed careful stories on the Egypt–Israel talks, threading facts through the haze of speculation. The peace process was fragile, guarded by couriers and threats, and Cairo was suddenly the world's pivot.

By late August, to escape the heat and the tightening web of Cairo's intrigue, Amol sometimes took the train north to Alexandria. The cool breeze off the Mediterranean, the salt tang in the air, the relaxed pace of the Corniche – it offered a temporary balm.

He would swim at Maamoura Beach in the early mornings, the water still and glassy, the horizon endless. The lifeguards knew him by name after the second visit, and he sometimes shared mint tea with them after his exercises in the water – long deliberate strokes, letting the tide pull at him before turning back towards shore.

In the evenings, he'd put on a linen shirt and walk to the Cecil Hotel. The Cecil had history; whispers still clung to its worn leather armchairs and faded drapes – echoes of wartime spies who had traded lies and secrets over lukewarm gin. Rumour held that the hotel's concierge during the war years had run an entire espionage ring single-handedly, passing messages hidden in cocktail napkins, listening more than he spoke – a shadow diplomat for a shadow war.

Amol sometimes wondered if those half-forgotten whispers were the real ghosts of Alexandria – more tangible than the apparitions tourists chased down darkened alleyways. There, under its slow-turning ceiling fans and the ghosts of wartime spies, he played roulette. Once, on a whim, he placed a bet on Seventeen Black and won a 100 dollars. He treated himself to a bottle of wine and a seafood platter and sat on the terrace, listening to the waves lap the seawall below. It felt, briefly, like a life far from microphones and briefings – a pause in a larger story.

Another weekend, he flew to Luxor and took a battered minibus into the Valley of the Kings. The heat was blistering, but he was hypnotized by the tombs – every corridor a journey into layered centuries. He stood alone in the antechamber of Seti I's tomb, staring at the painted constellations overhead, and thought about mortality, memory and what endures.

When he emerged, a hawker tried to sell him a replica scarab. He declined, then doubled back and bought two. One stayed in his desk drawer for years.

In early autumn, restless and curious, he made the long journey to Siwa, an oasis whispered about in books and old diplomatic files. He went by shared taxi, then camel; the desert vast and silent around him, yellow dunes rolling endlessly. The town was a mirage of olive groves and salt lakes, its air dry and charged with mystery.

Siwa was where Alexander the Great had come, centuries earlier, to consult the Oracle of Amun. Some said he had walked into the temple and emerged no longer merely Macedonian, but Pharaoh – blessed and cursed with divine insight.

Amol visited the crumbling ruins, stepped into the shadows of the Temple of the Oracle and placed his hand against the sun-warmed stone. The silence felt old and aware.

He spent two nights there, dining on grilled goat and dates, watching the stars explode across the sky. A Siwan guide, barefoot and unhurried, took him to the edge of the Great Sand Sea and quoted Herodotus: 'The farther one travels, the nearer one comes to myth.'

It was, for Amol, a pilgrimage – not to faith, but to story. A place outside the reach of wires and whispers, where even spies seemed irrelevant.

The invitation came on the third day after he had set up in Cairo. 'Thursday. Groppi's. Noon.'

It was unsigned, handwritten on cheap hotel notepaper. He smiled. They hadn't wasted time – whoever they were.

Groppi's was a colonial echo, all faded gilt and chipped marble. Once the haunt of spies and socialites, now a nostalgic café where the air smelt of cigarette ash and rosewater. Amol's gaze drifted to the honeycomb tiles lining the wall, the hexagonal patterns a silent tribute to industriousness and hidden order amid the faded grandeur.

Waiting for him was Miro – a tall, broad-shouldered man with the classic swagger of a Balkan officer and the impeccable tailoring of a Milanese couturier. He had the kind of face that made people turn twice – not out of recognition, but envy. A typical Serb, he claimed; though Vasna, his Croatian wife, liked to mock him for spending more on his linen shirts and Italian shoes than she did on groceries. 'Peacock,' she'd call him in three languages.

Miro was always immaculately dressed, as if he had stepped out of a fashion magazine between deadlines. Even when the Cairo heat pressed down like wet velvet, he wore pressed cotton, crisp collars, pocket squares. And yet, he moved with the casual grace of someone who expected to be watched. Like an actor playing a part he'd long since memorized – not for the audience, but for the mirror.

He was a manic smoker. Cigarettes curled constantly from his fingers, lighting one before the other was finished. 'In my country,' he said, 'every journalist is a spy.' Amol shrugged, 'In mine we just call that freelance.' The smoke thickened between them, a silent understanding settling in. Sometimes, uninvited, he would appear at Amol's apartment – at ten in the morning or three in the morning, it made no difference.

'You heard the Saudi foreign minister's been seen in Damascus?' he might begin, or 'You think Fawzi Khalil's on the payroll?'

At first, it unsettled Amol. Then it amused him. Then, without him quite realizing it, it became a kind of friendship. The first real camaraderie he had felt since school – unguarded, teasing, full of late-night laughter and half-spoken truths.

'You don't look like a journalist,' Amol said at their first meeting.

'Thank you,' Miro said and grinned. 'That is best compliment. You, my friend, look too much like one. You are too serious.'

They spoke of Afghanistan, Amol carefully, slowly gave him selective details. Captured on the road from Kabul to Kandahar. Blindfolded. Bamboo rods. Days of interrogation by the Mujahideen – trained, he suspected, by the CIA (the US Central Intelligence Agency). Then there was the torture, bashed around the head with a Kalashnikov, stripped naked, hung upside down on a makeshift cross and, after that, held down by five men who each took their turn to bugger him while the others held him down. The rest was left unsaid. The pain, the humiliation, the bleeds that returned years later, those remained locked away. What Miro heard was only the outline, never the horror. The full story would come years later, when Amol could finally speak the words aloud. Instead, they moved on to safer subjects like tennis, journalism, politics. The darker truths were buried again, beneath heat and laughter and Vasna's ice-cold Czech beer.

He didn't give Miro all the gory details at their first meeting. The information was teased out of him much later – after they started playing singles tennis and visiting each other's homes for drinks and food. It was usually Miro who played host, with Vasna providing the ice-cold Czech beer and the food that followed.

'They beat you?' Miro asked at their first meeting, eyes alight.

'Off and on,' Amol replied. 'It was more about control.'

Miro stirred his coffee slowly. 'It is all the Americans' fault,' he said. 'They want Afghanistan to join the North Atlantic Treaty Organization. You know? The NATO in the mountains. Madness.'

In the pre-drone era, he briefed Amol about the heavy armour that the Americans slipped across the border from Pakistan – missiles and machine guns that could target Soviet bases from the high mountains.

'And for what?' Miro asked, after one drunken evening. 'Who cares a damn about Afghanistan, landlocked misery hole in the middle of Asia. Install a puppet government, suck out all their precious minerals, bring them into an extended NATO, show the world who's in charge.'

Cairo was different. It had its own taxonomy of operatives. The British were gardeners – patient, precise. The Soviets, stone masons – hard lines, brutal cuts. The Americans? They were honey farmers.

And Paul Alexander was their smoothest export.

He appeared at a regional water conference in Giza.

Paul posed as a water purification consultant. His business card listed an American NGO and a dead landline. He was handsome too. Amol noticed how Camille, the French girl perched on his motorbike most evenings, glanced at no one else.

He wore aviators and desert boots and hung around the American University's Arabic night classes, which the newspaper paid for. They all kept running into each other.

First at the University, then drinks at the British embassy doctor's flat in Zamalek, where the doctor's wife – tipsy and sharp – mocked Paul as 'the CIA jewel that grows more valuable with every passing day'.

'So, Paul, how much do the Americans pay you to test Cairo's water supply?' Miro asked.

'Enough to afford a Belgian girlfriend and a second-hand Yamaha. You?'

'We Balkan types prefer Czech beer and Serbian wives. Less expensive. More dangerous.'

'And infinitely more stylish,' Amol added.

They clinked glasses. Camille rolled her eyes. She'd heard it before. The mock rivalry, the posturing. But something about the way the men laughed – tight, knowing – hinted at shadows beneath the charm.

Paul said, 'You both wear linen like it's armour.'

'Better than camouflage. You'd be surprised how many secrets fall from lips admiring your cufflinks,' Miro retorted.

Paul didn't flinch. He just smiled. Amol clocked the way Paul deflected. Not denial, not confirmation – just a practiced neutrality, polished like an old coin.

One afternoon, Sonya, Amol's Egyptian secretary, knocked on his office door. Fiercely loyal and quietly resourceful, she had a knack for navigating both bureaucracy and danger with equal grace. She'd been with him since his first month in Cairo, more bodyguard than assistant in moments that mattered.

'Paul's overhead phone line goes from his apartment through the US consul general's switchboard,' she said. 'Everyone can see it and I checked.'

Amol blinked. 'Checked how?'

She smiled. 'I know people.'

She left, humming. Paul's cover was crumbling.

The confirmation came at Amol's Christmas party. A modest affair, mostly journalists and diplomats, but Sonya had typed up the guest list for the building's security desk. Paul declined the invitation, said he was busy.

He turned up at midnight with two bottles of Californian

red and his French girlfriend Camille in tow. She doted on every word he said, rode pillion on his Yamaha, spoke longingly of their midnight feasts below the Gaza pyramids. Everyone was entranced.

'Did MI6 forget to dress up tonight or did you come straight from a Milan catwalk?' Paul quipped.

Miro replied saying, 'We dress well so your girlfriend stays interested. You should try it.'

Laughing, Camille said, 'He tried once. The shirt had a crocodile on it.'

'He thought it was a secret signal,' Amol added.

'It was. To the laundry,' said Paul.

The next morning, Sonya came in early. 'The Mukhabarat called. Asked for the guest list again.'

'And?'

'They wanted to know why the American's name wasn't on it.'

Amol stared at her. 'They knew he was there?'

She nodded. 'They always know.'

He laughed, not too loudly. Egypt wasn't subtle when it felt insulted. And the Mukhabarat didn't care if the joke was someone else's.

He later told Miro, 'So Paul's line goes straight to the consul general. That's commitment.'

'Or laziness. Real spies use laundromats and church basements,' said Miro.

'He probably thinks encrypted means whispering on a rooftop.'

'With sunglasses. At night.'

Paul left Egypt forever the following day. He'd received new orders overnight – urgent ones it seemed. Every now and then Amol would run into him unexpectedly, once at a press conference in Islamabad; another time at an NGO briefing in Larnaca, where he'd bought himself a beautiful Ottoman-style house built around a central courtyard, blue tiles on the inside walls.

Camille was a regular visitor, so he said, and Amol was invited to stay whenever and for as long as he ever wanted. The Mukhabarat's inquiries were never mentioned, though Paul made a point of mentioning how he'd spent several days proofreading Amol's book about the nuclear rivalries of Iran, the Arab countries and Israel.

One Larnaca afternoon, just as the sun was setting, he asked a key question, 'How on earth did the Israelis let you into their Dimona complex, allowed you access to their reactor and the outbuildings? Even we Americans can't get access.'

Amol looked away without responding. The answer went back to his Oxford days, to his half-Jewish tutor Michael Howard, regius professor of modern history, with all-powerful connections to Israel. It only required one telephone call from Oxford to Tel Aviv and all the Israeli doors had opened. He wasn't going to share that information with Paul, but made sure he thanked him profusely for his help with the proofreading.

Back in Cairo, Miro came to his house again, this time with beer and a copy of *The Brothers Karamazov* in Cyrillic. 'Dostoevsky is like *rakija*,' he declared. 'Too strong for children. But very good for nightmares.'

They sat on the balcony as the muezzin's call drifted across the river.

'You know,' Miro said, lighting another cigarette, 'the Americans think journalists are like bees. They land everywhere. Spread things. Sometimes sting.'

'And you?'

'I'm the beekeeper. I watch the hive.' He smiled without warmth.

Amol wondered what that made him up to be – the drone or the sting. Maybe just the honey. The sweet bait everyone circled without ever tasting.

He couldn't know it yet, but sketches like those – tight loops, wires, numbers – would one day return to him in another man's hands. How many children had those diagrams already buried? The sweet bait had a blast radius.

A few days later, Amol was invited to a dinner hosted by the Indian ambassador, Ashok Chabra, at his elegant residence in Zamalek. That particular evening was intimate – just a dozen guests seated under the terrace pergola. The night air was cool, carrying the faint rustle of bougainvillea leaves and the soft murmur of conversation drifting from the shaded pergola. Somewhere, the low thrum of an oud played a melancholy tune, threading through the clink of glass and laughter. There was biryani and aubergine stew, and a long conversation about Mahmoud Darwish's poems. It was there, among slow laughter and murmured lines from al-Ma'arri, that Amol first met Theo.

Theo's presence was understated but distinct. He quoted a line from Labīd, with the kind of care only non-native speakers give to sacred texts. When the ambassador smiled in approval, Theo merely shrugged and said, 'I've had good teachers.'

Chabra, a seasoned foreign service professional known for his polished mahogany voice and discreet love of Urdu couplets and Arabic verse, had hosted such evenings before. Though he outranked most diplomats in Cairo, he was neither pompous nor remote. It was well known that he and Theo, despite representing different nations and very different systems, shared a quiet bond over language and literature.

Amol had heard stories of the evenings Chabra hosted aboard the Indian Embassy felucca – a faded, elegant craft that drifted up and down the Nile under soft lantern light, its cushions worn smooth by diplomats, poets and spies alike. Theo and Maggie, his wife, had been frequent guests on those nights, sipping jasmine tea and discussing pre-Islamic poetry as the city blurred into river.

Privately, the British Embassy set ridiculed Theo as a throwback, calling him 'Lawrence of Arabia Lite' or sometimes 'Captain Shakespear without the poetry'. His colleagues would smirk behind their gin glasses, whispering how he took his Catholicism too seriously – a 'choirboy from Newcastle' more loyal to Rome than Whitehall. Yet, here he was, effortlessly conversing with Chabra, oblivious or indifferent to the whispers trailing him from embassy corridors.

Embassy mockery seemed suddenly small and jealous.

Amol sat across from him, studying the quiet intensity behind the politeness. There was something about the way Theo watched a room – as if recording and categorizing, weighing words not just for content but for intent. When they were introduced, Theo said simply, 'I've read your pieces. You have an ear for the world.'

Weeks passed. Later, they met again at a rooftop falconry evening hosted by the British at the Gezira Club. That's where Amol saw the other side of him. It deepened the impression and, perhaps, the illusion of friendship.

Tall, rangy, with a face like a geography teacher and the tan of a colonial ghost, Theo introduced himself through his falcon Marigold, a saker. As Theo held Marigold, Amol noticed his left wrist and hand – marked with tiny scars and fresh scratches from talon and beak. They spoke of hours spent patiently training the falcon, enduring quiet wounds in pursuit of trust. It was a quiet rebuke to those embassy voices that dismissed him as pretentious or affected.

Real commitment, Amol realized, always left marks.

His voice was soft, almost apologetic, and his handshake firm but fleeting. He'd spent years in postings across the Gulf, most recently Amman and Muscat, before Cairo. There was a quiet authority about him, the kind that came from having read too much and spoken too little.

His wife Maggie, a former secretary at the British Embassy in Abu Dhabi, stood beside him with a tray of mint tea, her manner warm and efficient. She had met Theo over visa paperwork, and the story of their whirlwind courtship had become something of a joke in embassy circles. Their two children, Philip and Emmie, chased each other barefoot along the rooftop tiles, their laughter mingling with the distant hum of traffic and the occasional squawk from the falcon's perch. Theo watched them with a faint smile that didn't quite reach his eyes.

Later, Theo invited Amol to the Nile Delta.

They left at dawn in Theo's dented Land Rover, winding through sugarcane and sand, passing roadside tea stalls and kids on donkeys. The highway ran east of Alexandria, tapering into rougher tracks, then gravel, then nothing but shifting desert scrub.

After several hours, they reached a Bedouin encampment nestled at the edge of a dry *wadi* (riverbed), its low black tents held down by rope and stone. The men greeted Theo with cautious nods. One elder stepped forward, lean and weathered, his *keffiyeh* a faded crimson. He and Theo clasped hands with slow deliberation. They began to speak in classical Arabic – Fusha – with a fluency that surprised Amol.

The Bedouin Arabic sounded like music: formal, poetic, from another century. Theo responded in kind, careful and precise, his pronunciation shaped by years in the Gulf.

Amol was struck by Theo's fluency, but there was something else too, an intensity behind the way he listened. Not just to language, but to hierarchy. As if every sentence had a subtext he was quietly filing away. Later, Amol learnt that Theo had spent extended periods among the tribes while stationed in Oman and southern Jordan. What he hadn't known was that Theo's father had been a headmaster in Durham, a Latinist and lover of maps.

Theo had grown up surrounded by books and atlases, raised on Pliny and Ibn Battuta, encouraged to memorize both the declensions of verbs and the names of deserts. It was his father who had instilled in him a fascination for old trade routes and tribal structures. When Theo had joined SIS, it hadn't been out of ambition but inheritance – a boy shaped by maps, who chose to walk the margins between them.

The elder with the crimson keffiyeh was named Sheikh Khalaf. He welcomed Theo like a distant cousin, and the younger men followed his lead. Khalaf explained, through Theo, that his family had once traded camels across the Sinai and watched the British retreat after Suez. He had no illusions about governments, but had respect for men who kept their word. Amol sensed quickly that Theo had earned that respect years ago and never spent it cheaply.

Falcons were brought out and uncapped – regal, sharp-eyed creatures with hoods of dyed leather and bells at their talons. Theo's Marigold perched calmly on his gloved hand, her feathers trembling slightly in the breeze. The tribesmen whistled, called commands Amol barely understood and released the birds into the sky.

Marigold soared upwards in great spirals, followed by two other sakers. Theo's eyes tracked her calmly, while Amol watched the

Bedouin with growing admiration. Their language was measured, their silences intentional. These were not people easily impressed.

Theo sat cross-legged in the sand as the falcons returned to the lure. Amol noticed how naturally he fit into the rhythm of the gathering – observing, responding, listening more than he spoke. It was a far cry from embassy cocktails and diplomatic receptions.

As late afternoon light warmed the encampment, the men brought out wide platters and mats. Theo gestured for Amol to sit beside him, instinctively making the sign of the cross before joining in. Dishes appeared: grilled lamb kebabs rich with cumin and garlic, mountains of rice flecked with saffron and pine nuts, fresh khubz torn by hand and passed around with murmurs of 'bismillah'. They ate communally, fingers deft and practiced. Amol followed Theo's lead, folding lamb into flatbread and scooping rice with his right hand. The food was exquisite – smoky, tender, spiced in ways that reminded him of Delhi.

The afternoon slipped into early evening as the whisper of sand shifted under emerging stars. The rough wool of the tents brushed against his skin, and the smoky scent of burning resin hung heavy in the air as faint Bedouin songs floated on the wind.

Children giggled behind a tent, a kettle hissed over the fire and one of the elders recited a line of Nabati poetry that made the others laugh softly. Theo translated: 'A falcon does not fly towards a storm, but rides the wind that carries it home.'

As Theo conversed in flawless classical Arabic, Amol recalled another cruel jibe from a junior diplomat, 'Theo's Arabic is better than his English; that's why he never makes sense at meetings.' Listening now, Amol saw clearly – perhaps for the first time – what Theo's embassy colleagues refused to acknowledge: there was a genuine, unpretentious poetry in Theo's careful speech, an honesty his detractors couldn't or wouldn't grasp.

After the meal, strong cardamom coffee was poured into tiny cups. Amol felt the wind shift slightly, a whisper of cooler air rolling down from the high desert ridges. The sun lowered itself behind a rust-coloured hill.

Theo turned to him and said, quietly, 'This is the only diplomacy that matters.'

But what Amol didn't grasp then, what only came into focus much later, was that Theo wasn't just a guest, or even a trusted friend of the tribe. He was studying them. Not with malice. With method. Each exchange, each turn of phrase, the seating arrangement at lunch, the direction the herders moved their camels at dawn – Theo registered it all. Who deferred to whom. Which sons led. Where the rifles were stored. The routes they used to fetch water. The gaps in their camp's perimeter.

To Amol, the day had felt sacred. To Theo, it was data. Observation dressed as intimacy. And every detail found its way – quietly, faithfully – back to Whitehall. Sometimes through coded memos. Sometimes through direct channels, passed to the Americans, shared with the Israelis. Preparation disguised as peace.

Amol didn't see it. Not then.

His presence, he realized much later, had been part of the camouflage. A journalist's notebook was a convenient cover. It made the whole thing look like reporting. What he thought was kinship had been cover. He hadn't been invited; he'd been deployed. Theo wasn't there to learn the tribe's poetry. He was there to know where they would run when the next war came.

Amol didn't speak. He was still chewing on the poetry, the scent of roasted lamb, the way the falcons had risen into nothingness. On the drive back, headlights picking out jackals and thorn brush, Theo said almost absently, 'You ever think about nuclear weapons?'

'Most people try not to.'

'You studied them. Oxford. India's programme. Raja Ramanna.'

Amol tensed 'That was a while ago. He was India's chief nuclear scientist but he was a friend of my grandfather.'

'And Ramanna introduced you to Fawzi Khalil?'

'Yes.'

'He showed you Inchas?'

'I saw the reactor. From the viewing platform.'

'You gazed into the core?'

'It looked like a swimming pool filled with fire.'

Theo said nothing. Marigold slept in her travel box behind them. The rest of the ride back was silent. Yet, something about the silence lingered – and in it, Amol heard a sentence Theo hadn't said but somehow still conveyed: 'You were never a child.'

He closed his eyes and returned to Delhi.

Twelve years old Hiding under a rattan table at one of his grandfather's salons. Whisky glasses clinking above his head. Douglas Keir's voice – dry, knowing – cutting through the evening heat.

'You must learn to listen, young man. Not just to what is said. But what is not said.'

Keir had given him books – Malleson, Mountbatten, Maugham. Maps of Central Asia. Oblique advice about observing power.

Later, in London, Sean Gallagher had done the same – assigning him to Tehran, Algeria, Istanbul. Compliments from strange quarters. Invitations that felt too strategic to be accidental.

The signs had always been there.

Delhi. London. Now Cairo.

Three cities. One line.

They hadn't discovered him. They'd been waiting.

The postings, the praise, the invitations, they weren't accidents. They were breadcrumbs. And now, in Cairo, he was standing at the door they had built for him.

Back in Cairo, Sonya gave him an envelope. 'No return address,' she said. 'Smells like glue.'

Inside: a photo of him and Miro on the balcony. Taken from across the street. He didn't speak for a long time.

Miro dropped by uninvited.

'You ever think we are just characters in someone else's story?' he asked, cracking open a beer. 'And that someone else is laughing?'

He didn't stay long.

Later that month, Amol met Theo at the Gezira Club. Children played tennis nearby. Theo had arrived early, choosing a chair under the jacaranda shade. Amol joined him without a word.

'You're wasted on newspapers,' Theo said.

'I like being wasted.'

'You're comfortable in a lot of worlds. That's rare.' There was silence.

'You remember those Delhi parties?' Theo asked.

Amol froze. 'What about them?'

'We were watching then too. Keir sent word. He thought you were promising.'

'I was a boy.'

'No,' Theo said quietly. 'You were never a boy.'

The words settled like dust. Not new, just finally spoken aloud. A line he'd carried since the desert, now given shape.

That night, Amol sat on the balcony with a glass of Egyptian-made Omar Khayyam, watching the city blur. The memory of the Delta still lingered – the falcons, the poetry, the scent of grilled lamb. It had been the most human encounter he'd had in months, maybe years.

And so, the following morning, he wrote.

He changed Theo's name, altered a few identifying details and put together a story. It wasn't exposé; it was tribute. A careful evocation of a moment, a gathering, a man who lived in the seams of diplomacy. Still, Amol knew it was a risk. But the story demanded to be told. As a courtesy, he printed a draft and slipped it under Theo's front door with a short note: 'Let me know if you're happy with it.'

An hour later, Theo turned up at Amol's flat, eyes blazing. But for a split second, before his anger flared, Theo's gaze softened, a flicker of regret crossing his eyes as if part of him wished things could have been different. It vanished almost instantly, swallowed by the weight of duty and betrayal.

'You bastard,' he said, voice low and shaking with fury. 'How dare you. After all the courtesy and kindness we showed you.'

Amol opened his mouth to explain, but Theo cut him off.

'You don't get it. You think changing names makes it safe? This isn't fiction. You crossed a line.'

Amol's throat dried. 'I thought you'd understand. That I was honouring the moment. It wasn't about you, it was about the world you showed me.'

Theo's laugh was short and bitter. 'The world I showed you isn't yours to narrate.'

He turned and began walking out. At the door, he paused. 'You think your peace-talk coverage makes you valuable. It makes you visible. There's a difference. Be careful what you illuminate. Some shadows serve a purpose.'

A sickening realization settled over Amol. In trying to capture Theo's essence, he had unknowingly validated every shallow, mocking barb from Theo's colleagues. His attempt to honour Theo now felt indistinguishable from the embassy gossipers' sneers – just more elegantly packaged. 'Catholic choirboy,' they'd whispered. 'Pretentious explorer.' Had he, in writing about Theo, inadvertently become their ally rather than Theo's friend?

What cut deepest wasn't the shock, it was the knowledge that even in the desert, under stars, even among stories half-traded for tea, the game had still been on. And Amol had played it blind. It wasn't the anger that gutted him – it was the finality. Like watching a bridge, that had once felt like home, burn.

Amol stood frozen in the silence. The paper was still in Theo's hand. The Americans think journalists are bees. But Cairo wasn't the hive. Amol was. And the honey wasn't information. It was trust.

The fallout was swift. Somewhere, Amol suspected, notes were being taken. Not just by embassy staff or the Mukhabarat, but by others, those who operated in the cracks between postings, the watchers of watchers. He didn't know their names, only that they existed.

Files were being built; patterns logged. The city buzzed around him, a hive full of watchers and stingers. And somehow, he was both.

One day, perhaps, someone would step forward and speak as if they had known him all along.

He would later come to know that man as Dexter.

Theo didn't return calls. Nor did Maggie, though Amol left a carefully worded apology in an envelope at the front gate of their apartment. The next day, Amol's invitation to the British Embassy's National Day reception was rescinded. Without explanation.

Two weeks later, his regular lunch companions at the Press Syndicate had thinned out. Conversations now ended as he approached. A few offered forced smiles, but most avoided eye contact.

A fixer he relied on in Alexandria stopped returning his calls. One of his submitted pieces on Nile water rights was quietly pulled from the paper. No explanation, just silence.

Even Miro grew quieter, watching him with a more appraising gaze. 'You broke something,' he said one night over rakija. 'Not just with Theo. With all of us.'

'I told the truth.'

'No,' Miro said. 'You told a story. That's not always the same.'

'Funny thing,' Miro said, swirling his *arak*. 'You remember that Kurdish contact? Word is there was some business on a Greek island – a job gone wrong, maybe. No one seems to know who pulled the strings.

Amol didn't flinch, but his jaw tightened. He couldn't know it yet, but the words would come back to him later.

He did remember. Not just the man exactly, but the story and how its warnings had sounded too theatrical at the time and now echoed everywhere.

Miro noticed. 'Don't look so surprised. Cairo talks. Embassy walls are thinner than you think.'

'Rumour is he turned up in Thessaloniki. UN escort. Then vanished. But not vanished – *vanished*, if you follow.'

'You're saying he's alive?'

'I'm saying someone's keeping him safe. That's not nothing.' Miro exhaled smoke. 'Just be careful. Some ghosts are protected. Some are radioactive.'

Amol nodded, but a different realization was surfacing. There was a pattern, he realized – Theo, Miro, each fluent in a different grammar of threat. And he, Amol, had become the common noun.

The variable that everyone studied, manipulated, measured against silence or smoke.

He tried to carry on as usual. Filed pieces about water scarcity in Upper Egypt. Wrote a column on Soviet–Egyptian technical cooperation. Attended briefings at the American University. But the unspoken tension weighed heavier each day.

One morning, Sonya walked in and laid a note on his desk. 'From Theo,' she said. 'Delivered by hand.'

It read:

I'm not angry anymore. But I am done. You won't see me again.

– T.

Amol folded the note carefully, then glanced up. A shadow detached itself from the alleyway across the street, pausing just long enough to catch his eye before melting into the crowd. The city's endless eyes were watching.

That evening, Amol walked to the Gezira Club alone. Marigold's perch was empty. The falconers were gone. He stood for a long time near the courts where Philip used to play, the sky darkening over the Nile. Then he returned to his flat, poured a glass of arak and read the story one last time.

Sometimes, Amol wondered if they were all just copies – different faces cast from the same mould. Miro was Efimov in sharper clothes. Theo spoke like Keir, if Keir had grown up reading Pliny and flying falcons. And Paul – Paul was a cocktail of Langley's greatest hits, shaken with charm and poured over secrets.

Amol paused, considering his own role. Journalist or spy? Sometimes it was hard to tell which mask he wore. Different flags, same game.

It was a beautiful piece. Careful. Thoughtful. Honest.

And it had cost him everything.

Maybe Cairo had never been the hive. Maybe he hadn't been the observer at all. He'd been the lure – the one everyone circled, trusted and used. The honey in the trap. The hive buzzed on, with or without him. Cairo didn't care what you thought you were – friend, reporter, spy. So long as you came close enough to taste the honey – and leave a little blood behind.

Years later, in Amman, they crossed paths again. Amol was there covering Syrian refugee negotiations. The Sheraton was full of suits and whispers. When he checked into his room, the receptionist hesitated, then handed him the key with a note of polite urgency.

'We've been instructed to notify Mr Rowan,' she said.

Rowan – Theo.

That night, a plainclothes embassy guard was posted outside Amol's hotel room. He opened the door once to ask why, and the man simply said, 'Orders.'

The next morning, Theo appeared at breakfast, already seated at a table near the windows, reading a Jordanian broadsheet. He didn't look up as Amol approached. Didn't smile.

'Batty,' he said, not lifting his eyes. 'Still writing fairy tales?'

Amol sat down. 'Good to see you too.'

Theo folded the paper. His hair was greyer now, the tan deeper, but the eyes had the same cold clarity. 'You think what you did in Cairo was noble. It wasn't. It was theft, a personal insult.'

'I changed your name. I honoured the experience.'

'No,' Theo snapped, voice sharp. 'You made it about you. About your enlightenment. Your transformation. That day, that place, that trust – it wasn't yours to mine. We let you in because we thought you could handle nuance. Turns out, you're just another romantic with a deadline.'

Theo leaned back, eyes narrowed. 'You know what hurt most? You gave them ammunition.' He shook his head slowly, a bitter edge to his voice. 'All those snide little jokes in Cairo – Shakespear, Lawrence, choirboy – I'd lived through it for years. But you, Amol, you wrote their final punchline. And you never even realized it.'

Amol said nothing. There was no winning this.

Theo stood, tossing a few dinars on the table. 'Enjoy Amman. And the guard stays. Just a precaution. You're not as invisible as you think.'

He left without another word.

Later, as Amol returned to his room, the embassy man nodded silently. The line had never been repaired. Only buried deeper. And Amol, once the buzzing observer, now felt like a drone cut off from the hive.

9

Endless Fighting

Spring 1980, Beirut

After Cairo, Beirut felt like exile – or promotion, depending on who was speaking. No one said it outright, but the posting came too quickly after Theo's silence. Amol wasn't sure if it was a reward for his access or a way of burying him deeper.

He didn't ask. The paper framed it as natural progression: a veteran of South Asia and the Levant reassigned to the region's next crucible. He accepted without protest. Beirut, at least, offered work – real work. A city boiling with factions and stories, where neutrality was both liability and currency.

He packed quickly and didn't say goodbye.

Amol arrived in Beirut on a grey morning thick with mist and static. The Middle East Airlines' Boeing landing on a runway that seemed to stretch into the sea. Even the windows of the airport shuttles were fogged, and through the smears he glimpsed a fractured skyline – crumbling towers, cranes frozen mid-build, the old Holiday Inn riddled with bullet holes.

There was no welcome, no customs queue, just a clip boarded man calling his name, then a battered Peugeot to ferry him through the city's wreckage. Amol pressed his face to the window and tried to read the city like a source – its contradictions laid bare in torn posters, tangled wires, flags in every direction. Beirut was not one city but five, coexisting by force and fear.

He was to be based, nominally, at the Commodore Hotel in Hamra – journalist haven, bar with a whisky shelf like a war wound – but in practice, he'd move between that and the Hotel Alexandre in the Christian-held east.

Each crossing of the Green Line, through sniper alley, was a negotiation with death. It was one of the most terrifying roads in the world – an exposed stretch near the Beirut Museum where you took your life in your hands with every step. The strip between the two worlds was lined with burned-out cars and sandbags, their shattered windshields and broken mirrors scattering fragments of sunlight onto the cracked pavement.

You had to dart from doorway to doorway, zigzagging between the tall buildings like a hunted animal, hoping the sharpshooters on the rooftops had missed you. Even at night, those bastards amused themselves by targeting anything that moved. It didn't matter if it was a rabbit or a human. What mattered was the accuracy of the hit and the squelch of blood. The alley was sport to them, and terror to everyone else.

Sometimes, he crossed on foot, holding his notebook in one hand and a pack of Marlboros in the other, the closest thing to neutral credentials.

Beirut in 1980 was already ablaze with tension. The Israeli Defence Forces were gathering along the southern border. The Palestine Liberation Organization (PLO) dug in across the city, ran their own neighbourhoods. Christian militias held the east. Syrian tanks lurked in the hills.

Every journalist spoke of escalation in the passive voice, as if war were a weather system. Amol had seen war before, but this was something else: a city with too many fronts and no rear. His job was to cover it all.

Amol interviewed PLO commanders in alleyways thick with graffiti and cordite. One of the longest was a tense sit-down with Yasser Arafat in a fortified office near Sabra. The interview had barely begun when the building shook. Israeli jets screamed overhead, followed by the boom of impact. Plaster rained from the ceiling. Shards of glass tinkled to the floor like shattered stars. The lights died.

Amol was thrown to the ground. As he lay there, chest tight and breath shallow, the dust settled over him felt like the weight of every story he'd yet to tell. His hands trembled slightly as he reached for his notebook, the distance between witnessing and surviving razor-thin.

When he staggered to his feet, coughing through dust, he saw Arafat being helped out by aides, still calm, still issuing instructions. As they emerged into the rubble-strewn corridor, Arafat turned briefly to Amol and hissed through clenched teeth, 'See? See? This is what they do, the Israelis. See for yourself – and they claim they want peace. Actually, they are the real killers.'

One of the other journalists there – Lally Weymouth, daughter of the *Washington Post*'s owner – had blood on her cheek from flying glass. They all escaped. Later, Arafat would joke that it meant the Israelis were listening.

George Habash, head of the PFLP (Popular Front for the Liberation of Palestine) and one of the more austere Palestinian ideologues, was careful and cold, full of conviction but wary of exposure. 'Every step we take,' he told Amol, 'they track. We do not fear death, but we will not deliver it to them gift-wrapped through careless mouths.'

Walid Jumblatt of the Druze was equally guarded – thin, impeccably polite, with bulging eyes that gave him the look of a startled saint, or perhaps someone struggling with thyroid problems. Slippery as a diplomat, but united in hatred of Israel.

Amol felt the room's temperature drop as words turned to implications. His throat closed, and for a moment, the journalist inside him wavered beneath the weight of what he was being asked to witness and become. Jumblatt's English was flawless, his tone always measured, almost apologetic, as if each sentence were being edited in real-time.

'They offer promises with one hand and cluster bombs with the other,' he said, fingers tapping the armrest. 'The Americans fund them, the French pretend not to see and we are expected to be grateful when we are not yet dead.'

Amol pressed him gently on Syria, and Jumblatt leaned forward, lowering his voice. 'Syria is a knife you must learn to dance with. Too close and it opens your veins. Too far and they slit your throat anyway. We need them. But we never forget they're watching.' He smiled faintly, eyes widening further. 'I say this to you, but deny it tomorrow. That's how we survive.'

Ahmed Jibril of the PFLP – General Command (GC) was a different story. Deadlier. Harder to reach. Amol finally met him in a concrete bunker outside the city, led blindfolded the last 100 metres. Jibril sat behind a desk cluttered with radio parts, flanked by two silent men with rifles.

'Talk is distraction,' Jibril said flatly, eyes unreadable. 'We act. Others write. That is the difference.'

He granted Amol exactly ten minutes. No photographs. No recorder. Just a notepad and nerves. When Amol asked about the future of Lebanon, Jibril smirked.

'There is no Lebanon,' he said. 'Only territory not yet liberated.'

It was the Maronite Christians who stood apart – Bashir and Amine Gemayel. Notional presidents of Lebanon, who smiled for cameras but ruled like kings in a crumbling palace.

In 1982, Amol had arranged an interview with Bashir, but a few weeks before it was to take place, Bashir was killed in a bombing at the Phalange headquarters. The appointment shifted to his brother Amine, whose smile was polite and practiced, but who gave nothing away.

'Lebanon's future,' Amine said blandly, 'is for the Lebanese to determine.' He refused to discuss the Israelis, though everyone knew his slain brother had signed a secret accord with them. Amol left the meeting with pages of notes and no usable quote. Their alliances were local, their rhetoric sharp and their disdain for the Palestinians obvious.

Amol drank thick coffee in East Beirut with Lebanese Forces officers who spoke of survival and betrayal in the same breath. He reported on Israeli bombardments from rooftops where shells had landed minutes before.

Once, while standing on the rooftop of the Hotel Alexandre, he noticed a flicker of movement nearby. An Israeli Army Major, positioned two rooftops over, was calmly scanning the city through high-powered binoculars. Amol realized he was watching real-time targeting unfold – the officer muttering into a radio, then seconds later, the shriek of jets and the crump of impact on the PLO-held western side of the city.

Amol stayed still, notebook in hand, heart pounding. For a moment, the Major glanced his way. They held each other's gaze across the war-split skyline – two men doing their jobs in radically different ways, neither quite blinking.

Amol stepped back slowly, careful not to appear startled. The moment unsettled him in ways that surprised him. Not because he feared being targeted – he was used to danger – but because of the calm efficiency he saw in the Major's eyes.

It was a reminder that this was no chaos; it was control. Somewhere, someone was watching. Calculating. Delivering death with professional detachment.

He went downstairs and filed nothing. What was there to say? He felt like he had been caught peeking behind the curtain at a magic show, and what he saw wasn't illusion – it was engineering. The war wasn't a storm. It was architecture. He filed stories about civilians who spoke five languages and trusted no one.

When the invasion began – Operation Peace for Galilee, they called it – he was in West Beirut. Israeli tanks rolled in from the south, cutting through Lebanese defences like paper.

The siege began in June 1982. For weeks, the city shook with artillery. Buildings collapsed like bad metaphors. At the Commodore, they drank whisky and played cards under candlelight, filing copy from a single phone line that never stopped ringing.

In late August, under international pressure, the PLO began evacuating. It was around this time that he met Layla.

Amol stood on the Corniche and watched as flatbed trucks filled with fighters wound their way to the port. He made his way down to the harbour, where a chaotic procession was unfolding, fighters clutching rifles and duffel bags, women in hijabs weeping beside crates of equipment, children with solemn eyes.

Amid the crowd, he glimpsed Yasser Arafat – Abu Amar, his nom de guerre – at a distance, standing near the gangplank of a ship. The trademark keffiyeh, the fatigues, the raised hand in farewell. Beside him was Khalil al-Wazir (Abu Jihad), his second in command, giving orders calmly, clipboard in hand. Years later, Abu Jihad would be assassinated by Mossad in Tunis, but now he looked like the steadiest man on deck.

As the ships pulled away, a mournful silence settled. Layla, the Lebanese French journalist who had been working beside him through the final days of the siege, stood next to Amol, her hand slipping into his without a word. She was fluent in both the street politics of West Beirut and the cadences of French philosophy, filing dispatches in two languages and moving between factions with a quiet confidence that disarmed even the most hardened fighters. They had shared checkpoints, cigarettes and silence – more intimacy than declarations.

They said nothing – there was nothing to say. The silence wasn't just political. It was personal. As Arafat disappeared down the ship's gangway, Amol felt a knot form in his throat. Layla squeezed his hand. The Israelis began their withdrawal soon after.

Then came Sabra and Shatila. These were the refugee camps packed with Palestinians who fled their homes after the creation of the state of Israel and challenged the authority of the Maronite Christians who held the reins of power in Lebanon.

It started with rumours. Then radio silence. Then survivors who fought back against the Maronite militias sent in to finish them off. Indifferent Israelis looked away as the militias got on with their ruthless work. Few were spared. Amol got in late – too late. The massacre had already run its course by the time he arrived.

Layla came with him, refusing to stay behind. They walked together through streets soaked in blood, past bodies stacked in alleys, into homes where the air was thick with rot and silence. She didn't flinch. He felt her fingers tighten around his own as they stepped over rubble and glass.

A dog sniffed at a child's slipper. A man stood against a wall, keening without words.

He photographed what he could. Interviewed dazed survivors. Filed a story that got picked up across Europe. It brought condemnation from capitals and caution from his editors. He didn't care. The truth was the only thing he had left that felt uncorrupted.

This wasn't so different from what a man like Sedo would one day describe. The logic of the bomb, the death of the village, the silence that followed.

Each picture he took felt like a betrayal and a duty intertwined. His chest tightened, the familiar ache pressing deep – a silent reminder that some stories were too heavy even to carry alone.

April 1983

It was a bright morning, the American Embassy was bombed. Amol was meeting a fixer near the Corniche. The blast knocked him off his feet. When he stood – dazed, blood trailing from one ear – he saw the embassy façade had been peeled open like fruit. Sixty-three people were dead. Among them: Marines, CIA officers, Lebanese staff.

The scene was chaos – papers in the wind, fire raging in the stairwells, a woman screaming into a crushed phone.

A few months later, the French were hit.

On 23 October 1983, the same day a suicide bomber drove into the US Marine barracks near the airport, another exploded outside the French paratroopers' base in Ramlet al-Baida. Fifty-eight French soldiers died in the Drakkar building.

Amol arrived within hours. The roof had collapsed inwards. Helmets and rifles lay scattered in the dust. A French sergeant wept openly on the curb. It was the worst loss for the French military since Algeria.

The Multinational Force began to pull back. Westerners were now targets. There were whispers that a new group was rising – Hezbollah, or something like it. Hostages began disappearing. Journalists, aid workers, diplomats. Some turned up. Some didn't.

There was a pattern to it. Hostages were snatched off the streets of Beirut and its surrounding areas – journalists abducted at gunpoint, aid workers pulled from cars, professors dragged from apartments in the night. Then, after months or years of silence, they would resurface in Damascus, dazed and gaunt, released to a fanfare of Syrian publicity. The Syrians took all the credit – issuing statements, parading their diplomatic prowess.

But everyone in the know understood the choreography. The real deals were done elsewhere, in the shadows, through Tehran or Beirut's southern suburbs. Syria just made sure the cameras were rolling at the end. The West played along, grateful for a clean exit.

The hostages just looked tired. Amol kept the names in a notebook, like a tally. One day, maybe, he would write the story that tied them all together.

He filed what he could, but most of it was trimmed to ribbons in London. Editors preferred clean lines, not the blurred edges of fear and ambiguity that defined Beirut.

Still, he kept notes – names, dates, fragments. Every abduction felt like a rehersal for something larger.

At night, when the shelling paused, he would replay conversations in his head, trying to see what he'd missed. The city spoke in riddles: rumours of new militias, of foreign money, of the shifting hands that fed the war. Each clue felt like a breath drawn underground.

As Amol navigated the crowded Beirut streets, a shadow detached itself from an alleyway, lingering just long enough to catch his eye before vanishing into the crush of pedestrians. He shook his head, brushing off the unease, but the feeling clung like dust.

That was when Lt Colonel Chuck Johnson appeared. He was lean, tanned, with the easy charm of a man who didn't blink twice under pressure. He introduced himself as the British military attaché, a friend of Theo's number two in Cairo. They'd met over drinks at the British residence. Johnson had a way of dropping names and leaning close, like a conspirator.

One evening at the bar, he said, 'You're one of the few who can get through without raising flags.'

Amol raised an eyebrow. 'Get through where?'

'Baalbek.'

Johnson explained, with grave confidence, that a British relief worker had gone missing near Baalbek – last seen two weeks earlier, heading north with a driver. Officially unverifiable. But Johnson thought Amol might be able to find out what had happened.

'You've got the right face for it,' he added, almost amused. 'They don't notice you. Not the way they notice the rest of us.'

Amol didn't think twice. He wasn't in anyone's pocket.

He was simply chasing what might be the biggest story of the year, offered by a source with the polished certainty of a man who'd briefed others first. That's what he did: he listened, he followed, he reported.

The road was dangerous. Syrian checkpoints. Local militias. Amol hired a driver he trusted and left before dawn.

Baalbek was quiet that afternoon. Too quiet. The townspeople were bemused. They had heard no such rumour. A sheikh told him no Westerners had passed through in weeks. The graveyard Johnson mentioned existed, but there were no freshly dug graves. Amol stayed two nights, just in case.

There was nothing. He filed nothing.

When he returned to Beirut, Johnson was gone. 'No such person,' the embassy staff said. 'Must be a misunderstanding. Perhaps you meant someone else.'

Amol checked records. Asked quietly. Called a contact in London.

'No Chuck Johnson here. Never has been.'

He never got an answer. Only a growing certainty that he'd been used – sent north not to verify, but to observe. Measured. Watched. He'd chased a ghost into Hezbollah territory, and only later realized – the story had been about him all along. A test. Or bait.

He pieced it together slowly – the missing man, the phantom officer, the silence that followed. It dawned on him, with a cold clarity, that he hadn't been sent to find anyone. He had been sent to see if the air was breathable. Like a canary lowered into a mine, he was there to measure the danger, not to survive it.

Someone had wanted to know how far a brown-skinned journalist could walk into Hezbollah country before being noticed, stopped or shot. The result, whatever it was, would go neatly into a file somewhere. He felt sick, not with fear but with recognition. He'd been used as an instrument, not as an observer. And worse, he'd volunteered for it.

It wasn't just that Chuck had vanished. It was that he'd never been there to begin with. A man without a file – and Amol had followed him into the mountains. At the embassy, Baalbek was never mentioned. Oversight or intent, it made no difference. Baalbek vanished, like the man who sent him.

The new force taking shape in the south didn't fly the faded flags of Arab nationalism. Hezbollah moved in silence, wrapped in Qur'anic rhetoric and revolutionary zeal. Where the PLO had negotiated, Hezbollah abducted. Where the Leftists had issued manifestos, they issued ultimatums. It wasn't ideology – it was leverage.

Iran's long reach, filtered through Lebanon's fractured terrain. They weren't pro-PLO. They saw the old guard as compromised. This was something colder. More calculated. And far harder to trace. Later, Johnson's words came back to him. *You're one of the few who can get through without raising flags.*

He understood, then, what Johnson had really meant. Not that they trusted him. Not that he was part of anything. But that he was invisible. His skin, his face, his ease with language – these let him slip through doors others couldn't. Not because he was accepted. Because he was overlooked.

They had seen it. And they had watched.

The Commodore Hotel was unlike any other he had known. A kind of war-weary sanctuary for the global press corps, it was a place where deadlines collided with detonations.

Owner Youseff Nazzal ran the hotel like a patron of the press – he loved the reporters, kept the bar stocked and the phones working, and made it his mission to ensure the Commodore never lost its lifeline to the outside world, no matter the shelling.

The hotel was a virtual who's who of foreign correspondents – veterans from *The Times*, *The Post*, *Le Monde*, *Der Spiegel* – each clutching their notes, their grudges and their fifth drink of the night. Cracked mirrors hung crookedly in the lobby, catching distorted reflections of reporters whose faces seemed as fractured as the city outside

And then there was the parrot. A giant green Amazon parrot in a battered cage near the entrance, its feathers flashing like a tropical flag. It belonged to a British stringer named Chris Drake, who'd arrived with two suitcases and left years later for Cyprus, where he eventually died. The parrot outlived him. It shouted obscenities at anyone who passed, switching languages mid-sentence. 'Wanker!' it would squawk, then add brightly, 'Welcome! Goodbye!' – a chaotic, feathery greeter to a world that had long since abandoned rules.

At the Commodore, Amol stopped drinking. But around him, life pulsed in erratic bursts – stories filed over scotch, alliances formed over chess, love affairs begun and ended in the space of a week. There were rooms where typewriters clattered through the night, and others where voices dropped to whispers behind closed doors. Youseff Nazzal saw it all with a smile and a shrug, his loyalty not to any nation but to the mad fraternity of war correspondents.

Some journalists arrived shattered and found themselves again in the Commodore's chaos. Others unravelled slowly. Amol watched a French photographer fall in love with a Danish stringer one week, only to catch her weeping in the corridor the next.

Always crowded, the hotel lobby was filled with stringers, drunks, diplomats. He nodded to the manager as he prepared to cross from West to East Beirut, remembering Sedo and how easily he moved between worlds, leaving chaos behind like footprints in the sand.

Amol had learnt to cross Beirut with caution – carefully neutral, always watching. But one day he would meet a man who moved through places like this as if the world were porous, borderless. He made danger look ordinary. It struck him even then that people like that weren't merely elusive; they were protected. Shielded by the same systems that claimed to hunt them. And still, Amol couldn't decide whether that made them tragic or terrifying.

An American correspondent proposed marriage in the bar and took it back by breakfast. Beirut was merciless like that – compressed time, accelerated emotions. As one veteran put it, 'A week here is like a year anywhere else.'

One night, he and a few other reporters were nursing beers at a low-slung bar near Hamra, trading gossip and jokes with a group of sharp-eyed local girls – students, activists, daughters of diplomats or nobody at all. There was laughter, some flirtation, a moment of fragile reprieve.

Then the Saudi walked in. Unexpectedly.

Heavyset, alone, sweating through his starched thobe. He didn't speak. Just chose a table near the back, opened a soft leather pouch and laid out a fan of 100-dollar bills with the indifference of a man used to buying silence. The shift was instant.

One by one, the girls drifted away. Amol watched it happen like a tide going out. Smiles that had once been for them now sharpened for him. Voices softened. Ankles uncrossed. Within minutes, the Saudi was surrounded – laughing, gesturing, lighting cigarettes, a circle of warmth and beauty forming around his chair.

Amol didn't feel anger. Not exactly. Just recognition. Power didn't announce itself. It arrived. In a thobe. With cash. And gravity.

Beirut taught you that. The market wasn't always metaphorical.

Now the city felt colder, more abstract. Layla was the only compensation – her French passport proof of her sensual name, her presence a kind of reprieve from everything Beirut had taken.

There was so much destruction, so many ruins both fresh and ancient, that he couldn't bring himself to even glance at the famous beaches – once the Riviera of the Middle East, now pocked with debris and silence. The thought of skiing in the mountains near Broummana, once a favourite escape for Lebanese elites, felt absurd. What was once paradise now felt like hell – sunlight on rubble, olive trees beside cratered roads, jasmine blooming where children had died.

He remembered something his grandmother had once told him.

Years ago, she and Amol Senior had stopped in Beirut on an Air India flight – first class, of course – en route from London to Geneva, then Beirut and finally Bombay. They had been offered a lavish lunch by a well-placed friend, served in a terrace garden overlooking the sea. 'There were trays of strawberries,' she'd said, laughing softly. 'The biggest I've ever seen. Lebanese strawberries – deep red, wild and perfect.'

Then she'd paused. 'Kim Philby was there. Tried to stroke my knee under the table. Clumsy old goat.'

Amol had laughed at the time. But now the memory struck him differently. Beirut had once been a jewel. The people around that table had known it. And now? Filed fewer stories. Spoke less. The city felt colder, more abstract.

He sometimes thought back to the first time he saw Layla – in a tiny supermarket near the Commodore. He'd backed into her near the cold shelf, muttering an automatic 'sorry'. She turned, smiled – an easy, amused smile – and said, 'So you're English.'

He wasn't sure if it was a question or a judgement. But something about her stopped him cold. Olive-skinned, green-eyed, with cheekbones like sculpture and her dark hair twisted up carelessly – she was striking in a way that lingered. Half Lebanese, half French, she told him later.

Very soon she became the passion of his life. Her scent – jasmine and something he couldn't name – lingered on his clothes, in his bed, in his thoughts. Her long neck begged for kisses. Her body curved with impossible grace beneath linen dresses that clung in the Beirut heat. When they lay together, she whispered things in French and English, soft, unhurried. Sometimes, her voice caught as she said, over and over, 'I love you, I love you, I love you.'

It wasn't just lust. It was beginning to feel like home.

Layla's father lived in Lyon – an academic of some kind, distant but doting in his way. They spoke only occasionally, mostly by letter, though she claimed he still sent her French perfume each birthday. Her mother, by contrast, was ever-present: a divorcee who lived in a faded but elegant three-bedroom apartment in Ras Beirut, just ten minutes from the Commodore.

The building had been grand once – high ceilings, wrought-iron balconies, black-and-white tile in the entrance – but now its façade bore the pockmarks of war, and the lift worked only when it wanted to. Layla brought Amol there often, unannounced but always welcome. Her mother, Imane, was a slender woman with silver streaks in her dark hair, always wrapped in a cashmere shawl no matter the season.

She spoke softly, like someone used to listening before speaking, and greeted Amol as if he'd been expected all along.

The kitchen was small but rich with scent – sumac, parsley, garlic warmed in olive oil. Layla would open a bottle of arak while her mother assembled a spread on the small dining table: stuffed vine leaves, kibbeh, tabbouleh so fresh it made his eyes water, flatbread still warm from the *saj*. There were always olives, always labneh, always something she insisted he try 'just once' and then refilled before he could protest.

Amol sat there often, shoulders unclenching, watching mother and daughter trade remarks in French and Arabic, occasionally turning to include him in English with affectionate laughter. It was the only place in Beirut that felt like it had walls thick enough to keep the war out.

Later, when he and Layla lay together in her room – curtains drawn, jasmine on the windowsill – he'd think of her mother's steady hands, the quiet clatter of plates in the sink, the smell of lemon and mint drifting through the flat. It was a domestic calm that felt impossibly rare in Beirut, like a lullaby on the edge of a battlefield.

As Layla's fingers brushed his, the tension in his chest loosened just enough to remind him there was something beyond the chaos. Her calm presence was a balm, a fragile tether to a world still worth fighting for.

Sometimes, late at night, when the shelling paused and the city exhaled, they read to each other in bed. Amol recited from memory – Yeats, Auden, sometimes Donne – lines that made her smile in the half dark.

'Our two souls therefore, which are one,' he whispered once, brushing her collarbone, 'though I must go, endure not yet a breach, but an expansion.'

Layla would answer in turn, quoting Rumi with her lilting accent: 'The minute I heard my first love story, I started looking for you … Not knowing how blind that was.'

She'd shift closer then, bare legs tangled in his, her breath warm against his neck. 'You were inside me all along,' she whispered.

Other nights, she recited more: 'Don't grieve. Anything you lose comes round in another form.'

Or: 'You were born with wings, why prefer to crawl through life?'

Her favourite, murmured once with her head on his chest as shelling rattled the distant hills: 'Out beyond ideas of wrongdoing and rightdoing, there is a field. I'll meet you there.'

They were mirror images in more ways than either admitted aloud. Both of mixed blood, raised between worlds. Both drawn to words as a way to make sense of fractured histories. Layla had begun filing cultural pieces for a French magazine – interviews with filmmakers, short essays on life in wartime Beirut. Her prose, like her, was elegant but edged. She never called herself a journalist, but Amol saw in her a reflection: someone who could navigate between identities without losing the thread of herself.

Sometimes, after long days under fire or long nights filing in candlelight, she would ask him softly, 'Why do you go into these places, Amol? Why keep chasing the worst of it?'

He never had a simple answer. But once, he told her, 'Because someone should. Because they're always the ones no one listens to.'

She would look at him a long while and say nothing. Just kiss his fingers and press her forehead to his.

Sometimes he wondered what pulled him towards these stories. It wasn't just the thrill or the byline. There was something older, deeper – a kind of stubborn instinct to bear witness, to stand beside those no one else would. He wasn't fearless, not exactly. But he'd never known how to walk away from the underdog.

Back then, there was still a kind of honour in it. A time when journalists were trusted, even respected, for getting close to the fire. He sometimes wondered what had changed – when the act of telling the truth began to look like subversion. He thought sometimes of those who had never come back. Of the Japanese crew killed by a mortar strike in Qana. Of foreign correspondents in Phnom Penh and Santiago who vanished without trace.

Names whispered in newsrooms, framed on press club walls, etched into memory not by their deaths, but by the work they left behind.

He'd met Christopher Dickey once in a Cairo bar – too many whiskies and a shared sense of foreboding. Dickey was younger then, still chasing something unnamed. They talked of bylines and burnouts, of the strange loneliness that came with knowing too much. Amol never forgot it.

There was a time when journalists were considered the Fourth Estate – sentinels of accountability, not collateral. They wore flak jackets, not allegiances. But the lines had blurred. In Beirut, they still drank together, filed from the same payphone, crossed into sniper alleys with notebooks held high. But even then, even here, they were beginning to be seen not just as observers – but as participants.

He didn't know it then, but the whole terrain would shift. Years later, when truth-tellers became fugitives, when figures like Julian Assange were hunted for publishing what governments feared, Amol would think back to Beirut. To typewriters clacking under candlelight. To green parrots swearing in five languages. To a time when bearing witness still felt like a calling – and not a crime.

It was Layla who introduced him to Broummana – took him up the mountainside one weekend to breathe pine-scented air and forget the noise of the capital. The road twisted upwards through groves of cypress and olive, past ruined villas and roadside shrines. The air grew cooler as they climbed, and Amol felt his chest loosen for the first time in weeks.

They stayed in a crumbling guesthouse run by an old Druze couple who served thick coffee on a terrace that overlooked the valley below. In the mornings, the mist rolled in like a veil, curling around the pines. Layla wandered barefoot through the garden, plucking herbs for tea. At night, they wrapped themselves in woollen blankets and listened to the distant thump of artillery echoing up from the coast.

'If we stay here long enough,' she said once, her head resting on his shoulder, 'we could pretend none of it exists. Beirut, the war, the embassies. Just trees and sky and us.' He kissed the top of her head.

'And jasmine.'

'Always jasmine,' she whispered.

One afternoon they walked through the cedars in near silence, her hand in his. The trees were tall and ancient, the forest floor thick with needles and birdsong. At one point, she stopped and looked up into the branches, her face dappled with light.

'Do you think the trees remember all the blood spilled beneath them?' she asked.

He didn't answer right away. Then, quietly, he said, 'I think they carry it. But they keep growing anyway.' She smiled faintly and kept walking.

In Broummana, for a fleeting moment, they lived outside the war. It was a borrowed peace, but it felt real enough to hold onto. They made a striking pair – people turned to look. Amol with his quiet intensity, dark curls and thoughtful eyes; Layla with her perfect skin, green eyes and dancer's grace.

Together, they moved like a couple from a different world, untouched by the headlines they wrote or the carnage they filed. In the cafés and terraces of the mountain town, strangers sometimes mistook them for newlyweds. Layla would smile and roll her eyes when she caught the stares.

'We look too perfect,' she teased once, brushing a crumb from his shirt. 'It makes people suspicious.'

'Let them be,' Amol said. 'They don't know what we carry.'

Years later, whenever the noise returned – gunfire, grief or guilt – it was Broummana he remembered. But that came later. Long before that, there had been Oxford, plenty of flings – girls who threw themselves at him, brief entanglements that vanished with the next tutorial.

In Delhi, there had been talk of arranged marriages, serious suitors presented with genealogies and social standing. But none of it had touched him. This did. Layla did.

He didn't tell her everything. But he told her more than he'd told anyone else. She gave him something more dangerous than truth. She gave him hope.

The night before he left Beirut for good, they made love with a kind of quiet desperation. Her breath was warm in his ear, her body curved perfectly beneath his, every movement etched with finality. After, she lay tangled in the sheets, her hand resting on his chest, fingers drumming lightly against his heartbeat. 'Write me something beautiful,' she whispered.

'Promise me you'll remember it all.'

He didn't answer. He just pulled her closer, burying his face in the slope of her neck, inhaling the perfume she always wore – jasmine, and something darker, deeper. He knew even then he would never forget it.

Beirut, once a puzzle, had become a mirror. And in the reflection, he no longer recognized himself. Amol paused, fingers lightly pressed to his chest. The steady thump beneath his hand was a fragile rhythm against the noise inside his mind. Bearing witness was not just about telling stories, it was about surviving the ones that refused to leave.

10

Love and Death

Spring 1984, Jerusalem

After Beirut, Jerusalem felt almost antiseptic – tidy, watched, eerily calm. From Ben Gurion Airport, the road passed olive groves and checkpoints, then sprouted towers of steel and glass, defiant claims of permanence against the scarred hills.

The light was harder here, thinner and brighter than the Mediterranean haze he'd grown used to. A city on a hill, yes, but also a crucible. Amol arrived with his usual canvas bag – notepads stuffed inside pockets and the residue of Beirut still clinging to his clothes. He wasn't ready for this shift, not really, but the foreign desk had made it clear: the Arab–Israeli story was no longer about siege. It was about peace. Or the performance of it.

His new bylines would carry 'Jerusalem' and sometimes 'Gaza' at the top. Arafat and the PLO were talking, not just fighting. Western diplomats hovered around olive branches like butterflies at a bloom. Amol's reputation from Lebanon – his interviews, his access, his discretion – had made him the obvious choice.

Even the Israelis seemed willing to talk.

Shamir held the premiership with his flinty reserve; Rabin, now defence minister, walked like a soldier. Peres – suave, cerebral – was circling the diplomats and journalists. Amol had already been invited to two press lunches and a discreet, off-the-record conversation on a shaded terrace near the Knesset.

'They say you're the one who got Arafat to whisper like a priest,' Peres had said with a dry smile, offering a glass of mint lemonade. 'Perhaps here, you'll get us to sound like poets.'

Amol smiled, but said nothing.

—

He took a flat in Talpiot, not far from the German Colony – a cream-tiled apartment made of old stone. The cracked tiles and a sliver of balcony were just wide enough for a folding chair and offered a view of the hills beyond Bethlehem.

It was one of a string of identical units, all rented to foreign correspondents: French, American, Italian, Dutch. The sharp tang of burnt coffee drifted faintly from a nearby café, mingling with the scent of old paper and ink.

The hallway smelled of dust and late-night cigarettes, punctuated by the constant clack of typewriters and muffled arguments in Hebrew and Arabic. Morning light caught on the cracked tiles outside his kitchen window, spilling faintly like honey over the hills beyond Bethlehem.

The location was practical, just far enough from the Old City to breathe, but close enough to file quickly. He liked the anonymity of it, the way the other reporters nodded but didn't pry. From his kitchen window, he could just make out the golden cap of the Dome of the Rock in the morning haze, rising like a mirage over a city that never agreed with itself.

Every morning, the muezzin's call tangled with the bells from a nearby church. It was a place layered in worship, war and weary hospitality.

There were other correspondents – some new, some familiar – filing from the King David Hotel or sipping black coffee at the American Colony. The press corps here was better dressed than Beirut, but less brave. Everything was cleaner.

The wounds here were historic, not immediate. But Amol knew better. Blood dries fast on Jerusalem stone. It didn't mean it wasn't still there.

He was to travel to Gaza next week, embedded not with soldiers but with the UN. The Israel Defence Forces (IDF) had opened a narrow corridor for aid and observation. The PLO presence was still underground – formal leadership long exiled to Tunis – but there were whispers of intermediaries, soft-spoken men in threadbare suits who handed out press packets stamped with olive branches and delivered quotes on behalf of a distant Arafat.

In East Jerusalem cafes and Ramallah offices, journalists gathered to parse these half statements like scripture. Something was shifting.

But Amol felt none of the excitement his colleagues did. Not yet. The shadows of Beirut were long. And Layla's silence, since Beirut, heavier than any gunfire.

He opened his old Beirut notebook, idly flipping past torn pages and field dispatches. One leaf, tucked near the back, held a rough pencil sketch – wires, loops, the outline of a child's toy. He didn't know it then, but another man's hand would one day draw the same shapes. Words he had not yet heard seemed to rise from the page: 'Make it sweet. Make it small. They pick it up before they know.'

Amol closed the notebook.

The pages still smelt faintly of engine oil and cigarette ash.

—

The silence broke a week later when Layla arrived.

She came in on her French passport, flying from Beirut to Larnaca, then on to Tel Aviv. The journey was convoluted, half-coded and tense at every stage. But she made it.

She appeared at his doorstep in Talpiot just after dusk, wearing dark glasses and a linen dress, her hair pulled up beneath a scarf. She looked tired, but her smile – when it came – unravelled something in his chest.

Her linen dress carried the faint scent of jasmine and gardenia, soft in the cool evening air.

The rustle of her scarf whispered secrets as it caught the breeze.

'You're late,' he said, not unkindly.

'You're early,' she replied, and kissed him before he could respond.

It was the first of several visits. Between the political gridlocks and overlapping claims to holy land, they carved out pockets of time for themselves. They wandered hand in hand through the Old City, ducking into incense-clouded churches, pausing at the Western Wall, whispering verses beside the mosaics in the Church of the Holy Sepulchre.

One late afternoon, they took a taxi to Bethlehem. The air grew drier as they climbed, the hills rusted gold in the setting sun. Shepherds still moved their flocks across the terraces, though now with radios slung over their shoulders and plastic water bottles clipped to their belts. The checkpoints were quiet. No one asked questions.

The air was thick with the smoky sweetness of burning incense, the crackle of crushed stones underfoot and the distant melody of prayer calls weaving through narrow alleys. Baklava's honeyed aroma mingled with the dusty tang of sunbaked stone, while soft murmurs of Arabic floated like ghosts.

They walked together through Manger Square, past the olive-wood stalls and sweet shops piping out anise and baklava. Then they moved farther east towards the Shepherds' Fields – where the story went that angels once appeared, radiant in the sky, and told the shepherds not to be afraid. The dry hills crunched beneath their feet, dust rising in golden clouds.

Thyme and wild herbs grew stubbornly from cracks in ancient stones, their scent sharp and earthy. Sweet spices – anise, cumin and cinnamon – perfumed the market air, blending with fresh bread and roasted coffee.

They passed into the grounds of the Franciscan Church, a modern structure built over ancient caves. Inside, the walls were cool and pale. Latin inscriptions circled the apse. A single candle burned at the altar. Layla lit one more and whispered something Amol didn't catch.

Outside, they wandered onto the rocky slope, past a crumbling low wall where thyme grew wild in cracks between the stones. The wind picked up as dusk settled. Below them, Bethlehem shimmered in the last of the light – its minarets catching fire, its alleys curling back into shadow.

They sat in silence, backs against a rock, watching the sky turn a deeper blue. And then, just above the hills – faint at first, then steady – a single star pierced the dusk.

Layla pointed. 'Look.'

Amol followed her hand. 'Venus?'

She shook her head. 'No. That's not a planet.'

They said nothing for a while.

'That star,' she said softly, 'must've been brighter back then. To carry so much hope.'

He looked at her, unsure if she meant the Bible story or something else.

'I've never been so close to peace,' she said, 'as I am with you in this city built for war.'

Amol reached for her hand across the rock. Their fingers touched, stayed there, quiet and warm. Later, walking back through the sleeping town, he turned once more to look up. The star was still there.

Sometimes, they said very little. Sometimes, they talked until dawn. About the war. About the stories they didn't file. About what waited on the other side of all this. Once, on a terrace in East Jerusalem, Layla quoted Rumi and Amol responded with Yeats. Her eyes glistened in the candlelight.

The clink of coffee cups on mosaic tables punctuated their conversations, the bitter warmth grounding them amid the city's restless pulse. At night, jasmine scented the open window, mingling with the distant hum of traffic and the call to prayer.

But those moments, like all things in that land, passed like wind through stone.

One early evening, he watched as she lay on her side, reading a battered French novel.

He noticed the way her fingers curled slightly when she turned the page, the way her brow furrowed as she read. It led to a tightening in his chest; affection or fear, he couldn't tell.

Layla's warmth unsettled him. Something in her eyes left him raw, a rawness that, years later, would return on a Greek island, in the voice of a man speaking of dreams and detonation. She caught his gaze and smiled, not asking what he was thinking. That was the danger – she never asked.

She left quietly two mornings later, before dawn. The plane was from Ben Gurion to Larnaca, then on to Paris. She kissed him once in the hallway, her bags already packed, her eyes unreadable.

'Write me,' she said.

'I always do.'

He stood at the door long after the elevator had closed. The flat felt newly hollow. For days, he moved like a sleepwalker – through briefings, wire copy, corridor conversations about ceasefires and confidence-building measures.

He tried to write and couldn't. The clack of his typewriter echoed too loudly in the apartment. Everything he put down felt thin. Jerusalem was not a place that welcomed loneliness. It exaggerated it.

On the fourth morning, a card appeared in his mailbox. Heavy cream stock. No return address. Just five words in looping, deliberate handwriting: *Café Atara. Wednesday. 10 a.m.*

No name. No explanation.

He almost tossed it. But didn't.

Café Atara was a diplomatic outpost disguised as a coffeehouse – mosaic tables, strong Turkish brews and the quiet tension of too many watchers pretending not to watch. Amol arrived early, his notebook in his pocket, unsure whether this was a tip or a trap.

The man at the window table stood as he approached – navy blazer, white shirt, open collar, silver hair combed neatly back. His eyes were pale and assessing.

'You're punctual,' he said.

'I've been trained.'

'Of course you have,' the man said. 'Call me Malkin.'

There was something oddly elegant about him – not slick, not polished, but cultivated. His voice carried the faint cadence of Mitteleuropa, smoothed by years in foreign tongues. His hands were long-fingered, the nails kept clean.

They talked for nearly an hour. Books, mostly. Cities. Amol mentioned Delhi; Malkin replied that he'd been; a long time ago.

'I knew your grandfather,' he added, lightly. 'A remarkable editor. He hosted me for a dinner once. Said spies made the best sources and the worst guests.'

Amol blinked. 'You were a guest?'

Malkin smiled faintly. 'Of a kind.'

Before they parted, Malkin said, 'Would you come to Tel Aviv sometime? For tea. My wife bakes. I paint.'

'Paint?'

'Landscapes. Argentina, mostly. The colours there won't leave me alone.'

That Sunday, Amol drove down the coastal road. The light was sharp, the Mediterranean flat and silver. Malkin's apartment was behind a pale stone wall near Hayarkon Street, shaded by jacaranda trees. Quiet. Sparse. Observant.

Malkin opened the door in a pressed linen shirt and slippers. 'You're on time again.'

Inside, the apartment was cool and neat. On the walls: watercolours. Wide skies, lonely roads, the blue glow of Patagonian glaciers. One showed a man alone on a platform with no train in sight.

'She only lets me hang the quiet ones,' Malkin said. Amol turned to see Roni, silver-haired and linen-clad, watching from the kitchen doorway.

'I made you something,' she said. 'Fruit-and-nut loaf. English cake. In deference to your imperial ancestry.'

Amol laughed. 'We don't deserve such mercy.'

They drank Darjeeling from white porcelain cups. On the record player, a tango turned slowly, the needle popping softly like distant gunfire. The flat smelt faintly of cardamom and old paper.

Amol noticed a shelf lined with books in four languages. On it sat a carved wooden Mate Gourd and a black-and-white photograph of Malkin with another man – faces close, almost blurred by time. Both bare headed. One had a cigarette, the other a look Amol couldn't place.

In the background, a cluster of sombreros.

'Argentine?' he asked, without knowing why.

Malkin nodded. 'Everyone passes through. Some stay longer than they should.'

They talked for hours, mostly in ellipses. Malkin asked about Amol's grandfather, about Beirut, about poetry. Roni said little, but her gaze missed nothing.

As Amol rose to leave, Malkin handed him a thin parcel, wrapped in brown paper. 'For your shelf.'

It was a copy of Hannah Arendt's *Eichmann in Jerusalem: A Report on the Banality of Evil*; its cover worn, the margins lightly pencilled.

'You'll like this,' he said, tapping the cover. 'Though she got more wrong than right.'

Amol raised an eyebrow.

'I know,' Malkin said, deadpan. 'I was there in Buenos Aires when we grabbed him.'

He let the silence hang, as if deciding how far back to go. Amol leaned forward, listening.

'Ben-Gurion signed the order himself. It was a line we hadn't crossed before – snatching someone off foreign soil. Harel ran the operation from a rented house. We were ten agents. No backup. No official protection. We were told if we failed, we'd be disavowed. Classic.'

'And your role?'

'I was the guy who grabbed him,' Malkin said quietly. 'That's not bravado – it's just fact. We waited by the bus stop. He came home like clockwork, always walking the same road. I stepped out. Asked if he had a moment. Then I pulled him down, fast, into the grass. My partner jumped on top. He never screamed.'

He paused. 'In training, they told us to expect resistance. But Eichmann just … folded. As if he'd been waiting.'

Amol watched the man's hands – not trembling, not boastful. Steady as glass.

'We kept him in a safe house for nine days. When we flew him out, he was in an EL AL uniform, drugged. We told the Argentines he was a drunk crew member. The air crew knew nothing. Neither did the ground staff.'

Amol said nothing, letting the detail settle. Then: 'Did he ever speak?'

Malkin nodded. 'Plenty. He said he wasn't a monster. That he only managed logistics. Rail timetables. Cattle cars. We were just moving people, he said – like shipments of grain.'

'And what did you say?'

Malkin's eyes narrowed. 'I said I was just doing my job too. But I lied.'

A long pause. 'He cried when we showed him the black-and-white photos. The children. The mothers. That part she got right,' he said, tapping the book again. 'Even monsters weep. Doesn't make them less monstrous.'

Amol thought of the kind of man who built bombs and gave warnings in the same breath. There were monsters, and then there were men who knew how monsters were made.

Malkin stood up, brushing crumbs off his coat. 'Don't trust uniforms, Amol. Or excuses. Or men who tell you they're only part of the machine.'

As Malkin was walking away, he turned once more. 'Isser Harel said that bringing Eichmann to trial would be our people's second independence. He was right. But it also taught us something harder: even when you win, the work doesn't end.'

Back in Talpiot, Amol shelved it between Kipling and Ambedkar. He didn't open it.

Not unread. Just waiting.

It was a week later that Amol returned to Malkin's apartment.

The invitation had come casually, almost offhand, in a note slipped through the mail slot in Talpiot.

Come see what the brushes have been up to. – M.

This time, Roni didn't serve cake. She greeted Amol with a kiss on the cheek and disappeared into the back room with a stack of laundry. No tango on the record player. No tea poured.

Malkin led him into the small study. The light was dimmer here. Against one wall leaned half a dozen new canvases – smaller, rougher. No landscapes.

'These are new,' Malkin said.

Amol stepped closer. What he saw were figures – thin, angular men rendered in stark black lines, their limbs stick-like, their faces barely marked. They stood in rows. Or marched. Or stared, faceless, through iron gates. Behind them, always, a horizon: flat, grey, endless.

'They're not from Argentina,' Amol said.

'No,' Malkin replied. 'These are Germans.'

He said the word with care – not anger, not pain. Just precision. Amol studied one painting: four men, nearly identical, standing in a line before a low concrete wall. Each had a number scrawled faintly above their head, like a tally in a notebook.

Malkin stood beside him, arms folded. 'I try not to paint faces,' he said. 'It's better that way. The imagination makes them more honest.'

Amol said nothing. The silence in the room pressed closer. 'You were in Germany?' he asked at last.

Malkin didn't answer directly. 'I was … near. Later.'

In the next canvas, a single stick figure knelt, its shadow stretching twice its size behind it. No other figures. No horizon.

'They look like shadows,' Amol murmured.

Malkin nodded. 'That's all they ever were.'

Roni returned silently with a folded shawl, placed it over the back of Malkin's chair, then left again without speaking. Malkin watched her go, then turned back to the paintings. 'She doesn't like these ones. Says they don't let the room breathe.'

Amol lingered by the last canvas, where one figure seemed to be held – not by chains, but by two black lines gripping its wrists.

Malkin stepped behind him. 'I once held a man's wrists for twelve hours,' he said quietly. 'So he wouldn't kill himself before justice could reach him.'

Amol turned, slowly. Malkin met his gaze. He said nothing more.

Layla returned in July.

This time, there was no kiss at the door, no casual banter about being early or late. She arrived just after midnight, worn and wary, her scarf darker, her eyes sharper. The war in Lebanon had shifted again – smaller now, meaner. She carried a canvas bag that smelt faintly of damp paper and airport metal detectors.

'I only have four days,' she said. 'We'll make them last.'

But they didn't. Not really.

Their walks were shorter. The silences longer. They still held hands through the alleyways of the Old City, but the feeling was different now – less discovery, more defiance. She spoke of deadlines, of editors growing nervous. Her last story on the camp survivors in Sidon had been pulled. 'Too much grief,' her Paris Bureau Chief had said. 'Too little hope.'

They spent one evening on the roof, watching the muezzin's call roll like smoke across the stone. Amol read her Heaney aloud. She answered with a line of Darwish, and for a moment, their worlds touched like fingers beneath a table.

For dinner, they drank Cremisan red brewed by monks at a monastery located between Jerusalem and Bethlehem. Amol even cooked them a cheese souffle from a recipe taught to him by his mother in Oxford. Four egg whites, three egg yolks was the mantra she had drilled into him.

Layla loved it. 'I could marry you just for the souffle,' she laughed, as they transitioned from poetry to music, listened to Ella Fitzgerald singing 'Mac The Knife'.

On their second-to-last day, the air in Jerusalem had felt unusually heavy, as if something unsaid were pressing against the glass.

Instead of speaking, they escaped to Bethlehem, needing a break from the edges of politics and press briefings.

The city was quieter than Jerusalem, softer around the edges, its lanes shaded with overhanging vines and the scent of cumin and carob.

Layla wanted to buy a carved olive-wood baby Jesus for her mother. Amol rolled his eyes but went along, teasing her all the way to Manger Square.

They sat together in the corner of Manger Square, sunlight pooling on the warm stone like honey. She wore a sleeveless cotton frock – soft, pale, immaculately cut – that moved gently in the breeze. Her long brown hair spilled below her shoulders, catching flecks of gold in the light, and her blue eyes held the same impossible clarity as the sky above them or the sapphire on her finger.

Locals paused. Tourists slowed their steps. Even the old men playing backgammon at the café gate looked up and briefly forgot their dice. The ring – a single, deep-blue stone – had once belonged to his mother, Asha. It was her only real gift from David Batty, Amol's father, who had found it decades earlier in a dusty corner shop in the Pink City, Jaipur, nestled between bangles and sandalwood.

Amol, beside her, was unmistakably his own kind of beauty. Tall, but not imposing; slim, with the lithe stillness of someone used to watching rather than being watched. His skin was warm-toned, sun-kissed like hers, and his black curls seemed to defy gravity, slightly tousled from the walk. He wore brown chinos, yellow deck shoes and a soft blue linen shirt with the sleeves rolled to the elbow. There was something effortless about him – something clean, alert, boyish – that made strangers glance again. They looked right together, as if drawn from the same palette. As if, in that moment, the square had been made for them alone.

Later, he would wonder if that had been their still point – the moment before the wheel turned, before everything that came next.

The next morning, she began folding her things into the suitcase with quiet efficiency, as if the world hadn't shifted. Amol offered to drive her to the airport. She shook her head.

'There's a hotel shuttle from East Jerusalem. Safer,' she said, and then smiled. 'You forget. I'm French. We're boring targets.'

She kissed him at the door, lingered for a second and then left without turning back.

The bombing made the noon news bulletin.

A bus outside Damascus Gate, en route the airport. Twenty dead. One unidentified. The footage showed scorched glass and a single shoe in the road.

Amol didn't move. He watched the screen repeat three times before switching it off.

An hour later, the bureau phone rang. It was a fixer in East Jerusalem. 'I think … I think she was on that bus.'

He put down the phone. Then he walked into the bathroom, locked the door and screamed.

It wasn't a cry, or a shout or a word. Just a tearing sound from somewhere in his chest, loud and guttural, until he ran out of air.

His body collapsed forward over the sink. He stared at his own reflection, the face unfamiliar – slack with pain, rage and loss.

They found her the next day, or what was left of her, in the charred wreckage near the back of the bus. Most of the bodies were unrecognizable – limbs strewn, skin scorched black, faces erased. But someone had carefully set aside a woman's arm, severed clean at the elbow.

On its ring finger, still intact despite the fire, was a single blue sapphire in a plain gold band. It caught the light even then, absurdly beautiful in that heap of ash and ruin. Amol didn't need to see anything else.

That was the same ring. His mother's ring. The one she'd worn in Manger Square, tucking her hair behind her ear as she laughed at the olive-wood carvings. The stone was still sky clear, but the sky was gone.

He didn't cry. He couldn't.

The condolence calls began the next morning. Some sincere. Others performative. A Palestinian media friend sent a typed note of 'solidarity'. A French consulate official called with bureaucratic sympathy. The British Embassy sent flowers.

The last knock came just after sunset. Amol opened the door to find a man he'd never met, holding a slim bottle of whisky in one hand and a folded envelope in the other.

'Keith Josling,' the man said. 'British consulate. Can I come in?'

Amol stepped aside.

Josling was short, bespectacled and soft-spoken, with the clipped vowels of a man who had once taught at a decent school and never quite forgot it. He poured two drinks without asking, sat by the window and handed Amol the envelope.

Inside: Layla's press card, burnt at the edges.

Josling poured the drinks without asking, the ice clinking too brightly. Amol felt the chill of Naxos return, the way Sedo had warned him, flatly, about the cost of staying quiet too long.

'We found it near the debris,' Josling said gently. 'Your name was on the back. Next of kin, in her handwriting.'

Amol swallowed hard.

'She was brave,' Josling added. 'Too brave, maybe.'

They drank in silence for a while.

'You knew her?' Amol asked.

'Not well,' Josling said. 'But we read her. She had clarity. That's rare.'

The light faded. Somewhere in the street below, a cat yowled and a boy shouted in Arabic.

Josling rose to leave. At the door, he paused. 'We're a small group here. People who notice things. If you ever need … someone to talk to, or just some space to breathe – come by. No questions. We're just down the hill.'

He handed Amol a card. No title. Just his name and a phone number.

Then he left.

The consulate handed him a small urn. Ceramic, grey-blue, sealed with a brass clasp. 'There was no family request,' the French official said, almost apologetically. 'She listed you.'

He woke before dawn in Talpiot, the call to prayer faint in the far distance. Amol sat in silence beside the sealed urn – matte bronze, impersonal, yet unbearable to touch.

Layla's presence pulsed in every corner of the flat, as if she'd just slipped into the bathroom or left a book open for him to finish. The floor creaked the way it had when she danced barefoot across it, humming to herself in French and Arabic.

Her death had been cleanly recorded: a Jerusalem bus, two stops from the airport, a package left beneath the second row. The forensic report read like a crossword: ammonium nitrate, ball bearings, pressure switch. Nothing of the soul, nothing of the woman who once whispered Rumi verses to him in the dark.

But the details clung like dust. Ammonium nitrate. Ball bearings. Pressure switch.

Not just crude, too clean for that. A neat mechanism, tucked out of sight.

He didn't know why but an image rose unbidden, calm hands sketching loops and circuits in Naxos, saying: 'Make it sweet. Make it small. They pick it up before they know.'

Amol closed the folder. It wasn't proof. But it was enough to wonder whether silence had finally detonated and whether he'd helped light the fuse. He waited until noon. Then he carried the urn in a cloth satchel to the coast.

Driving north, he passed Herziliya and turned off the highway just before Caesarea, the sea stretching out like glass. The ruins stood quiet – Roman arches, fallen pillars, the ghost of a theatre that once echoed with empire.

Past a narrow path the cliffs gave way to a stony shore. The breeze was warm, tinged with salt and wild thyme. No one else was there.

He stood for a long time, the urn in his hands.

The sea air was sharp and briny, carrying the sting of salt and the faint scent of wild thyme growing in crevices. The stones beneath his feet shifted with a dry crunch as waves lapped softly, pulling the ashes away in slow, ghostly swirls.

The water in front of him was still, unusually so, like glass stretched across the past. He remembered a line she had once quoted – something about the ocean never forgetting what it swallows.

'You think the world can be held together by stories,' she'd said once, teasing him after he filed a piece from Sidon. 'But even the best story ends.'

'I'm still telling it,' he whispered now, to no one. 'You're still in it.'

'Do you believe we live many lives?' she had asked once, lying beneath his olive-green linen sheet.

'I believe we live one, badly.'

'Rumi said we're born many times until we return to the Beloved.'

He let the words return to him now, slow and private. 'Don't grieve. Anything you lose comes round in another form.'

The wind stirred, like an answer. Or like breath.

Now, alone on the rocks, he stood with her ashes as waves lapped and withdrew like breath. He didn't cry. That had come earlier, in violent waves that dropped him to his knees in the kitchen, then again in the stairwell of a friend's house and again at Ben Gurion, when the clerk casually asked, 'Is that your wife's luggage?'

Instead, he spoke softly into the wind. 'Layla. Forgive me. I thought the world could be fixed with stories.'

As he called out to her, the wind tugged at his clothes, whispering like a breath across the vast, glassy expanse. The silence was so complete, it pressed on his ears like velvet.

The ashes scattered oddly. Some clung to his fingers, refusing to leave. Others flew back onto his shirt. It felt cruel, as if she wouldn't let go, or he wasn't letting her. He stepped into the water, deeper than he meant to, shoes soaked, shins stinging. Only when he knelt – the urn nearly empty – did the sea take her fully.

He let the salt sting him. Let the weight of it pass through. Somewhere, in another future, a man would say something about love. But perhaps that too was a kind of detonation – softer, but just as irreversible. The sea took her. He did not.

He thought of Miro's words. Some ghosts are protected. Some are radioactive. And there would come a time when he would think of one in particular, the kind you called only when you were ready to bleed.

He stayed like that for hours. Later, he wrote a note in his diary: 'We are all temporary custodians of love and violence.'

As he was preparing to leave Jerusalem, the telephone rang in his flat.

A male voice said, 'Sir, Benazir Bhutto would like a word. She's calling from London.'

Her tone was warm, urgent, instantly familiar.

'Amol, this is Pinky.'

The nickname had followed her from Karachi to Oxford, where they had once argued about politics and poetry over bad wine. She was now in opposition exile, running her father's party from London and learning to live between diplomacy and defiance.

'I need a favour,' she said. 'You still have contacts with Arafat? I want to meet him quietly, in a personal capacity. He's in Tunis, and while Pakistan has formal ties with Tunisia, I'd rather not go through the embassy. Perhaps Cairo, or nearby. Could you pass a message?'

Amol hesitated. 'I can try,' he said.

She thanked him, and the line went dead.

The next morning he sent word through a friend at the PLO information office in East Jerusalem – a telex in careful language, routed through Cyprus to Tunis.

By the week's end, a reply came back through the same channel, unsigned but unmistakable:

Tell your friend the Chairman thanks her interest. He conducts his own diplomacy.

Arafat's temper, Amol heard later through a mutual contact in Cairo, had flared when the note reached him.

'Tell him to stay out of politics,' the Chairman had said. 'He's a journalist. Keep to his trade, as I keep to mine.'

It was the only time Arafat's anger touched him directly. They never spoke about it again.

He folded the telex, slipped it into his notebook, and shut it.

That was 1984.

Returning that day, he walked alone through East Jerusalem, the scent of cardamom and diesel in the air.

A muezzin's voice rose – cracked, beautiful – and Amol paused outside a shuttered antique shop where Layla had once bargained for a silver locket.

He touched the glass with his fingertips and whispered: 'You said: "We are where we're needed, not where we're wanted." But I never asked – who decides that?'

The city was quieter than usual, as if holding its breath. In the shop's reflection, he almost imagined her beside him – arms folded, lips curled in faint mischief.

'You brood too much,' her voice teased from memory. 'Even your silences have footnotes.'

'You liked my silences,' he replied to the glass.

'I liked that you listened inside them,' the voice returned.

He dreamt of her that night. Not as a ghost, but as she had been in Beirut: wild curls, ink-stained fingers, teasing him for misquoting Neruda.

'I want to do with you what spring does with the cherry trees,' she recited, touching his collarbone.

'Even the war can't touch this.'

He reached for her in the dream, but she stepped back into shadow. 'Finish the poem,' she whispered. 'Even now.'

But the line was gone. All he could say was her name.

In the weeks that followed, he returned to visit the garden at the American Colony Hotel, where they had once met a Palestinian poet who gave Layla a pressed flower and called her 'a bird from the firewood'.

Amol left a photo of them beneath a pomegranate tree, folded into a page from her favourite notebook. The faint scent of pomegranate blossoms lingered in the garden, mingling with the dry stone and faint smoke from distant fires.

No name. No message. Just a shared silence with the earth. He sat on the same bench they'd once shared and opened the notebook to the last page she'd written in.

One line stood out, written in French:

Je partirai avant la fin.Mais tu continueras l'histoire. [I will leave before the end. But you will continue the story.]

He copied it into his own journal and added only:

I am trying.

Then he closed the book and let the wind turn the rest of the pages.

But there was no healing, not even the recall of her voice. 'I've never been so close to peace,' she had said, 'as I am with you in this city built for war.'

Grappling with his pain, Amol drifted …

The condolence whisky with Josling had left a bitter taste, not from the drink but the knowing. Something had shifted – in him, around him. Files were probably being written. His name now lived in other people's mouths.

Later that week, Malkin appeared unannounced. It was the only time Malkin ever came to Jerusalem. He made that clear with a shrug when Amol opened the door to his flat in Talpiot.

'I don't usually come up here,' Malkin said, brushing city dust from his coat. 'But this one's personal.'

They walked without speaking to the edge of Armon Hanatziv promenade, the wind high and bitter. Below, the Old City spread out like a memory.

The chill wind tugged at his coat, carrying the distant calls of the Old City below.

'You remember now,' Malkin said, standing beside him. 'Pain teaches better than persuasion.'

He lit a cigarette with a windproof lighter. Amol stayed silent, hands deep in his coat.

'She was the real thing, that girl,' Malkin said. 'People like her make you believe in what's worth saving.' Still no reply.

Malkin turned towards him. 'Be careful with Josling. He's not from the old school. He sells people like used cars. Mossad knows his type.'

As Malkin spoke, Amol found himself thinking of eyes he had not yet seen – calm, cracked, already beyond bargaining. Whatever men like Josling are selling, those eyes had stopped buying long ago.

A week earlier, an unmarked envelope had slipped through the flap in Talpiot. No note, just a blurred photograph – a man loading crates outside a Balkan warehouse. The face was turned, indistinct. But the posture, the half-wrapped wrist, even the way he leaned into the lift; it echoed Naxos. Amol burnt the photo without thinking, but the image stayed with him like an unfinished warning.

'You're watching him?'

'We watch everything.'

There was a long pause. Then Malkin reached into his coat and pressed something into Amol's palm – a small, worn coin.

'Bronze prutah,' he said. 'From the Second Temple. You can still dig them up not far from here.'

Amol turned it over, the ancient grooves still sharp against his skin. 'Reminds you,' Malkin said, 'empires fall. Even this one.'

He didn't stay long. Just turned and walked back towards the city, vanishing down a side street with no farewell. Later, as Amol packed for London, he tucked the coin into his passport sleeve without thinking. He would forget about it for years.

Not long after the condolence whisky with Josling and the unexpected visit from Malkin, and a day after scattering Layla's ashes, Amol flew to London.

The seat beside him stayed empty. Amol kept the window shade half open, watching the clouds fracture and fuse as the plane climbed over the Mediterranean.

He touched the inside pocket of his jacket. The notebook was there. So was the coin Malkin had pressed into his hand. It was warm from his body, though it felt ancient and cold in the palm.

The drink cart rattled past. He waved it away.

Outside, the sea unfurled below – vast, indifferent, the same sea that had taken her. Somewhere far behind, her ashes stirred in currents he could no longer trace.

He opened the notebook. Just once. On the page where he'd copied her final line, he wrote:

Even now, you are the pause between my thoughts.

Then he closed it and watched the light flicker on the wing. No prayers. No poems. Just the hum of distance. And a name held quietly, like breath.

11

The Orchard Factory

Seven years after Layla's death, 1991, London

Everything felt too clean. Too ordered. The lights changed on time. The milk arrived cold at the door. The newspapers said nothing. Even the silence was efficient. It left no room for grief.

Amol wandered his flat like a man retracing the steps he'd once escaped. The ache was old now, dulled by years of work and travel, yet Naxos had re-opened it. The same questions, the same shadows.

Naxos had peeled back the seal on an old wound; it was not new grief, just newly awake.

Layla was ash now, scattered into the Mediterranean wind near Caesarea. He still remembered whispering her name to the sea, touching the waves with his fingers. 'I release you,' he'd said. 'But not from me.'

The silence had never really lifted. No outrage. No claim of responsibility. Just the usual official murmurs – a Shin Bet denial, a PLO statement denouncing 'rogue actors' and the quiet grind of normalization.

Even after all this time, it didn't add up. The Jerusalem bombing had been clean. Too clean. Not a PFLP–GC signature. Not

Hamas. The triggering mechanism, the blast cone – too refined. Whoever had made it had resources. Knowledge. Intent.

He had never spoken to Sedo about Layla. Not then. In Naxos their words had been about payloads, not people. But tonight, even silence felt like collusion

—

One night, unable to sleep, Amol tore through his old field notebooks. He wasn't looking for anything specific, but his fingers knew before his mind did. A scrap of paper from a hotel in Skopje fluttered out: a number scrawled in blue ink, slightly faded, but legible. No name. Just the number. He stared at it for a long time.

When he finally dialled, the line clicked and buzzed for several seconds. Then: 'You're calling me now?'

Amol didn't reply right away. 'I need to understand,' he said.

'Come to Beirut. Meet me near the Indian embassy. There's a café with pictures of Bollywood stars. You'll be safer there. So will I.'

The line went dead. Amol never asked which one. He didn't need to. He hadn't seen Sedo since Naxos. But the voice on the line still knew the rules.

He remembered the place – dim, dusty and overlooked by everyone except the ghosts.

It was tucked into a narrow side street off Rue Bliss, not far from the Indian embassy. Modest, unassuming – the kind of place that didn't ask questions. It was, according to local journalists, the last functioning Indian restaurant – part safe haven, part ghost of Partition. A dusty awning flapped in the breeze, and a faded poster of Raj Kapoor smiled down from the wall inside.

Sedo looked older but less guarded than Amol remembered. He stood when Amol arrived, 'I'm sorry,' he said, without preface. 'The girl. The bus. Word travels – especially the kind no one puts in print.'

Amol nodded, too tired for ceremony.

They sat. The waiter brought them masala chai in small chipped cups – heavy with cardamom, faintly sweet, poured from a dented brass kettle.

'You're thinner,' Sedo said.

'You're quieter,' Amol replied. They didn't shake hands. They never had.

After a pause, Amol leaned forward.

'The bus bomb in Jerusalem. What kind was it?'

Sedo took a breath. 'Not Syrian. Not freelance. Professional.'

'So?'

He traced a small circle in the condensation on the table. 'Copper-lined signature. Modified cell trigger. Directed blast – upward. Designed to kill the front rows.'

Amol's hands clenched.

Layla had been near the driver. She wasn't political. She wasn't even supposed to be on that route – she'd switched buses last minute, trying to get to the airport early. Just a writer, a dreamer, someone caught in the wrong story. Like so many others. Innocent lives made footnotes in someone else's game.

'Could it have been … one of yours?'

Sedo gave a rueful smile. 'No. But it looked like something I helped perfect once – under duress. Shared with people who had other priorities.'

Amol slipped the envelope into his jacket, feeling the weight of it press against his ribs like a second heartbeat. Across the street, the Indian flag stirred – barely – as if in warning. He didn't speak.

There was nothing left to say. Sedo had already stood, his water glass still half full.

No handshake. No farewell. Just a line tossed over his shoulder as he prepared to leave: 'They won't come for me first. They'll come for you.'

'Who?'

'You're asking the wrong question. Don't ask who made it. Ask who needed it. Who profits from a poisoned peace? Look there – not at the circuitry, but the timing. The PLO is splintered. Hamas is rising. The PFLP wants to stay relevant, and Jibril's PFLP–GC just wants to be feared. Add Hezbollah, al-Saiqa, remnants of the old Black September. Even Jumblatt's Druze have their own networks. And that's just Lebanon.

'In Israel, you've got Shin Bet factions playing off the settlers, rogue military elements and foreign handlers from five countries walking the alleys of East Jerusalem like they own the dust. Everyone wants control, but no one wants peace. That bomb was a message – but the signature's in the silence afterwards.'

Amol looked past Sedo, out the window, but saw only memory.

Amman 1970. The images still lived in the archives of his mind. He'd been a boy, watching from Delhi, but his grandfather had clipped the headlines: Leila Khaled's arrest, the hijackings to Dawson's Field. He remembered the grainy footage – the carcasses of planes smouldering on the tarmac, the way the press described it as 'a lesson to the West'. His grandfather had simply muttered, 'The world is learning all the wrong things. And soon it will forget who taught them.'

'You think that kind of thing just happens?' Sedo continued, voice low but steady. 'Look at history. The Jordanian monarchy under siege. The PLO splintering under pressure. Palestinian factions using spectacle to speak – not to kill, but to make themselves unignorable. The Popular Front pioneered it, but then it splintered and every splinter wanted its own moment. Arafat tried to pull them in. Failed. Or succeeded too well.

'Now everyone wants a piece of the spectacle – Hamas, Hezbollah, the new Iranian-trained networks in the Bekaa. You think the Americans stay clean in this? The French? Mossad?

'Everyone wants deniability, not distance. Chaos is fertile ground. And sometimes a bomb isn't planted to kill – it's planted to frame. To provoke. To reshape the next forty-eight hours of narrative. That's what we're in now. Narrative war.'

A long silence followed. Then: 'You gave me a question. I get one now.'

Amol nodded.

'What do you know about Jibril's people now?' Sedo asked.

Amol shrugged. 'Still operating in Syria, I think. Maybe Lebanon.'

'Jibril's old men – they were never like Fatah or the Marxists. They trained in North Korea, not Prague. And now? Just another proxy force, feeding off Iranian money and Russian weapons. The cause is gone, Amol. It's just pipelines and puppets.'

Sedo's eyes were scanning the shoreline now, but his thoughts were elsewhere.

Amol said, 'Lebanon reminds me of the Afghan border. Too many flags, not enough loyalties.'

Sedo gave a short, grim laugh. 'Same principle. Every commander with a beard and a Kalashnikov thinks he's the resistance. Till he gets a better offer. Or a CIA stipend. Or a Saudi *madrasa*.' He paused. 'You were in Khost, right? Or was it Spin Boldak?'

Amol nodded but said nothing. His jaw clenched.

Sedo observed him for a moment, then looked away. 'The only

difference,' he said, 'is that in Lebanon the puppeteers wore suits. In Kabul, they wore robes. Same games, same blood.'

Amol didn't respond. The air between them felt briefly heavier, charged with memory neither of them wanted to name.

Then he said quietly, 'Tell me about Ahmed Jibril's orchard.'

Sedo lingered, almost like watching his own reply. 'You want to understand the Orchard?' he said. 'Then you need to understand the soil.'

The name was deliberate. Disarming.

'You think Afghanistan was fragmented? Lebanon was a mirror, but sharper. Here the factions wore cologne and the buyers had embassies. They called it the Orchard because it sounded harmless. A place where apples grow, not isotopes. North of Zahlé, tucked behind the hills. Jibril brought in engineers from Bulgaria, maybe even Pakistan. One of them spoke Russian like a native.'

He looked up at Amol. 'You think it was a reactor? It wasn't. Just parts. Materials. Manuals. But enough to make people nervous.' A pause. 'Mossad knew. The Syrians knew. Even the Americans – eventually. But no one hit it. Not like Deir ez-Zor. Too many hands in the basket.

'You filed a story about it once', Sedo continued. 'Obliquely. A line here, a metaphor there. The Orchard stayed with me. Now I want the whole picture.'

Amol responded slowly. 'It was a facility, outside Damascus. I met Jibril there once, near Zahle in the Bekaa Valley. He greeted me like a revolutionary patriarch – black shirt unbuttoned to the chest, heavy with gold chains, the kind of man who wanted to be both feared and adored. Behind him hung portraits of Che Guevara, George Habash and an old, water-damaged photo of Nasser. The walls smelled of damp stone and cigarette smoke.'

He paused, remembering.

'It wasn't a lab. It was a warehouse with ambition. Clay floors. Reinforced rooms with soundproof padding. He said they could replicate any bomb in the world – Western, Israeli, Gulf. But it was the Orchard behind the compound that stays with me. Rows of trees, citrus and fig. I'd once described it to Layla, in half-joking tones – Jibril's secret orchard of lies. She had laughed. "Apples, figs and detonators," she'd said. "Some harvest."'

The memory stung now, sweetened by time and spoiled by context.

'Beneath them, buried caches: timing devices, casings, Soviet detonators packed in crates marked as fertilizer. Each type was stored with care. Jibril had a kind of pride about it – he called them his "combs", each one meant to give a different parting to the narrative. Blendable. Customizable. Some he claimed were designed to implicate Mossad. Others to echo IRA tech.'

Maps of Israel hung there too – like the ones Layla used to trace slowly, her fingertips moving as if the land could feel it. Amol had thought Jibril was bluffing. Now … he wasn't so sure. He hesitated, then spoke more plainly. 'Dates, components, names. Things no one had printed yet.'

Maybe he just needed to be believed, to prove that all his witnessing hadn't been for nothing.

Sedo didn't interrupt. He just listened, deliberately, like someone weighing a debt already owed.

Sedo looked at him. 'Did you believe him?'

Amol hesitated. 'I didn't. Not then. But now … ' He trailed off. The doubt had already answered.

Sedo nodded, saying nothing at first. His eyes didn't accuse, they calculated. Not suspicion, but something colder: evaluation. Then, almost softly, he said, 'Useful.'

Amol hesitated. The memory felt heavier now, not just reported but complicit. Had he unknowingly pointed the way? Had his old reports been mined like maps?

But it was more than that and Amol didn't see it.

Didn't see the slight narrowing of Sedo's eyes, the way he filed the Orchard details away, not like gossip but like ammunition. In another world, another meeting, it might have been a routine anecdote from a war correspondent.

But here – now – it was something else entirely. A data point Mossad had long suspected but never confirmed. A facility with replication capability, with provenance, with Jibril's imprimatur.

This was the moment Sedo decided. Not to recruit him – Amol would never wear anyone's colours. But to shield him. To protect the source of truth when so many others peddled lies. It was the invisible handshake, the unwritten bargain. No ceremony. No allegiance. Just value. The kind that endured.

And from that point on, Sedo never truly deserted him. Not in London. Not in the Balkans. Not even when Amol thought he was alone.

As Amol spoke, Sedo didn't write anything down. He didn't have to. The Orchard story was real and Amol had just confirmed it – calmly, plainly, without embellishment. It was the kind of detail that got passed up the line. The kind that made intelligence officers lean forward. Not because it was explosive. Because it was true.

Now Sedo tilted his head slightly. 'You know what Iran wants most of all?'

Amol said nothing.

'Not territory. Not even influence. They want the bomb. Not just for deterrence – for status. Permanence. And to get it, they'll back whoever offers them a shortcut.'

Amol's mind flashed to a conversation in Damascus years ago – a rumour whispered by an Iraqi exile. Modified centrifuge components traded through Eastern Europe. A Belgian physicist who disappeared outside Burgas. A crate labelled 'medical refrigeration' diverted at Latakia. He hadn't understood the significance then.

'Hamas feeds Tehran ideology and bodies,' Sedo said. 'But Jibril? He offers hardware. Blueprints. Smuggling routes. And with what you've just told me – about the Orchard, the casing types, the replication capabilities – you've just given one of them an edge. You think you're just remembering,' he said, holding Amol's gaze. 'They'll see it as a briefing.'

But his tone was softer now, not transactional, more reflective.

The café around them offered no hint of the conversation it was housing. A child wailed faintly in a back room; the waiter reappeared to wipe a table with a newspaper; the smell of turmeric and burnt ghee hung in the air, mingled with incense from a crooked shelf of plastic gods near the till.

A Bollywood melody crackled through an ancient speaker – Kishore Kumar, if Amol wasn't mistaken – barely audible over the street horns and scooter engines beyond. Somewhere behind the kitchen curtain, someone coughed like a history teacher nearing retirement. It was, by all appearances, a forgotten corner of Beirut trying to remember Delhi.

'Do you ever think about Hiroshima?' Sedo asked quietly, as if plucking the thought from steam.

Amol glanced at him. 'My friend James Cameron reported from Nagasaki. He said the survivors didn't talk in anger. Just … weariness. As if the shadow still follows them.'

Cameron had been old-school – tall, stooped, always in linen, with a voice like gravel in butter. His Indian wife, Moni, short for Monisha, came from Coorg. He wrote longhand on onion-skin paper and smoked slender Sobranies he claimed only Cairo could supply.

Once, early on, he had pulled Amol aside and said: 'The only rule, young man, is don't pretend you know more than the mothers of the dead.'

It had stayed with him ever since.

'It does,' Sedo said. 'Even when it's not cast in your direction. The Japanese lost two cities. But the world – the rest of us – lost something else. A limit.' He stirred his chai slowly. 'When I was younger, we still believed there were boundaries. That certain lines wouldn't be crossed. Nuclear weapons were the outer ring. The final gate. But now? Now they're just … items on someone's wish list.'

The light in the café flickered, briefly.

'You know,' he continued, 'an atomic bomb the size of the one dropped on Hiroshima – fifteen kilotons – wouldn't just level Tel Aviv. It would burn Haifa, crack the glass towers of Herzliya and send radioactive dust curling over Cyprus, even parts of southern Turkey. If you time it right – prevailing winds, coastal inversion – you could poison the whole eastern Mediterranean.'

Amol said nothing. Sedo's voice wasn't theatrical. If anything, it felt like a dirge.

'Most people think death comes instantly,' Sedo went on. 'But it doesn't. Not always. In Hiroshima, there were men who walked for miles with their skin hanging in sheets from their arms. Children who tried to drink from fountains with no mouths left to hold the water. Some vomited blood. Some went blind in seconds. Others wandered the rubble in silence until their organs gave out – not from trauma, but from radiation.'

The waiter placed a fresh bowl of curry on the next table. The smell of fenugreek mingled with talk of lunch specials. Outside, a man sold second-hand books from a cart.

'And that was one bomb. One. Imagine something larger. Modern. The kind designed not just to destroy, but to erase. You wouldn't even need to hit a city. Detonate it in the air above Haifa and the EMP alone would blind Israel's systems. Hit Tel Aviv, and you'd see bodies turn to vapour mid-step.'

Sedo looked down at the rim of the cup. 'And those who don't die instantly? The children, the elderly – they'll die slowly. Vomiting. Bleeding from the gums. Their skin peeling, nerves burning from the inside. It won't be a war. It'll be a sickness, a season of death. And the world will watch on mute, debating legal definitions.'

Amol swallowed hard. Not at the horror. At how plainly Sedo described it, like a weather forecast.

'Iran doesn't want to use a bomb. That's not the point. They want the option. And to get it, they play the long game – collect scientists, blueprints, broken casings, pieces of the puzzle that no one notices until it's too late.'

He paused.

'You mentioned centrifuges in Burgas. I heard another rumour. Pakistani triggers. North Korean experts passing through Damascus under agricultural visas. It sounds absurd – until you look at who dies suddenly. Who disappears.'

Amol leaned back. 'I always thought it would be a flash. A bang. But maybe you're right. Maybe it starts like this, whispers in forgotten cafés, buried under traffic noise.'

Sedo nodded. 'That's how these things begin. Quietly. With colour-coded wire and plausible deniability. With stories. The bomb isn't just metal. It's narrative. Once it's shaped, it becomes inevitable.'

Sedo reached for his chai again.

'We all live in the blast radius now. Some of us just haven't noticed yet.' He paused. 'And where would they go, the ones who survived? The ones they say will inherit the desert once the fire passes? The Jews? What will they do if the worst happens? Back to their wanderings, maybe. Back to the remembered hellholes of Europe – the damp basements in Kraków, the train stations in Lyon, the old alleys of Salonika.

'Will the great-grandchildren of Holocaust survivors be rehoused in tented cities within shouting distance of Auschwitz, Treblinka, Dachau, Buchenwald? History has a way of turning full circle. This time not with yellow stars, but with silence. That's what the bomb would bring. Not extermination – expulsion, disbelief, forgetting.'

Sedo sat still for a moment, then said, 'We Kurds have a saying: the mountain is our only friend. It means you learn to survive alone. No cavalry. No comfort. You read weather, not treaties. Trust only what casts a shadow.'

He glanced at Amol. 'The Jews live with something deeper. Not just statelessness. Precarity, generation after generation. And not because of faith. Judaism is as old as Islam, as foundational as Christianity. If this were about God, they'd have reconciled centuries ago.'

He shifted slightly, voice quieter. 'It's because they're a small people. Easy to mark. Easy to blame. That's what makes a minority, not just numbers, but usefulness. You become the explanation for other people's failures.'

He ran a hand across his forehead, as if wiping away more than sweat. 'How the world treats the Jews,' he said, 'is a litmus test. A moral barometer for the age. That's always the weather report, the one history forgets to archive.'

His tone hardened just slightly. But killing Jews doesn't solve anything. That's not how it works. It's never the end. It's the beginning. A rehearsal. Once you prove it's possible to erase them, you've built the architecture for something larger. The machinery remembers.'

Now he looked Amol directly in the eye. 'You know the quote. Niemöller. German pastor. People always skip it or misquote it. Let me say the whole thing.

"First they came for the Socialists, and I did not speak out – because I was not a Socialist.

Then they came for the Trade Unionists, and I did not speak out – Because I was not a Trade Unionist. Then they came for the Jews, and I did not speak out – Because I was not a Jew.

Then they came for me – and there was no one left to speak for me."'

He let it hang.

'Everyone thinks they'll be spared. That the line stops before it reaches them. But it never does. Silence never saves.'

As Amol rose to go, Sedo said: 'Still in Islington?'

Amol stopped. 'You know Islington?'

'We all read *The Guardian* in holding. Even the footnotes.'

Amol stiffened, just slightly. He hadn't mentioned his London neighbourhood. But then again, maybe he never needed to. Sedo's reach, like the past, seemed to arrive uninvited but always on time.

A small smile passed between them.

'You're not safe, Amol,' Sedo added gently. 'Not because of what you know – but for what they think you do.'

'Is that a warning?'

'That's a kindness.'

—

Amol turned away. Behind him, the café's rusting fan hummed. The street felt quieter than before, too quiet. As he stepped out into the sunlight, he had the sudden, weightless sense of being observed, not by Sedo, not by the waiter, but by something more patient. A camera lens. A window. A name being underlined in a file. He was back in the open now, and whatever game this was, he no longer controlled the rules.

The embassy flag fluttered across the street.

He didn't feel lighter. Only looped back into something – not friendship, not betrayal, but a continuity neither of them had chosen.

In the war for memory, even grief had a price. Amol was still paying it, not with blood but in memory. And somewhere beneath the weight of it, something had hardened. Not certainty, not yet, but the shape of resolve. He wondered if his certainty was only pride in disguise, a habit of judging and calling it conscience.

12

Spirits of the Past

The flight back to Heathrow was uneventful. It was late summer now, the kind of grey English August that made Beirut feel half-imagined.

Before leaving London, he had told no one where he was going. Not the office, not his friends and least of all the Foreign Office. Just bought a return ticket, packed nothing but a book and boarded the late flight.

London was waiting, but so was something else – not comfort, but gravity.

Leaving Beirut, the airport felt like a stage set after the play was over. No one looked at him. Not the guards. Not the flight attendants. Not the woman who asked if he wanted tea.

In Oxford, it rained. The same grey stillness, the same sense of something finished.

He took a taxi to the house on Woodstock Road, where the hedges had grown too long and the brass number on the gate had begun to tarnish. The garden was full of wet roses and uncollected newspapers. The porch light was off.

His mother answered the door in slippers, a shawl around her shoulders. She looked smaller than he remembered.

'Amol,' she said, as if surprised.

'I didn't know where else to go.'

He hadn't cried in weeks, but something inside was beginning to crack, not loudly, just enough to make him seek shelter.

She nodded once and stepped aside.

The house smelled like old paper and turmeric. Books everywhere, as always – his father's empire. Shelves lined with academic journals, monographs, marginalia scrawled in soft pencil. The ghost of David Batty hung in every room – his jackets on the pegs, his fountain pens in the blue ceramic pot by the phone. A cup sat untouched on the desk in the study. Dust had started to form on the rim.

Amol stood in the doorway.

'He died quietly,' Asha said behind him. 'In his sleep. In May.'

'I should've come sooner. I'm sorry' he said, shame laced in his voice.

'You were at war,' she said, not accusingly.

They sat in the kitchen. Rain tapped the windows. She poured him tea but didn't touch hers.

'I thought maybe you could help me understand what just happened,' Amol said. 'There was this girl. Layla. She was –' He stopped. 'She's gone.'

Asha reached across the table and touched his hand. 'I'm sorry.'

He waited for more. For the comfort of a mother who had once wiped his forehead through monsoons in Delhi, who had sung ghazals under her breath while marking exam papers. But she was still somewhere else, turned inward. Her eyes were dark, tired.

'I've been dreaming of your father,' she said after a while. 'He walks through the Bodleian stacks, but he doesn't stop. I try to follow. But he disappears into the books.'

Amol looked at her – really looked. She had aged quickly. The grief had hollowed her, not loudly, but completely. 'I thought I'd come here and feel less alone,' he said softly.

Asha didn't flinch. 'You are never alone. But we don't always know how to carry each other.'

He nodded.

That night, he slept in his childhood room. His old cricket bat still leaned in the corner. There was a poster of Gorbachev peeling off the wall, and beside it, a photograph of his grandfather – suited, dignified, smiling beneath a neem tree in Delhi. He seemed to watch over the room like a relic from a vanished republic.

The next morning, the phone rang.

Asha answered, then brought the receiver to his room. She didn't speak. Just handed it to him. It was Delhi. His grandfather was gone. He stared at the receiver long after the line went dead. Outside, the rain began again.

1982, Delhi

The air in was hot with monsoon breath – thick and expectant. Even before the rain fell, the walls sweated. Amol arrived from London on a late July flight, still wearing the same blazer he had worn at his mother's kitchen table in Oxford, when they'd sat wordlessly over tea.

He hadn't planned to come so soon after Layla, but the call had come while he was still in north Oxford, a cousin in Defence Colony, his voice curt and formal.

His grandfather was gone. Delhi had called him home. The house in Golf Links had not changed. Bougainvillea curled like muscle across the gate, and the garden was half-wild with monsoon growth. Inside, it smelt of old paper and sandalwood and was filled with the sound of ceiling fans. His grandfather's presence was still everywhere – faint, exacting, invisible only in the way stone monuments pretend to be scenery.

The old man's Remington typewriter sat beneath the window, carriage askew as if the last sentence had been paused, not ended. A pair of battered slippers still lay beneath the desk, toes aligned. On the shelf beside the clock, a folded copy of *The Hindu* had yellowed at the edges.

The funeral was quiet but densely attended. Former ministers, old editors, university friends, two retired ambassadors and at least three men Amol knew to be spies. No one wore black. The room was a sea of khadi and linen. The marigolds bled orange on the veranda.

Amol lit the lamp. The priest droned the verses from memory. His grandfather's portrait stood framed against the mantle, captured in his last decade – tie loose, mouth set mid-judgement, eyes glinting with a writer's lifelong disbelief.

After the prayers, guests came in waves. Someone pressed lemon rice into his hand. Another gave him a rolled clipping of an old editorial. No one stayed long. Grief here was kept like a notebook: close, private, never read aloud.

He stood alone by the neem tree, the rice cooling in his hand, when Douglas Keir appeared beside him.

'You look older,' Keir said gently.

'So do you.'

'I hide it better.'

They shook hands. Keir wore his usual linen suit, white shirt open at the collar and that air of effortless observation. 'He was one of a kind,' Keir said. 'Your grandfather. He could cut a man down with a footnote and make him thank him for the correction.'

Amol smiled. 'He made the world seem decipherable.'

'And now it isn't?' Amol didn't reply.

Keir reached into his pocket and handed over a folded slip of paper. 'A message,' he said. 'An invitation.'

Amol opened it. No letterhead. Just a time, and a single line:

Rashtrapati Bhavan. 07:30. You are expected.

He looked up; Keir gave a mild smile. 'Arafat is in town. Official visit. State dinner last night. But he asked for you. Said you'd know why.'

Amol folded the paper slowly. 'Did he attend the funeral?'

Keir shook his head. 'He doesn't do crowds. But he remembers the house. And the man in it.'

The car arrived at dawn.

A white Ambassador with a government driver, the emblem on the number plate discreet but unmistakable.

It rolled up to the gate at Golf Links just as the birds were beginning their second chorus, the air still soft from last night's rain.

Amol wore a white shirt, pressed trousers and the narrow black tie his grandfather had once scolded him for wearing too often. He carried nothing but his notebook, though he knew he wouldn't use it.

The driver spoke no English, only nodded and drove through the half-waking city towards Rashtrapati Bhavan.

The ceremonial guards were already in position when they arrived – red turbans, white gloves, polished boots. One of them saluted and opened the door without a word.

He was led through a side entrance, not the public colonnade, into a smaller wing of the estate where the ceilings were lower and the curtains heavier. The carpet underfoot was a faded Persian design, its reds worn to rust. The aide who escorted him only said, 'He's already seated.'

The room was small by Rashtrapati Bhavan standards – a breakfast salon with high windows, pale upholstery and a single long table laid with silver and porcelain. No other guests. No visible staff.

Yasser Arafat sat at the head of the table, keffiyeh in place, fatigue jacket perfectly pressed, spoon in hand.

He looked up and smiled.

'You are early,' he said.

'You expected me?'

'I invited you.'

Amol bowed slightly. 'On behalf of my grandfather, thank you.'

'I respected him,' Arafat said, gesturing to the seat beside him. 'He asked questions that were meant to clarify, not humiliate. That is rare.'

Amol sat. The silence between them was warm, not strained. Arafat returned to his breakfast: a white porcelain bowl filled with cornflakes, already softening in milk. Without hesitation, he reached for a jar of honey, unscrewed the lid and poured a golden stream over the top.

'I don't trust sugar,' he said. 'But honey … honey has always been with us. From the Prophet to the *fedayeen*.'

Amol smiled, quietly memorizing it.

They spoke little as they ate. Arafat offered tea – strong, black, slightly bitter. Outside, the lawns of the Presidential estate shimmered with dew. Somewhere far off, a peacock cried.

When they finished, Arafat leaned back, folded his hands on the table and looked at Amol without blinking.

'Your stories matter,' he said. 'Not just because they are read. Because they are remembered.'

Amol inclined his head.

'I am not asking for coverage,' Arafat continued. 'I am asking you to remember how this place felt. What you saw in your grandfather's house. What you heard at his funeral. That is how we survive. Not with armies. With memory.'

There was nothing to reply. At the door, just before Amol was led away, Arafat turned back.

'If you ever visit me in Tunis,' he said, 'bring honey. They have none worth speaking of.'

He packed the jar of honey last. Not for Gaza. For whatever came next.

Three weeks later, September 1991

Amol crossed into Gaza under the white flag of the UN. The Israelis had reopened a narrow corridor for observation teams and journalists – though everything was slow, pre-cleared and curated to exhaustion. Amol was embedded with a group of international monitors, mostly Swedish and Dutch, who spoke in clipped moral language and sweated in linen suits.

The IDF officer at the checkpoint had glanced at his passport, noted the stamps and smirked.

'Back again? Thought you'd moved on to nicer trouble.'

'I follow the silence,' Amol replied.

The soldier didn't laugh.

Inside Gaza, the streets were quieter than he'd expected. No bomb craters, no screaming. Just the hush of disrepair. The walls were layered with slogans, some in Arabic, some in English:

'Our resistance is our existence. Jerusalem is the capital of Palestine. Glory to the martyrs.'

But the paint was fading. And so was the message.

Children played barefoot in the dust outside a shuttered school. A man sold flatbread from a rusted trolley, while a transistor radio crackled static. Most people didn't look up. Amol walked with a translator named Omar, a Palestinian man in his fifties with a French education and UN credentials pinned loosely to his lapel.

'This isn't what the world thinks it is,' Omar said as they passed a half-repaired clinic.

'What is it then?'

'Not a battlefield. Not a prison. Not a cause. Gaza is an X-ray. What you see here is the fracture before the diagnosis.'

Amol jotted it down.

They visited a local office of what was nominally the PLO's civilian bureau – two rooms, a broken fan and a secretary with purple nail polish who offered warm Pepsi. A man in a threadbare suit introduced himself as 'a liaison to the central committee'. He handed Amol a press packet with Arafat's face and a short statement about dignity, resilience and the path to peace.

'Do you speak to him directly?' Amol asked.

The man smiled. 'No one speaks to him directly anymore. He is now a place.'

Later, over strong tea on a rooftop, Amol watched the sun sink behind a row of satellite dishes. The Mediterranean beyond was flat, colourless. Gaza City hummed beneath him, not with energy, but fatigue.

He had been here before – years ago, during the many wars, when rockets and tank shells made the air vibrate. Now, the silence was heavier.

He scribbled in his notebook: They speak in metaphors because the truth has become too distant. Gaza has become a performance of Gaza. The flags wave, the slogans echo, but the audience has left the theatre.

That night, he couldn't sleep.

He spent five days in Gaza.

He interviewed aid workers who lived in UN compounds behind blast walls, drinking instant coffee under ceiling fans that barely turned. They spoke in press-release English, cautious and over-rehearsed. A Geneva official jabbed at a map of broken pipelines. 'They sabotage the system and hand us the wreckage. Then wonder why it leaks.'

In a boys' school turned shelter, he met a man named Marwan – once a university lecturer in Kuwait, now sleeping on a mat with his two sons and a cracked radio.

'I taught Foucault,' he said, unprompted. 'But now I sell cigarettes. I can no longer remember what it was I once resisted.'

Marwan didn't want his picture taken. 'The world prefers us as symbols. Not people.'

Amol understood. He filed nothing that night.

At a makeshift press conference in an NGO compound, a man in a grey suit, Comrade Walid, stood beside a plastic flag, issuing the same words they'd all heard before. No one wrote anything down.

In the hallway, Amol asked, 'Who do you really speak for?'

'No one,' Walid replied. 'We only pretend to.'

There were checkpoints everywhere – Israeli, Palestinian, unofficial militias.

One night, a boy offered to show Amol a 'real' tunnel, dug behind his uncle's house. The translator intervened.

'It's not safe,' Omar said. 'Not for him. Not for you.'

By the fourth day, Amol stopped taking photographs. He stopped recording. He just watched: the endless queue for cooking gas, the children kicking a punctured football through the alleyways, the plastic sheeting fluttering where roofs had once been.

What disturbed him most wasn't violence. It was the ritual of visibility. Everything curated. Every statement pre-cleared. Every display of poverty arranged like a museum of grievances.

The only truth he trusted came from Omar.

On their last afternoon, they sat on a low wall near the shore, eating falafel from a paper bag, watching the waves roll in like clockwork.

'You're too quiet,' Omar said.

'I don't know what I'm supposed to write.'

'Then don't write. Just remember.'

That word again. Memory. Everyone was carrying it like contraband – unspoken, heavy, unsellable.

Amol looked up. 'You're not here for the UN, are you?'

Omar didn't answer. He only said: 'In Gaza, everyone works for someone. The trick is not forgetting who you started out working for.'

Amol returned to Jerusalem with dust in his lungs and his notebook heavy with contradiction.

Before sending his story, he flipped through old clippings with his own bylines beside anticipating exclusives he barely remembered. Pieces filed in haste, edited by strangers, shaped for narratives he hadn't endorsed. Truth was no longer pursued – it was managed, like risk. He wondered if Sedo had felt the same, passing blueprints to a man who couldn't even guarantee a headline.

He filed enough copy for a single, spare column and the subs gave it a simple but brutal headline: 'Living With Death'

His editor didn't know what to make of it.

The next day, a diplomatic courier dropped off a plain envelope. Inside was a folded slip of paper. No letterhead.

Tunis expects you. Bring what matters. – K

He stared at it a long time.

Then he opened a kitchen cabinet, reached for a jar of golden, thick Indian honey and packed his bag.

October 1991, Tunis

It was blistering and bureaucratic. The air shimmered with heat and the hum of diplomatic engines. Amol was collected from the airport by a man in mirrored sunglasses who said nothing, not even his name.

He held open the door of a black Mercedes and gestured for Amol to get in.

The drive was smooth and swift, past pale villas and shuttered cafés, deeper into the city's hush. They arrived at a compound behind high hedges – no flags, no signage, just the shape of importance.

Inside, the air-conditioning hissed. Amol was led through a side door into a narrow salon with cool tiles and drawn curtains. A pot of mint tea steamed quietly on the table. The fan clicked above like a metronome.

Arafat entered a few minutes later, dressed as ever – keffiyeh, fatigue jacket, sharp eyes under tired lids. He extended his hand without smiling.

'You're punctual,' he said.

'You're hard to find.'

'That's the idea.'

They sat. The mood was formal. Tea was poured. The conversation brisk, updates from Jerusalem, impressions of Gaza, Amol's thoughts on how the Western press was covering the PLO. Arafat took it all in without notes, occasionally raising an eyebrow, rarely commenting. It was not an interview. It was a temperature check.

As the meeting began to slow, Amol – half in jest, half out of instinct – asked, 'Is it true what they're saying? That you've just got married?'

The silence was instant and sharp.

Arafat stared at him, blinking once, slowly. Then, in a sudden hiss of fury: 'You ask an Arab Muslim about his wife?'

He stood. The meeting was over.

Amol rose, stunned. 'I apologize. It was careless.'

Arafat turned his back.

At the door, Amol hesitated. From his satchel he removed the jar of Indian honey – the gift he had brought with him from Delhi – and placed it quietly at the corner of the table.

Then he left.

An hour later, as he packed in his hotel room, there was a knock at the door. The same man from the airport stood in the hallway.

'Come,' he said. No explanation.

They drove through side streets to a low white bungalow outside the city, nestled between citrus trees and flowering hedges. The sea shimmered beyond the wall.

Inside, in the cool hush of a high-ceilinged room, Arafat stood smiling – dressed in short sleeves, relaxed. Beside him stood a young woman in a pale summer dress, her eyes steady, her hair uncovered.

Amol hesitated.

'This is Suha,' Arafat said. 'My wife.'

The woman inclined her head, her smile faint but kind.

Arafat stepped forward, touched Amol lightly on the arm. 'You remembered the honey,' he said.

That was all. For a man surrounded by silence, it was the one thing he could still taste.

And somehow, it was enough.

Back in his hotel room, Amol sat by the window and watched the dusk roll in over Tunis. The call to prayer drifted from a distant minaret, soft as birdsong. The jar of honey was gone. In its place, he carried a new kind of silence – less the absence of sound, more the weight of things left unsaid. Grief had taken many forms that summer: smoke, marble, wreckage, ritual. But now it wore a smile and stood beside a man who had once been myth.

—

Somewhere in Jerusalem, his typewriter waited.

He hadn't planned to return. But the night after Tunis, after the honey, after Suha's pale smile in that seaside bungalow, Amol boarded a *sherut* from Jerusalem and rode west into the Tel Aviv heat.

He hadn't planned what came next. But the thread had already been pulled.

It was after nine when he reached Malkin and Roni's building. The street was quiet. A lone cat slinked between parked cars.

Lights still burnt behind Malkin's shutters. He rang once.

Roni opened the door. She took one look at him and said, 'He's in the study.'

She didn't ask questions. She disappeared down the hallway, shawl over one shoulder, her bare feet soft on tile.

Amol stepped inside. Malkin was seated at a desk, one lamp casting long shadows across a stack of canvases and two glasses of whisky. One glass was full. The other, untouched.

'You've been somewhere,' Malkin said.

'Tunis.'

Malkin nodded slowly. 'Did he smile?'

'Yes.'

'Then he liked you.'

They sat in silence for a minute. The fan ticked above them. The window was open and the Mediterranean wind pressed gently at the shutters. Malkin pushed the full glass towards him.

'I owe you a story,' he said.

Amol didn't reply. He just waited.

Malkin took a sip, then leaned back, his voice low, stripped of performance. 'Remember what I told you about Eichmann? We were actually sent for Mengele. That was the point. The doctor. The butcher. The genius of anatomy. He was the one they wanted. I still have the order. His name printed in block letters.'

Amol blinked in surprise.

Malkin went on. 'Eichmann was the insurance. The bureaucrat. The filing cabinet of genocide. But we thought Mengele was still there – hidden in Argentina, protected, sloppy with his routines. We had sources. Shadows. Patterns. We thought we could pin him.'

He exhaled. 'Three days before we arrived, he vanished. No trace. Someone tipped him off, or he just felt the wind change. I like to think he felt something. Some pulse in the earth.'

Amol stared at him. 'So Eichmann was the –'

'Consolation prize,' Malkin said. 'Not officially. They'd never say it that way. But he wasn't the monster we wanted. Just the one we could catch.'

He finished his drink. The ice had melted. Roni returned quietly and placed a folded blanket on the back of Malkin's chair. She touched his shoulder. Then she left again.

Malkin turned back to Amol. 'You've seen war,' he said. 'Seen the headlines. The briefings. But there's another part of it. You go looking for the devil. Turns out he took early retirement.'

Amol stared at the wall, where a new canvas leaned, half finished – dark greys, empty corridors, a barely visible door in the background.

'Do you regret it?' he asked.

Malkin shook his head. 'I regret that Mengele died in Brazil of a stroke. That no one held his wrists.'

It was the only time Amol saw him speak with something close to hatred.

Then he stood up slowly, as if dismissing himself. Amol didn't try to stop him.

As he left the apartment, the Tel Aviv night wrapped around him like a warm shroud.

He didn't even write any notes but remembered every word and wrote up the entire story from memory.

Back in Jerusalem, Amol lay awake until dawn. The city's white light was already seeping through the shutters – clean, clinical, the kind of light that flattened everything into certainty. He didn't file copy. He didn't call his editor.

The summer had taken Layla, his grandfather and something quieter – his certainty. Now, all that remained was memory and the men who fed on it.

He had crossed into the realm of watchers and keepers, not just a witness anymore, but something harder to define. Somewhere between Caesarea and Tunis, between Gaza and that quiet Tel Aviv room, the border had vanished. He was in it now, whatever it was, and there would be no safe place left to stand. Only the burden of memory and what sweetness might survive it.

13

The Man Who Wasn't There

Late November 1991, Jerusalem

The light was losing interest in the day by mid-afternoon. Shadows draped the stones like silk.

Amol had begun walking every evening without direction, through Talpiot and into Rehavia, or sometimes down to the Old City – moving through streets half remembered and half forgotten. He wasn't sure what he was looking for. The walks were less about distance than dislocation. In motion, he felt less trapped.

So many years had passed since Layla's death. He remembered the week that followed, a stretch of silence thick as fog, some press cables, blurred condolences. There was never any body identified. The bus bombing near the airport left only smoke, ash and a partial list of the dead.

A mistake at first, he thought – someone else, same name, same flight. Then came confirmation. Bus bombing en route to the airport. Claim of responsibility from some group he'd never heard of. 'Unfortunate civilian collateral.' That phrase clung to his ribs like a stone.

He hadn't told anyone how he'd screamed when he read the faxed death notice. The sound had torn from him like cloth.

That evening, just after sunset, he received a small, blue envelope – the same colour of blue as the Israeli flag. No stamp. No return address. Hand-delivered. Inside: a single note in looping handwriting.

Come to the terrace at the American Colony. Six o'clock.
A friend who admired her.

No signature.

For a moment, he thought of Sedo – not because the handwriting matched (it didn't), but because the tone did: cryptic, purposeful, stripped of sentiment. Sedo always had a way of turning grief into invitation. This felt like the same currency – summons disguised as condolence.

He stared at the paper for half an hour before setting it down beside the cold cup of tea and unopened notebook. He hadn't written a word since her death. Words had become inert things, stripped of meaning, too crude for the complexity that churned inside him. What could he write? That her laugh still rang out when he reached for sugar? That he now hated his work, his editors, his notebook? That he hated himself?

The street outside was almost empty now, the evening light bruising the stone walls. But she was everywhere. In the shapes of windows, in the cadence of boys' voices, in the way the light turned corners.

A boy passed on a bicycle, humming something that reminded Amol of another place, another time. Layla, Sedo, both gone in different ways, both shaping the silence he now carried.

It was Sedo who once told him, after Naxos, 'We are where we're needed, not where we're wanted.' At the time it had sounded noble. Now it felt like evasion.

At 5.30 p.m., he put on his long coat and walked towards the hotel. The air was cool and dry, the kind of chill that clung not to the skin but the spaces between thought. As he neared the amphitheatre in Hinnom Valley, music floated up into the darkening sky. A concert. Sting perhaps. One of those songs about faith and loss.

The sound spilled out into the night, gentle and clear: 'If I ever lose my faith in you … ' The voice hovered in the air like incense.

A small crowd stood outside the walls, listening for free. Families, young couples. Children sitting on shoulders. Amol paused. The crowd was mostly young – students, soldiers on leave, girls in sundresses and boys in white shirts, their faces soft with optimism and late sunlight.

They swayed to the music, arms brushing, smiles easy and unguarded. It reminded him of a time he could barely recall, when belief in the future hadn't yet become foolish.

Why was Sting here, he wondered. Was it part of that brief window of hope? When Arafat shook Rabin's hand on the White House lawn, and people clung to the illusion that something new could grow out of the rubble?

Music, Amol thought, was always first to arrive when peace seemed possible. And last to leave when it wasn't.

'You could say I'd lost my belief in our politicians … They all seemed like game show hosts to me … ' The lyrics struck a nerve. He stood still, his hands deep in his coat pockets, letting the chords wrap around his grief. The voice, precise and plaintive, carved a space inside him that had been numb for days.

He noticed a girl near the fence, no older than twenty, mouthing every word. Her fingers traced invisible shapes in the air with each verse. She reminded him of Layla at twenty – that mix of fierceness and wonder. The kind of girl who would argue with professors and then cry during poetry.

'If I ever lose my faith …'

By the time he reached the American Colony, the song had changed. But the voice stayed with him.

The terrace was nearly empty, except for a man sitting beneath an olive tree – thin as a stone, waiting without impatience.

Elegant suit, unfashionable tie, wire-frame glasses that caught the low glow of the outdoor lanterns. His command of English was good, but he was not British, not like Josling, possible East European, and imbued with the kind of calm that made people speak more than they meant.

The man looked up as Amol approached. 'Mr Batty.' Not a question.

Amol nodded. 'And you are?'

The man smiled. 'Eric.'

Amol raised an eyebrow.

'Just Eric.'

He gestured to the chair opposite. A waiter appeared without being called. Two espressos arrived.

'I knew Layla,' Eric said. 'Not well. Not for long. But well enough to admire her.'

'From Paris?' Amol asked.

'No. Here. Once or twice. We spoke about poetry. She was fond of Neruda.'

'She was fond of many things.'

Amol studied him. There was nothing threatening about the man – no visible weapon, no security presence. Just a sense of stillness. Like he belonged in a different time.

Eric sipped. 'You've been told not to go to Sudan.'

'I haven't decided yet.'

'You will.' The tone was not prophetic. It was observational.

'I'm a journalist,' Amol said.

Eric didn't smile. 'Are you?'

Amol opened his mouth, then closed it. He hadn't filed copy in weeks. The notebook stayed blank. Was he still a reporter, or just someone walking through ruins, bearing witness too late? He felt heat rise. 'Meaning what?'

'Meaning that journalists ask questions. Lately, you've been answering them.'

'What do you do?'

'I observe.'

'For who?'

Eric's eyes glinted behind the lenses. 'Let's not spoil things.' He paused, then added: 'I knew Malkin. We shared … proximity. That's often more revealing than friendship.'

Amol's chest tightened. That name again. It carried too much weight. The night in Tel Aviv, the confession over whisky, the exhaustion behind the legend. Malkin had shown him what pursuit really cost. Some debts couldn't be spoken about, only endured.

'You never saw him again, did you?'

Amol shook his head.

Eric gave a small nod, as if confirming something he'd long suspected. 'He read what you wrote. Said you had a precision we don't often see anymore.'

They sat in silence. The clatter of crockery, distant laughter, the whisper of olives in wind. Amol's eyes drifted to the courtyard

– memories of Layla came unbidden. Her voice in French. Her bare feet on tile. A smile traced from memory.

'You've written well,' Eric said. 'Too well.'

'What's that supposed to mean?'

'Sometimes a story is dangerous not for what it reveals, but for how clearly it does so. You write in a way that makes certain people nervous.'

'Good.'

Eric nodded. 'Good can be dangerous.' He took something from his pocket – a photo. Black and white. A boy, maybe sixteen, armless, standing in sand. One arm lost at the shoulder, the other at the elbow. He was smiling.

'Sudan,' Eric said. 'Village near Kassala. They called him the Singer. Beautiful voice. They took his arms for stealing maize.'

Amol looked at the photo for a long time.

'I want to go there,' he said, surprising himself.

'No, you don't.'

Amol handed the photo back. 'You said you observed,' he said. 'But you're doing more than that.'

'I'm intervening, yes. Quietly.'

'For who?'

Eric's eyes narrowed. 'For those who still think silence has value.'

They left the terrace together but did not walk side by side. At the hotel gate, Eric stopped.

'I'm sorry about Layla,' he said. 'She made you better. Don't let that go to waste.'

Then he turned and disappeared into the traffic. Amold didn't know then that Eric's warning would be the hinge on which his next story turned.

—

He stood still for a long time, then walked home in silence. He stayed up most of the night. It had been nearly three months since Tunis. But Jerusalem no longer felt like a sanctuary.

He couldn't write, not in any way that made sense. Instead, he walked his flat in slow loops, barefoot, the silence broken only by the occasional creak of old pipes and distant horns.

Around 3 a.m., he opened a notebook and wrote a single line:

The grief doesn't go away. It changes shape, but it stays.

He underlined it twice. Closed the notebook. Opened it again. Wrote:

Maybe that's why I take risks. Not because I want to die. But because I already did, a little.

He tore out the page, folded it and tucked it inside his wallet.

At dawn, as the muezzin's call rose in the distance, he stared out across Jerusalem's rooftops and whispered Layla's name like a prayer. He loved Jerusalem with a passion that surprised even him. For all its scars, all the blood it had soaked up over centuries, it remained unlike anywhere else. The light had its own cadence. The air carried echoes. There were days when he swore he could feel the weight of history pressing into his shoulders. Romans had marched here. Ancient Jews had sung here. Crusaders had wept and bled and vanished into dust.

Had Solomon really built a temple on this rock? Had Cleopatra visited with Mark Antony? Was this truly the world's greatest city, as some still claimed – the navel of the earth, the city of peace, forever trembling on the brink of war?

Even now, with loss curling inside him like smoke, Amol believed it might be true. Jerusalem was an ode to noble ideals – defaced, graffitied, defiled – but still sung. And he loved it.

He did not yet know that this grief – dense, undigested – would be the quiet engine behind his next assignment. That Sudan, and what followed, would be his way of stepping into fire, hoping to feel again.

But part of him already suspected. And part of him welcomed it.

He ran his hand along the spines of books Layla had touched. Her favourite was still there, a slim volume of translated Sufi poems with dog-eared pages and notes in the margins – her handwriting, chaotic and confident. He opened it and found one that she had marked with a small heart: 'Don't grieve. Anything you lose comes round in another form.'

He closed the book slowly. Layla believed that. He wasn't sure he did. But he carried the thought with him, fragile as a pressed flower, into the coming days.

He would leave Jerusalem soon. The world was calling again, not with answers, but with danger. He was no longer chasing stories. He was chasing memory. And memory was a dangerous thing to carry.

Twice in two days, the same man brushed past him in different cities. Once in Cairo, once in Athens. Amol noticed the shoes first. Polished, wrong for the weather. Like a signature left for him to find. The man passed him again. Not a word. Not a glance. Just presence, like smoke, like memory.

The man who wasn't there, always was.

Was it coincidence? A warning? Or just another way of reminding him that observation had no off switch?

In the Saudi city of Taif, the silence was thicker than the heat. Locals claimed this was where the Prophet found rest. Cool air, clean hills, perfumed breezes – a summer retreat for royals and generals escaping the furnace of Riyadh. But to Amol, it felt like a city where nothing could be seen directly. Everything was shielded – by hedges, by silence, by the secret agents of the local mukhabarat (the feared secret police).

He'd gone to Taif on a quiet lead, following the displaced Yazidis who'd fled northern Iraq and now lived on the margins of a state that didn't acknowledge them. A fixer had promised introductions. 'It's safe,' he'd said. 'As long as you don't write anything down.'

Amol arrived cautious but curious. The hotel was sparse and antiseptic – plain white walls, scent of bleach, air conditioning that whispered like gossip. He checked in under his real name, which already felt like a mistake.

Three Yazidi men came at dusk. Only one spoke with edge – older, missing three fingers.

'They call it Al-Maidan,' he said. 'The Square. Come Friday, after prayer, they bring them out – thieves, apostates, dissenters. The sword falls clean.'

Amol hesitated. Then nodded.

That night, he barely slept. Morning came, hushed and gold. They walked at dawn, past shuttered shops and manicured hedges. The square was just a patch of sand framed by low walls. A bloodstain, faint but undeniable, darkened the centre like a watermark.

A wooden post stood alone – cracked, blackened at its base. No one else was there. Just birds, flitting.

Amol didn't photograph it. He didn't sketch it. He simply wrote four lines in his notebook:

Execution Square. Taif. Friday prayers.
Blood still visible.
Locals avoid eye contact.
Mukhabarat presence implied.

He closed the book. Said thank you. Walked back.

The hotel manager was waiting outside the gate. He wasn't smoking. He wasn't smiling. He looked like a man who'd just received a phone call he didn't want.

'Mr Batty,' he said, voice low. 'You need to leave.'

Amol blinked. 'Excuse me?'

'Now.' The man pressed a folded receipt into Amol's hand. 'I prepared your bill. Room is paid. No refund.'

'I still have –'

'They are asking,' he interrupted. 'Secret police. The ones you don't see. You went near Al-Maidan. You made notes.'

Amol's breath caught. 'How do they – ?'

The manager shook his head. 'They know. They always know.'

Behind him, across the street, two men stood by a black Land Cruiser. One leaned casually against the bonnet. The other stared, unmoving.

Amol didn't move. He'd seen this play out before – not in Taif, but in Tehran, in Khartoum, in Algiers. And he'd read the bulletins. So-and-so was detained and never seen again. So-and-so died in a car crash no one investigated. They were never close friends – just names on the wall, bylines in old magazines, colleagues who lived on the edge and stepped an inch too far.

He didn't want to be the next name. Amol didn't go back to his room. Didn't pack. He walked to the rear entrance, slipped out through the kitchens, flagged a passing taxi and told the driver he would give him a bonus to take him to Jeddah international airport, 176 kilometres to the south.

'Which airline?' the driver asked out of curiosity.

'It doesn't matter,' Amol said. 'Just get me there.' He didn't look back.

—

That night, on a layover in Cairo, he opened his notebook in the airport lounge and crossed out the lines about Taif. Then he rewrote them in smaller script on the inside flap of his passport, beneath a fold no one would see.

He'd remember. Even if no one else did.

The Saudis called it justice. The world called it sovereignty. But Amol had seen what happened to people who didn't stay invisible. In Taif, the sword still fell clean – but the silence that followed was what cut deepest.

After Taif, after the silence that followed the blade, he returned to Jerusalem. The flat felt stale, as if it had been holding its breath. On the doormat, an envelope waited.

No return address.

He knew the hand. Sedo's script, restrained, deliberate. Still growing.

Inside: a photocopy of the orchard they'd spoken of in Beirut, grainy and torn, with a handwritten note: 'Still growing.'

Amol stared at it for an hour. No signature. Just the same handwriting he remembered from Skopje. Still growing. Like a threat. Like a memory.

14

New Dangers

Grief had made Amol reckless. Jerusalem's white light no longer felt cleansing – it felt surgical. He woke each morning in silence. Filed his stories. Ate little. Slept less. What he craved now was friction. A test. Some line to cross and not come back from.

He didn't know Sudan would be the door Tehran would open.

He defied Eric's warning. Yes, without thinking. He didn't yet understand that recklessness could masquerade as purpose.

It was early December when the Sudan assignment arrived, the season where Jerusalem's cold light gave way to darker choices.

The details were vague, something about amputations, religious courts and punishment camps – he defied Eric's warning. Yes, without thinking. A voice in his head whispered: this one will hurt.

Mid-December 1991, Khartoum

Khartoum greeted him with dust and distrust. The hotel lobby was silent. The phones worked only in one direction. Elevators stuttered as if watched.

The Doctor arrived in a borrowed Toyota. British-trained, dry-eyed and anonymous. He handed Amol a surgical mask, a bottle of water and a look that said 'you asked for this'. Four hours east of the capital, the road dissolved into dust.

The village came into view like a hallucination: huts of scorched cement, canvas roofs torn at the corners, shadows that didn't move like they should.

'This is what's left,' the Doctor said. 'They call it the village of the legless.'

Amol stepped carefully through the scorched grass, the minefield just beyond. The men in the camp stared with blank, amputated eyes. It reminded him of another story – one that hadn't yet been written. About trees, not bones. About fruit, not flesh.

He pushed the thought aside. The men and boys came slowly. Some rolled on wooden carts. Others dragged themselves forward on their elbows. There were no patterns to their injuries – only cruelty. Missing limbs, twisted stumps, a leg here, an arm there, sometimes both. All punished for small crimes.

'He stole biscuits,' the Doctor murmured, pointing at a teenager missing both legs.

'And him?'

'Petrol. From a generator.'

Amol met a boy named Farouq, maybe thirteen. His right leg was gone till above the knee. His left arm ended at the elbow. He was drawing letters in the sand with a stick held between his teeth. 'What did he take?'

'Three tins of Fanta.'

Amol asked permission to record. The boy nodded. His voice was soft but unwavering. He spoke of being tied down, of the blade, of the screaming that stopped only when it was over.

Dozens of others gave testimony. Some described the rituals. Others spoke of silence. One simply pointed at a pile of rope under a corrugated roof.

'This,' a man said, 'is what justice becomes when God is turned into a gun.'

Amol thought of another man once – calm, measured, drawing lines between faith and fire. Sedo had called it resistance. The villagers here just called it survival. He wondered if Sedo would have understood this place. Probably. Sedo understood violence the way cartographers understood borders: as temporary things drawn by force.

Before they left, the Doctor gestured towards a low enclosure.

'There's another camp,' he said. 'Women.'

Behind a curtain of brush and twisted wire sat twenty or so women – some young, some hollow-eyed, most silent. A few had children clinging to their robes. Amol was ushered to one who let the Doctor lift her sleeve. Burnt into her forearm was a brand – three vertical bars under a crescent.

The skin had puckered around it like melted wax. 'She refused marriage to a militia emir,' the Doctor said. 'They said Allah had chosen. She said Allah gave her choice. So they marked her.'

Amol asked if he could record her. She nodded. 'They told me I was impure,' she said, her voice flat. 'But I have never touched a man.'

He recorded for an hour. Story after story. Some whispered. Some sung like hymns. One woman repeated the five pillars of Islam, then said: 'I followed them all. And still they burnt me.'

Amol clicked off the recorder and slipped it into his bag. He did not take photographs. That night, he returned to Khartoum under a different name. It didn't matter. The hotel phone rang once and fell silent.

In the lobby, two men read newspapers upside down. A bellhop followed him to his room without knocking.

He booked the next flight to Cairo.

Two days later, 1991, Khartoum Airport

At the airport, two Sudanese agents met him at the gate. They wore short sleeves and carried nothing. One stepped forward. 'You need to come with us.'

Amol didn't move. Behind him, two other foreign journalists appeared – one American, one Egyptian. They didn't speak his name. Just stood beside him like anchors.

'If you're taking him,' the Egyptian said calmly, 'you're taking us too.'

The agent hesitated. Looked around. Then wordlessly stepped back. But they weren't finished.

Fifteen minutes into boarding, as Amol sank into his seat near the back of the plane, the same two agents entered the aircraft. The cabin hushed. They walked the aisle with the slow precision of men who knew they were being watched – and didn't care. They stopped beside him.

One leaned in close and said, 'You should know, we read everything.'

Then, without waiting for permission, he reached into the seat pocket, took Amol's reporter's notebook and flipped through it page by page. Slowly. Mockingly. Then, just as slowly, he tore it cleanly in half. He walked to the nearest emergency exit window, slid it partway open and with two fingers, flicked the shredded remnants out into the Sudanese wind.

A few passengers gasped. A stewardess froze in the aisle. The agents turned and left the plane without another word.

Amol sat motionless, hands curled into fists.

His notebook was gone. But the cassette recorder, with every voice from the village, every testimony from the branded women, sat buried deep in the inside pocket of his jacket. Still running. Still intact.

The aircraft taxied, rose into the air, and turned north.

Only once Khartoum disappeared from the horizon did Amol allow himself to exhale. Yet, tensions among the crew and other passengers remained palpable. When the plane finally landed in Cairo, there was spontaneous applause – a clapping of hands, from all the passengers and the now smiling stewardesses.

Late December 1991, Jerusalem

Back in Jerusalem, Amol barely spoke.

He filed the Sudan story in a daze. It ran quietly – page ten, beneath a wire brief about grain shortages in Algeria.

No one called. No one asked for more. A junior subeditor emailed once: 'Disturbing stuff. Keep us posted.'

That was it. He wandered between the American Colony and his flat. Slept little. Smoked too much. The days bled together.

Then, without warning, an old contact reached out. Farhad Amini – a fixer from Tehran he barely remembered meeting in Cairo years before, sent him a telex via London.

'Your Sudan piece made it to Tehran. Some here took note. One man in particular. He wants to speak to you. He was close to Saddam once. Now he isn't, he is an exile in Iran and he's willing to talk. Interested?'

No flattery. No details. Just coordinates.

Sudan had been a test – he just didn't know who was marking the paper.

Amol stared at the screen. He didn't ask who 'some' referred to. He didn't care. The answer had formed before he'd even read the message twice. He sent back a signed message with one word: Yes.

Mid-January the cold in Jerusalem had deepened, but further east the air was sharper still.

January 1992, Tehran

Three days later, he was on a plane to Tehran.

No fanfare. No briefing. Just his old leather bag, a notebook and the tape recorder, rewound and emptied. This time, he had packed spare cassettes.

The air in Tehran was sharp with late winter. Bare trees lined the boulevards, their branches etched like black ink against a white sky. Amol arrived just after dawn. A diplomatic visa tucked into his passport. A contact number for Farhad Amini scribbled on the back of a calling card.

Farhad met him in the lobby of the Hotel Laleh. A small man, neatly dressed, smelling faintly of cloves. He offered tea but no small talk.

'Thank you for coming,' he said. 'They were right to trust you.'

Amol raised an eyebrow. 'Who's they?'

Farhad didn't answer. 'He'll see you tomorrow.'

The next day, Farhad collected him at 10 a.m. sharp. They drove north into the hills above Tajrish – away from the city's noise and fumes. The streets grew quieter, lined with shuttered villas and apricot trees just beginning to bloom.

They arrived at a house set back from the road – modest, clean-lined, fronted by a wrought iron gate. No guards. No visible security. But Amol sensed he was being watched long before they rang the bell. The door opened before they knocked.

Hasan Askari greeted them himself. He was taller than expected. Silver-haired, in a grey wool suit, open collar, no tie. His face had the sculpted calm of someone who had long ago separated anger from usefulness. Behind his glasses, his eyes were flint.

'Mr Batty,' he said, not smiling. 'You may call me Askari. Thank you for coming.'

His voice was low, formal, precise.

The sitting room was austere: a large bookshelf, two armchairs and a *samovar* steaming quietly in the corner. On the mantel, a photograph of an old nuclear facility – cooling towers, men in hard hats, a younger Askari in a lab coat, his arms folded across his chest.

'You are here,' he said, pouring tea without ceremony, 'because you wrote the truth about something no one wanted to see.'

Amol nodded, uncertain.

Askari continued: 'Sudan was a test. Not for you, for them. You passed.' He sipped his tea. 'What I am about to show you is dangerous. But necessary. If the world does not understand what Saddam did, it will not understand what he is still capable of.'

Amol opened his notebook.

'No recordings,' Askari said. 'Not here. Not now. Only listen.'

For the next two hours, Askari spoke – calmly, factually – about Iraq's weapons programme. Its inner hierarchies. Its silences. The day-to-day terror of proximity to power. He spoke of poison gas and stolen uranium, of purges disguised as promotions.

'I was not the man who pushed the button,' he said. 'But I helped build the button. That is why I speak now.'

Finally, he turned to Amol and said: 'There is a place you must see. Halabja. The world remembers the headline. You will see the imprint.'

'And after that?' Amol asked.

'The marshes,' Askari replied. 'But Halabja first. It's the scar. The marshes are the still open wound.'

He stood. The meeting was over.

Farhad returned Amol to the hotel in silence.

The next morning, Halabja

They arrived in Halabja by helicopter – an old Iranian Air Force Bell 214, with its insignia painted over and the windows blacked out from the inside. It lifted from a base near Kermanshah just after dawn, slicing through the mountain air with a growl that never softened.

Amol had ridden military choppers before, but never in silence. No radio chatter. No shouting. Just the thrum of rotors and the soft rasp of Askari's breathing beside him.

He wore the same grey suit. Unflinching, even at altitude.

'There's no official permission for this,' he said. 'We are not here.'

The chopper descended into a clearing just beyond the ruins of Halabja. The pilot said nothing. Just pointed once, towards the town, and then rose again into the fog.

They walked in.

Halabja didn't smell like a town. It smelled like metal and rot – like something unnatural had soaked into the earth and would never leave. Whole blocks had collapsed. Others stood intact but lifeless – windows blasted out, curtains still fluttering.

Askari led him behind a collapsed mosque to a half-submerged basement. The temperature dropped instantly. Moisture clung to the walls. And the air – thick, unmoving – carried the weight of death.

Inside, they found the bodies.

They hadn't decomposed fully – not yet. The chemical agents had arrested decay in strange ways. The skin of the dead had turned a deep, unholy blue. Lips split. Eyes filmed over. Some sat upright, as if still waiting.

'They turn blue in the end,' Askari said quietly. 'First the lungs fill. Then the spasms. Then this.'

Amol wrote, slowly. His hand shook. He crouched beside a woman curled around two children, all of them with eyes open and mouths frozen mid-breath.

They moved from house to house – no interruptions, no survivors. Only the final positions of entire families: a boy hiding under a bed. An old man gripping the leg of a table. A dog, long dead, lying nose-first at the front door.

The silence was monstrous.

Outside, as they prepared to leave, a gaunt man in a long coat approached. His beard was white, his eyes unblinking.

'I come each Friday,' he told Askari in Kurdish. 'To remember that I lived.'

Amol recorded the line in pencil. He would use it to close the piece.

The chopper returned an hour later. The pilot never turned off the engine. Askari helped Amol in, then climbed in after. As they lifted off, Amol looked down and saw the town recede like a stain beneath the mist.

The rest of the flight was an exercise in silence. He had seen war. But this was rot from within, a silence so complete it rewrote him.

The story ran five days later under the headline: 'The Town That Died Breathing.'

It spread fast. Translations in Farsi, Arabic and even Turkish.

An Iranian academic emailed him: 'You wrote the dead back into the world.'

State radio read passages aloud. The Iranian Foreign Ministry called it 'a grave warning to all nations about the West's complicity in Saddam's crimes'. The regime found it politically useful.

Amol found it unbearable.

At a quiet lunch in north Tehran, a senior cultural adviser pushed over an illicit glass of Armenian cognac and said, 'You have told the truth that serves us. For this, we are grateful.'

But the warmth felt theatrical.

—

His hotel phone rang often, always once, never twice.

One evening, a man who claimed to be a journalist invited him to dinner but asked only vague questions about his schooling and family. The next day, a woman from a 'literary institute' pressed a card into his hand and said, 'If you ever feel unsafe, we can help.' Her headscarf was carefully loose, her nails immaculate, her smile entirely unconvincing.

At the Laleh café, Farhad Amini stirred his tea for a long time before speaking.

'They're watching you now,' he said. 'Don't mistake praise for protection.'

Amol said nothing.

'You wrote what they needed written,' Farhad continued. 'That buys you time. Not safety.'

He tapped his teaspoon once, sharply, against the rim.

'They call you the "safe asset." It means: foreign, compliant, disposable. They've used worse words.'

'And Askari?'

Farhad shrugged. 'He was never safe. Just harder to remove.'

They sat in silence. The TV in the corner played footage of schoolchildren waving flags. The caption read: 'Future of the Revolution.'

Farhad leaned in. 'He wants to take you to the marshes next. It's different there. No graves. Just water.'

Amol nodded. 'When?'

Farhad smiled. 'Soon.'

Early February 1992, The Marshes

When Askari visited again, this time in plain clothes, he issued instructions.

'You're ready for the marshes,' he said. 'Bring boots. And salt tablets.'

They crossed under cover of fog – on foot, then by boat, then foot again, stumbling uncertainly across the tarmac highway that links Baghdad to Basrah. The smugglers moved silently, wearing wool balaclavas and cracked plastic boots, their breath fogging in the dawn.

Askari handed Amol a worn anorak and a pair of knee-high rubber waders. The air stank of algae and diesel.

'This place,' Askari said, 'was once called the Venice of the East.'

Now it was silence, salt and ruin.

The marshes – once vast, shimmering and alive – had shrunk into a patchwork of stagnant pools and cracked silt. Boats sat beached like carcasses. The water that remained was oily, laced with green film. Buffalo bones jutted from the shallows like the ribs of sunken ships.

Askari walked ahead, feet sinking with each step. 'Saddam drained it in the nineties,' he said. 'To punish the Shia who sheltered the rebels. He dammed the rivers, built canals to reroute the Tigris. Then came the fires.'

'What fires?'

'He burnt the reeds. So the people couldn't hide.'

They reached a hut – barely standing, made of broken rushes lashed with wire. Inside, a family sat on cinder blocks. A man with one eye. A girl with swollen ankles. An old woman who coughed as if her lungs were made of dust.

Amol asked to speak with them. Askari translated. They said the water came only once a week now – filtered through plastic tanks dumped by NGOs. They said the fish were gone. That the birds no longer sang. That the reeds no longer grew tall enough to cut.

'Before,' the old woman said, 'we floated to weddings. Now we walk to funerals.' She pointed to a cracked teapot on a rusted stove.

'This,' she said, 'was once the heart of Iraq.'

Amol wrote it all down. They moved from camp to camp – scattered communities still clinging to islands of sludge. Children played barefoot in water that shimmered with petrol. A bearded man showed Amol a photo of his father holding a spear next to a canoe.

'He died building a canal for Saddam. They promised him a pension. He got a bullet.'

Askari led him into a collapsed madrasa where pages of the Qur'an lay soaked into the floor, unreadable. A buffalo skull sat atop the teacher's dais.

'This,' Askari said, 'is what happens when you try to erase a people by erasing their land.'

By the second night, Amol had filled two notebooks.

Mid-Febuary 1992, Tehran

Back in Tehran, he filed his next story, this time under a new headline: 'The Drowned Nation.'

As with the story about Halabja, it was translated into Farsi and Arabic within days. IRNA quoted it. Radio Tehran read excerpts on air.

The Foreign Ministry issued a statement blaming Western powers for supplying Saddam with chemical agents, then cited Amol's story as proof.

He became, overnight, useful.

A professor at Tehran University sent him a handwritten note: 'You have given voice to those who were erased. History will remember this.'

Next, he was invited to a private dinner at the Ministry of Islamic Guidance. Someone offered him pistachios and a glass of imported wine beneath a portrait of Khomeini.

'You are a friend to truth,' one official said, raising a glass. 'And therefore, a friend to Iran.'

Farhad pulled him aside afterward. 'They like you. They trust you. For now.'

By then, Tehran wasn't just watching; it was measuring him.

A week after the Marsh Arabs story ran, Askari called without preamble. 'I want to show you something,' he said. 'You've earned it.

—

Askari looked straight at Amol. 'No one else would be allowed in. Not even most of ours.'

They drove south from Tehran in a ministry car with no plates. Amol asked no questions. The road curved into desert – flat, ochre, vast. The mountains faded into haze behind them. It took five hours.

At the last checkpoint, a man in fatigues checked their IDs against a printout and made a quiet call in Farsi. Then the barrier lifted and they passed into a narrow valley flanked by scrub and rock. At the far end: a low, grey building, half sunken into the earth.

'This is Natanz,' Askari said softly. 'Or at least one part of it.'

Inside, the air chilled. Clean corridors. Surveillance cameras tucked into ceiling corners. Men in white coats moved quickly, not looking up. Amol was made to sign a document in Farsi. Farhad, who had reappeared like a shadow, murmured, 'Standard non-disclosure.'

The tour was brisk, controlled. Centrifuge housings. Control rooms lined with analogue dials. A decontamination chamber. Every object gleamed.

'No photography,' said one of the scientists. Askari ignored him.

He explained the shift in Iranian strategy post Saddam – how the marshes and Halabja weren't just memories, but warnings.

'We will never be that vulnerable again,' he said. 'If Saddam had succeeded, Tehran would look like Halabja now.'

They passed a viewing room with reinforced glass. Beyond it, rows of black canisters hummed softly. This wasn't just access. It was grooming. And he wasn't sure where the line was anymore.

Amol turned. 'Are these … active?'

Askari smiled. 'No one will ever confirm that. But they are functional.'

Later, over strong tea in a side office, a younger technician asked if Amol's next story would be on this facility.

'No,' Askari said before Amol could reply. 'He writes about what happens to people. Not metal.'

The technician looked disappointed.

The next morning, Amol packed in silence. No one called. No one knocked. Farhad had left a note with the front desk – 'You did well. Be careful.'

The message said nothing, but its existence said enough.

Later that day, he arrived at the hotel in person to hand over a tattered folder with scribbled names, dates and blurred photos.

'Intercepted traffic,' the fixer muttered. 'Mostly junk. But one name stood out – Sedo Hazan.'

Amol blinked. 'Kurdish?'

'Might be. The trail ends near Urmia.'

He forced a neutral expression, but his heart kicked. That was a name he recognized. Or one of them.

Someone was keeping him moving – or circling in place.

And that someone had eyes on Amol.

Naxos came back like static – the scratch of pencil on paper, detonator sketches folded into matchboxes, the faint smell of cold metal.

He hadn't thought of Sedo in weeks. But now, with Askari's stories swirling in his head and Josling circling like a hawk, the name felt less like a memory and more like a fuse, burning back towards him.

Outside, Tehran moved at its usual pace – horns, prayer calls, young men hawking bootleg CDs in the underpasses. A newsstand by the hotel carried a Farsi weekly with his Halabja piece on the cover. The photograph was wrong. It showed a collapsed house with a child's toy in the rubble. Amol hadn't taken it.

Someone had added drama where none was needed.

At the airport, a customs officer flipped through his passport, paused at the diplomatic visa and waved him through. No questions. No stamp. Just a look. The visa was still a mystery – neat Farsi script, a red seal, no expiry date. He didn't know who had arranged it. Maybe Farhad. Maybe someone in Vauxhall who still thought he could be turned.

Maybe it didn't matter.

Another man, further down the corridor, watched him pass without blinking. Amol didn't look back.

The flight boarded late. He didn't sleep. Just stared out the window at the desert falling away below, wondering when the shaking in his hands would stop. He drank nothing. Ate nothing. The voice recorder stayed zipped in his jacket the entire way.

By the time he left Tehran, gratitude had curdled into scrutiny. He felt the net tightening, though he couldn't yet see its pattern.

Early March 1992, Jerusalem

He returned to his flat in Talpiot just past midnight. It was spacious – high ceilings, chipped white walls, books everywhere. From the terrace, he could see the golden dome of Al Aqsa shimmer faintly in the distance, and on a clear day, Bethlehem – dry hills and silver rooftops – rose faintly to the south.

The silence felt different here. After Tehran, after the marshes, it was almost luxurious.

He made strong coffee. Smoked on the balcony. Tried not to think.

By the first week March 1992, he was back in Jerusalem, the cables still warm.

Mid-March 1992, Jerusalem, The American Colony Hotel

Three days later, a note slid under the door.

Lunch. Tomorrow. 1 p.m. American Colony. – K.J.

The initials were a signature. He didn't need to guess. He considered ignoring it. Instead, he pressed his one good linen shirt and booked a service taxi.

The American Colony Hotel was shaded and still. Reporters lingered in the lounge and Josling was already seated in the courtyard, blazer draped neatly, shirt cuffs rolled back just enough to suggest ease.

He stood as Amol approached. Smiled with warmth that didn't quite reach his eyes.

'You're back,' he said gently. 'I wasn't sure we'd see you again.'

They shook hands. Water was already on the table. So were olives and pistachios. The staff knew not to hover.

'I trust the trip back was uneventful,' Josling said, as though they'd seen each other just last week.

Amol didn't answer.

'Your Tehran work has made quite an impression,' Josling went on. 'Halabja. The marshes. That visit to Natanz.' A pause.

'Quite an impression indeed.'

He reached into a slim leather folio and produced a single sheet of paper. No letterhead. Just typed lines and two numbers at the bottom.

'This isn't a formal pitch,' he said. 'Let's call it a conversation. Between professionals.' He waited. 'You return to Tehran. Resume contact with Askari. Keep doing what you're doing. But with one small adjustment.' He tapped the paper. 'You record your conversations. All of them. Use whatever method suits you – cassette, digital, shorthand. 'Doesn't matter. We'll handle the rest.'

Amol picked up the page. Scanned it. $10,000 a month. No taxes. No questions.

'That's a consultancy rate,' Josling said lightly. 'Discreet. Flexible. Our books are quite creative.'

He leaned back, let it sit.

'This isn't betrayal. No one's asking you to spy. We're simply asking you to pay attention – and share what matters.'

Amol folded the page once. Set it on the table. Josling smiled again. This time, colder.

'We only ask that you keep doing what you're doing. Alone. With fewer friends. In a city where shadows move faster than truth.'

A long silence.

Then he stood.

'You've been through a lot,' he added, with a softness that made it worse. 'Don't shut out the people who understand what that does to a man.'

He adjusted his cuffs. 'Take your time, Amol. But not too much.'

Amol left with the weight of Josling's words pressing on him. For a while, there was no word, no invitation, no pressure.

A week passed. Then another. No follow-up, no pressure. Amol thought perhaps they'd moved on.

Two weeks later – late March 1992 – the matchbook arrived. No envelope this time – just a torn matchbook with the hotel's crest and a time written inside. Different ink. Same hand.

He lit a cigarette and didn't decide until the last moment.

Same place: the American Colony, the bar this time, wood-panelled and dim.

A few UN staffers murmured over glasses of arak. Outside, the muezzin was calling Maghrib.

Amol arrived late, coat unbuttoned, tired from another Tehran trip. Askari had been generous with information, guarded with predictions. Something in the air had shifted.

Josling rose as Amol approached. 'Still in one piece,' he said. 'Layla would've been proud, you know.'

Amol sat. Said nothing. Josling ordered two drinks without asking. When the waiter left, he leaned in.

'I won't spin this out,' he said. 'We need you. Still. Maybe more than before. You're inside Tehran in a way even their diplomats aren't. Askari trusts you. That kind of access doesn't grow on trees.'

He slid a fresh folder across the table. 'Same offer. Better rate.'

Amol didn't touch it.

'I told you last time,' he said. 'I'm not your man.'

Josling studied him. Something hard flickered in his eyes. Then softened, too quickly.

'You know,' he said, swirling his drink, 'my daughter's just moved out here. Gorgeous girl. Smarter than I ever was. She loves journalists. Always going on about them. Thought you two might hit it off. We don't just trust you, Amol, we rate you.'

Amol looked at him. Slowly.

'I beg your pardon?'

Josling smiled, a little too tightly. 'No need to look so shocked. I'm just saying – it's always nice to have friends. Real ones. The kind you can talk to at dinner. Maybe in private.'

Amol's glass stayed untouched. 'You're offering me your daughter?'

Josling didn't flinch. 'Don't be dramatic. I'm offering you the life that comes with belonging. It's not a bribe. It's … comfort. You've earned that.'

Amol stood. 'You used to sell paint, didn't you?'

That caught Josling. 'What?'

'Before this. Before SIS. You were in adhesives. Or colour-matching. Something small and oily.'

Josling's smile vanished.

Amol stepped away from the table. 'I report what I see,' he said. 'And what I see right now is a man trying to pimp his own daughter to save a dying case file.'

He didn't wait for a reply. Just walked out, past the Ottoman arches and the cool marble hall, back into the dry Jerusalem night.

He didn't sleep that night, or the night after. By the time the cables caught up with him in London, his disgust had hardened into a kind of calm. The world wanted heroes; he'd learned how they were made.

Early 1992, London

The applause didn't ring so much as linger, soft and polite, muffled by the clink of glasses and the distant clatter of crockery from the kitchens. Amol stood awkwardly near the floral centrepiece, hands clasped, the plaque in his grip already beginning to sweat under his fingers.

Some phrasing about 'exceptional foreign correspondence' had been engraved onto it, though he hadn't looked closely. He gave a short nod, mumbled a thank you and stepped down from the small, raised platform.

A round of pats on the back greeted him as he slid into his seat at the far corner table, already half forgotten by the time the next round of honourees stood up. He smiled thinly and reached for his wine.

This was the third ceremony in as many weeks. One had taken place at a Victorian hotel near Hyde Park, another in the upstairs dining room of a private club with red velvet chairs and service bells. Now this one – in a conference hall in Holborn that had been hastily decorated with ficus trees and fairy lights. He could barely tell them apart anymore.

There were bouquets in reception. Letters with government franks. A colleague told him, with some glee, that one of his stories had been quoted during a parliamentary debate. A young MP apparently held up a printout of Amol's report on the Marsh Arabs and declared: 'When we ignore the suffering of the voiceless, we make an ally of tyranny.'

'Oh Christ,' he said. 'Can you tell them, please, a tanker's just around the corner. It's heading this way.'

Sedo nodded, turned and relayed the message in flawless Arabic.

The crowd eased. Smiles returned. A girl waved. The soldier climbed out of the Land Rover, still rattled but grateful. A lanky corporal, barely twenty-two, with freckles and a Midlands accent flattened by exhaustion.

'Corporal Fielding,' he said, sticking out a hand. 'Honestly – thanks. I thought they were going to tear me apart.'

'They just wanted a drink,' said Sedo.

'Don't we all,' muttered Fielding. He glanced around. 'Look, if you're headed to the main palace complex, I can run you in. Safer that way.'

They climbed into the back. No paperwork, no clearance. The rules were loosening by the hour.

The Land Rover bumped across the cracked tarmac and through a once-grand gateway flanked by crumbling lion statues. The palace compound loomed ahead – sun-bleached colonnades, windows broken, but still under military guard. Inside, dust hung like incense. They passed shattered chandeliers, upending chairs, portraits leaning face-down against the walls.

One wing had collapsed entirely. Another was daubed with graffiti in three languages.

The colour scheme was unmistakable: gold and cream, everywhere – on the balustrades, the ruined chandeliers, the shredded brocade curtains.

Saddam, like a certain New York property tycoon decades later, had never met a gilded surface he didn't trust. The aesthetic of invincibility: tasteless, excessive, deeply insecure.

Fielding drove them right up to the entrance.

Inside, the silence was thick, like a museum after hours. They passed shattered windows, upended armchairs, the remains of a chandelier that now lay coiled like a dead insect.

'Guided tours don't usually come with corporal escort,' Amol said.

Fielding chuckled. 'You'll want the east wing.'

'Why?'

He grinned. 'That's where Uday used to sleep.'

No one spoke. They stepped through a door with a cracked gold handle and found themselves in a room larger than most London flats – pink marble tiles, one-way mirror, and what remained of a rotating circular bed.

Amol walked to the window. Outside, the palm trees swayed like they didn't care.

Sedo ran a finger over a bullet hole in the wall. 'He would've hated us being here,' he said.

Amol nodded. 'Which makes it perfect.'

The room was both enormous and ridiculous. A circular bed sat in the middle like a stranded lifeboat, its velvet upholstery scorched and clawed.

Mirrors lined the ceiling – cracked in places, spider-webbed with impact. The marble floor bore dark stains that didn't look like dust.

It was like Donald Trump's interior decorator had lost a bet in Vegas, then flown straight to Baghdad with a suitcase full of gold leaf and no shame.

There were syringes everywhere. Strewn across a bedside table, rolling underfoot, jammed into the plush carpet like silver darts. Some capped, others not.

The walls were a collage of contradiction. Dozens of images – mostly torn from magazines or printed on glossy Kodak – showed naked women in acrobatic poses, some amateur, some porn-star perfect. Thumbtacked, peeling, fading in the heat. And tucked between them – absurdly, tenderly – were photographs of Uday with his family.

A teenage Uday, grinning beside his mother, Sajida Talfah, both framed by gilded curtains. Another, more recent: Uday in military fatigues, arm slung awkwardly around Saddam, who stared into the lens with the blank confidence of a man convinced history would forgive him.

Amol stepped back, trying to take it all in.

'He had a theme,' he said.

Sedo nodded. 'Degeneracy?'

'Duality.'

He pointed – one wall, all breasts and legs. Another, with the Ba'ath Party crest and a framed quote from Qur'an. Below it, a minibar.

Fielding hovered awkwardly near the doorway, glancing at the syringes, the porn, the photos of mother and son. 'I don't get it,' he muttered. 'How does someone live like this?'

Amol was about to reply when Sedo crouched beside a toppled nightstand and pulled something from beneath the debris – a large hardback book, miraculously intact.

He turned it over.

The dust jacket showed a golden bowl of chicken korma, ringed by coriander leaves and rice shaped into a dome. The title was embossed in cheerful script: '*The Best of Indian Curries*' by Madhur Jaffrey.

All three of them stared.

Of all the things they'd expected to find in Uday Hussein's bedroom, a celebrity cookery book wasn't on the list.

Just then, a tinny speaker clicked on somewhere overhead. A voice – off-key, over-enunciated – belted out 'My Way' in heavily accented English. They froze.

'That's him,' Fielding whispered. 'We found a stack of cassettes. He used to record karaoke nights. Made his own backup vocals.'

Uday crooned through the chorus like a dying lounge singer.

Then the track skipped, repeated, and died with a hiss.

'What is this place?' Amol said.

'A ruin,' said Sedo. 'But curated by a psychopath.'

Amol raised an eyebrow.

'Well. He had range,' Sedo snorted.

Fielding cracked first, a short, confused laugh that quickly became something helpless. Then Sedo joined in, then Amol, until the room echoed with the sound of three men laughing too loudly in a place that didn't deserve it.

As the laughter ebbed, Sedo flopped down onto the edge of the bed with theatrical solemnity.

'Well,' he said, patting the velvet like it might purr, 'we've come this far.'

Amol raised an eyebrow. 'What are you doing?'

'History,' said Sedo.

He beckoned them over.

Corporal Fielding hesitated for a heartbeat – then, with a shrug, walked across the room and sat beside him, his boots crunching lightly over glass. Amol took the third spot, careful to avoid a suspicious stain on the bedspread.

Sedo held up his pocket camera.

'Smile,' he said.

The camera clicked.

Three men – a British soldier, an exiled revolutionary and a half-Indian journalist – sitting shoulder to shoulder on the wreckage of Uday Hussein's pleasure bed, grinning like tourists who'd taken a wrong turn on the palace tour.

For a second, none of it mattered: not the war, not the ghosts, not the headlines waiting to be written.

Just the absurdity of survival.

As Sedo checked the photo and muttered something about the angle of his jaw, Fielding stood and stretched.

'You've seen the armoury yet?' he asked, almost casually.

Amol shook his head.

'Two rooms down,' said Fielding. 'Last week we found a stash – five Kalashnikovs, custom-built. Solid gold plating. Not paint – actual gold. Heavy as hell.'

Sedo whistled. 'And?'

Fielding shrugged. 'Worth a bloody fortune. But try explaining that to customs at Heathrow. Bit tricky, you know, declaring weapons of war encrusted with national assets.'

Amol grinned. 'So what happens to them?'

'We never really unpack the crates. Just move them between wars.'

'Ultimately, they go to the Americans,' Fielding said. 'Or into the vaults. Or disappear.'

He paused, then added: 'One guy from the Welsh regiment tried to nick a gold-plated bidet. Got caught using it as a punch bowl at the regimental barbecue.'

Amol laughed. 'Let me guess, dishonourable discharge?'

'Promoted,' Fielding said. 'Mess decor's never looked better.'

They stood for a moment, surrounded by filth and velvet, syringes and scripture, staring into the hole where a dictator's son once slept, schemed and dissolved. Then they walked out together.

A few months later, mid-1993

Sedo travelled back to the Balkans, which were aflame in the early 1990s as the Yugoslav wars reshaped borders and loyalties.

It felt strange to return. Skopje had once been his halfway house, a bureaucratic purgatory where silence was traded for safety. Now he came by choice, not exile, and for a different kind of reckoning. Amol had arranged the meeting. An excuse, at last, to introduce him to one of his most trusted contacts. Miro had been many things: war fixer, journalist, sometime arms courier, occasional poet. Tall, handsome, always overdressed, he moved like a man who knew which rooms had microphones and which corridors to avoid.

Once, in Cairo, someone had whispered that Miro had UDBA (Yugoslav State Security Service) connections – the old Yugoslav secret police. Miro never denied it. He just smiled and said, 'I was loyal to Tito. After him, less so.'

They met outside Skopje, in a rented car that smelt of diesel and cigarettes. Miro drove them in silence to a warehouse on the edge of town, part-abandoned, part-guarded by rumour. Inside, behind sagging tarpaulins and crates labelled in Cyrillic, lay what looked like a stack of metal tortoises: squat, curved, faintly ominous.

'Nuclear landmines,' Miro said, almost cheerfully. 'Soviet-era. They dumped them here when Albania went rogue. No one's claimed them since.'

'Always,' Miro said, lighting a cigarette. 'Though not in court. I can sell you one for one hundred dollars, if you promise to declare it at customs.' Amol kept a straight face. 'Does that include delivery?'

Miro's laugh echoed off the concrete walls, the sound bouncing between cracked Soviet pillars and rusting crates. 'One hundred dollars,' he repeated. 'You want two, I give you discount.'

It sounded like a joke, but Amol knew he wasn't bluffing. These weren't props, they were decommissioned Soviet nuclear landmines – the real thing, once wired to detonate beneath tank battalions or key passes if NATO forces ever advanced too far.

Later, on the drive back through the ravaged outskirts of Skopje, Amol couldn't stop replaying the scene – the casual offer, the forgotten danger.

Years on, when a Bulgarian spy on trial in London coolly claimed that even nuclear weapons were available for the right price, Amol thought again of Miro's warehouse. What they'd laughed off in the debris of empire had curdled into prophecy. The real joke was how cheaply annihilation could be bought – if you knew the right people and didn't mind the radiation.

Amol remembered his DPhil days at Oxford – dense archival work, seminars with arms control theorists, long afternoons tracing footnotes through government white papers. The Cold War legacy of atomic demolition munitions had stayed with him: devices designed not to win a war, but to deny territory, poison rivers, irradiate valleys.

'Area denial', the manuals had called it – a chilling euphemism for turning fertile land into radioactive deserts. As if language itself could contain radiation. Forgotten, unsecured, rotting quietly in an abandoned warehouse, they were the nightmare the Cold War had left behind, ticking silently without clocks.

Amol's stomach twisted. He knew exactly what these could do. Entire cities, valleys – gone, irradiated, unreachable for generations. And here they sat, forgotten, waiting. 'You're serious?' he asked.

Sedo snorted. 'Do they still work?'

Miro blew a smoke ring. 'Depends what you want them to do.'

Late summer 1993, London

Back in London, Amol filed the piece. Tight, sober, explosive in every sense. He handed it to Sean with quiet satisfaction.

Sean barely looked up. 'We knew about that a long time ago,' he muttered, flipping a page. 'Peter wouldn't be interested.'

Amol stared. 'Peter Dexter?'

Sean shrugged. 'They had someone in the Balkans in the nineties. It's not new.'

'But it was never published.'

'That's different.'

Amol's voice rose. 'Are we writing for them now? Or for the people who actually read the paper? Doesn't the wider audience count?'

Sean's expression didn't change. 'It's a crowded news cycle.'

For a moment, Amol said nothing. Then he turned, walked out and left the door swinging behind him.

17

The Chess Game

Late 1993, London

Amol was livid. Two years later, after Naxos, the story had been spiked. Early autumn's chill seeped into the newsroom, matching the cold silence that followed the story's death.

The warehouse full of Soviet-era nuclear landmines, the photograph of the dented metal casing, Miro's offhand joke in the Balkans about selling one for a 100 dollars – Gone. Buried. Killed. He'd filed in mid-1993; by October it vanished from the schedule and then from the building.

In the newsroom, the usual hum continued. But he could feel it, a shift in tone, a sidelong glance, a sudden hush.

He hadn't seen Sedo in weeks. But his presence was everywhere.

Someone had pinned a cartoon to the office noticeboard – a man juggling bombs while blindfolded. The caption read: 'Foreign Desk Special.' Amol tore it down without a word. No one stopped him. No one asked. But he felt their eyes, not with curiosity, but caution. Like he'd wandered too close to the fault line.

At lunch, no one sat near him. Days slipped by unnoticed, marked only by the growing distance between Amol and his colleagues.

His regular slot in the editorial meeting was skipped over. Even the intern avoided eye contact.

Sedo hadn't called. But his silence felt heavier than any warning. The man who used to scribble diagrams on napkins had vanished into the folds of someone else's protection or erasure.

'You want to know what happens when you get too close?' the deputy editor muttered by the lifts. 'Ask the ghost of David Holden. Or David Blundy. We've lost better men than you.'

Amol knew the story wasn't dead. It had simply been absorbed, filed, cross-checked, buried in a drawer at SIS headquarters in Vauxhall, to be weaponized or forgotten depending on convenience.

Finally, three days later, Sean texted. 'King's Cross. Café by the florist. Noon.'

No explanation. No apology. Just that same brittle tone, like nothing had broken.

Amol read it twice, then closed his phone. He wasn't going for Sean. He was going because something in him, something left over from Naxos, from four days of quiet sketches and wary glances, refused to leave Sedo's fate in other people's hands.

They met in the corner booth where the hum of the coffee machine was louder than the conversations.

The place smelled faintly of boiled cabbage and mildew. A cracked Formica counter held a cake display case with nothing inside. Outside, buses sighed through puddles and pigeons fought over a soggy chip. A fly buzzed against the smeared windowpane, drunk on the ghost of sugar. A menu curled with age lay limp on the table, its corners greasy with forgotten breakfasts. The waiter was either deaf or pretending to be. The coffee was astringent.

Amol had drunk two by the time Sedo arrived, his usual limp softened by a long coat and an old man's dignity. He smelled faintly of cardamom and tobacco, and when he slid into the seat, it was as if the room tipped slightly towards him.

'They spiked it,' Amol said. 'Killed the whole damn story.'

His voice was tight, clipped. The sort of rage that didn't flare, but coiled under the skin like a pulled tendon. He'd slept badly, woken with his teeth clenched and kept seeing that warehouse in his mind. Miro's laugh, the cold metal shell, the way it all now felt like a dream that someone had paid to erase.

Sedo didn't react at first. He ordered tea, glanced at the damp newspaper on the table, then said quietly, 'That story could've bought your death. Maybe they just saved your life.'

'And before you ask' Sedo said, 'I wasn't boasting in Naxos. I *was* a designer. I built shaped shapes and chargers and timers for other men's wars, then spent the rest of my life trying to stop them'

Amol looked up sharply. 'Is that a threat?'

'No. A reflection.' He glanced sideways. 'You remember what happened to that French reporter in Basrah? Or the Greek stringer who went poking around the Serbian weapons routes in the mid-90s? Dead within weeks. One car crash, one overdose. No official link. Just a quiet consensus that they went too far. Got too curious. Journalism doesn't kill, Amol. Secrets do.'

'When they pushed me to the British Embassy in Athens back then, it wasn't curtesy. It was exfiltration – contain the leak keep me breathing, keep me owned.'

He sipped his tea. 'And intelligence agencies? They're not the scalpel they pretend to be. They're a butcher's blade in the wrong hands. They'll lie, smear, blackmail, even kill – just to stop a truth they don't like. If you're lucky, they ruin your name. If you're not, they ruin your body. And they always, always make it look like an accident.'

He paused, let the words settle, then added, 'You don't understand what you were walking into. That warehouse wasn't just some forgotten Soviet junkpile. It was a nerve ending. That stash links to Cold War caches, secret NATO and Warsaw Pact stockpiles scattered across Eastern Europe, meant to disappear but didn't.

'There are names tied to that place, Amol. Names that still carry rank. Black ops routes through the Balkans, old NATO deniability agreements, things London and Washington swore never existed. You print that story, and it's not just a scandal. It's proof. That we're still playing dirty. That our side lied. You would've embarrassed the Americans. Exposed their contractors. Pissed off every agency that signed off on the post-Soviet mop-up and then pocketed what they found. You would've made enemies with people who don't need to call lawyers.'

They sat in silence. Outside, the rain blurred the street like a censor's pen. Red brake lights bled across the pavement. A man with no umbrella stood under the awning of a pawnshop, staring at nothing. The rain began needling the windows.

Then Sedo spoke: 'You think you carried me all these years. Truth is, I carried you.'

Amol laughed, not kindly. 'You were the source. I was the one risking my name, my passport.'

'I told *you* because you weren't for sale' Sedo said. 'I needed a witness, not a handler.'

'And you think it was luck you weren't shot in Halabja? Or arrested in Taif? Or disappeared in Algiers?'

He paused. 'You thought you were handling a Kurdish rebel. The truth is, I'm a Kurdish Jew.'

Amol leaned forward, thinking he'd misheard. 'A what?'

'They exist. We exist. Not many of us left. My uncle left Zakho in 1951. My aunt's buried on the Mount of Olives. I stayed behind. Easier to move between worlds.'

'But your name – ' Amol started to ask.

'Isn't obviously Jewish,' Sedo completed for him, with the faintest trace of a smile. 'But be assured, we are from one of the seven tribes of Israel. When you belong to a persecuted minority, you learn to make adjustments. Changing a name was the least of my grandparents' problems.'

'You, you work for them, don't you?'

Sedo didn't answer. But Amol had seen enough.

If this wasn't Mossad, it was the shadow of it.

'Relax' he said softly, 'your friends at Vauxhall never knew who stood behind me. They filed me as a Kurdish *asset*. Let it stay that way.'

Amol blinked. Unspoken words milled around in his brain, felt like a door opening in a dream, unexpected, inevitable and somehow already known.

For a moment, he felt like a character in someone else's story. The pieces reassembled too fast – Sedo's casual disappearances, his strange access, the people who suddenly backed off after 'a quiet word'. The idea that he'd been protected all along was both comforting and insulting. He hated how grateful he felt.

Sedo didn't answer. He simply sipped his tea. But something flickered – pride, unmistakable and quiet, the kind carried by men who have walked through history without asking to be named. His eyes shone for a moment, not with vanity, but with the serene gravity of someone who had served in shadows and lived to see their work understood. It was the calm of someone who'd lived for decades in dangerous clarity, never needing to name the flag he served.

Sedo's gaze drifted towards the window, where rain streaked down the glass like slow ash.

'You know what happened to Eli Cohen?' he said quietly.

'The Mossad agent who infiltrated Syria's Ministry of Defence. Dined with generals. Memorized the topography of the Golan. They hanged him in '65 – from a scaffold in Damascus. Left his body swinging in the square for days. A message.'

He stirred his tea without looking up.

'That's what happens when you get too close to the fire and someone decides you've seen enough.'

Amol felt cold.

'So you were protecting me.'

Sedo shrugged. 'Sometimes you protect a man because he's useful. Sometimes because he's not like the others.'

Amol remembered something from years earlier – Naxos, maybe Athens. A question asked in a moment of uneasy quiet. He had asked, cautiously, if any of Sedo's devices had ever found their way to the West.

The older man didn't answer. Just lit a cigarette, stared out to sea, and said, 'You remember Pan Am? Over Scotland? 1988. People like me, we write the first chapter. Others finish the book.'

Amol wasn't sure what to make of it. But now, in this damp London café, the weight of those words settled differently.

'Why me?' Amol asked.

'Maybe I'm old fashioned. Maybe I liked that you still had a conscience. A real one. Not the kind SIS buys at The Ritz.'

'I read your Mosul piece,' Sedo added after a beat. 'The one with the old man and the broken radio.'

Amol eyes narrowed. 'That was years ago.'

'Doesn't matter. You let him finish his story. Most reporters would have cut him off. You wrote it like it mattered.'

Amol didn't reply. He remembered that interview – a man who'd kept a BBC World Service radio running with car batteries and spare parts, hoping to hear the Queen's Christmas speech one last time. He'd thought no one noticed that story.

Sedo let the spoon rest in the cup, silent now. 'That's when I knew. You weren't like the others.'

'Naxos was my idea' he said. 'I fed the location through their line, so they'd think they were running it. But I wanted you unbriefed.'

Amol studied him. The usual deflective irony was gone. This was something else – almost tender.

Amol didn't speak for a while. Then, almost as if to deflect, or confess, he said quietly: 'There was a time in southern Sudan. I'd been with rebel leader John Garang, afterwards in a two-jeep convoy, heading back. One of the jeeps hit a mine.'

Sedo stilled.

'A British TV man – Julian – was flung from the blast. When he landed, a branch had gone through his skull. Clean through. He was still breathing.'

Amol glanced at the table, then back at Sedo.

'We had no morphine. No comms. I sat with him for fifteen hours while he moaned and shook. Near dawn, he threw up a glob of blood and died.'

'You couldn't have helped,' Sedo said softly.

'No,' Amol replied. 'But I was there. That's what stays. Not the horror. The helplessness.'

Sedo stirred his tea slowly. 'Do you dislike us, Amol?'

Amol raised an eyebrow. 'Who's "us", exactly?'

Sedo let the question hang. 'You've broken bread with the Arafats. Cited Darwish in interviews. It raises questions among certain people.'

Amol's voice was steady. 'I respect arguments from both sides. Two nationalisms. Two traumas. I try to listen. That's not the same as taking sides.'

He glanced at the window. A bee was bumping against the glass, slow and stubborn.

Trapped. He stood and opened the pane just enough to guide it out. It hovered for a moment, dazed, as if shocked by the sudden sky, then darted away.

Amol sat again, a little quieter now. 'I try to listen,' he repeated, more to himself than to Sedo.

Sedo gave a slow, tired nod. 'That's unusually fair.' He stirred his tea. 'It unsettled them. You weren't picking a side. You weren't buying the script. I kept them off your back for that.'

He paused, then added with something closer to reverence, 'It's not just you, Amol. It's where you come from. That Indian spine. That ancient conscience, through centuries of fire – colonialism, partition, famine – and still remembered to carry water. We can smell that in a man. It's why some of us watch from afar, and step in when needed.'

Amol breathed out.

He thought, too, of Layla. One night in Bethlehem, under the hush of curfew, they had wandered down cobbled lanes lit only by moonlight. She had taken his hand and begun to sing softly, in French, her voice brushing the stone walls, a quiet, luminous echo of the old carol:

Ô petit village de Bethléem, dans l'ombre où rien ne luit, Combien paisible tu reposes tandis que dort la nuit.
Dans les ténèbres brillent les étoiles sans fin,
Les espérances du monde reposent ce soir en toi.

For a few fumbling moments, he had tried to sing back the English version:

O little town of Bethlehem, how still we see thee lie,
Beneath thy deep and dreamless sleep, a thousand stars go by.
We hear the Christmas angels, the everlasting light,
The hopes and fears of all the years …

Then he had lost it. Not because of the words, but because of her and her overwhelming loveliness. The way her voice echoed against the old stone. The way she believed in beauty, even here.

To cover his embarrassment, he'd laughed at her sentimentality, but she'd only smiled, saying the words weren't sentimental, just honest. 'It's a lullaby for the broken,' she whispered. 'Not a hymn for believers.'

It was the voice he feared most. The one that still knew how to reach him. The one that hadn't yet learnt how to say goodbye. He remembered how he used to ruffle through her hair, bury his face in the curve of her neck, breathe in that light, amber perfume she loved – something floral, faintly spiced, impossible to name. It wasn't expensive, but it stayed with him longer than any headline. In war zones and hotel rooms, in airports and interrogation cells, it was that scent he summoned when hope began to slip.

Not a flag. Not a god. Just her. The memory of skin and grace and the last good thing he believed in.

Now, in this grey café, her voice returned like a half- remembered dream. A song of hope, sung in exile. A small defiance against the dark.

Amol breathed in. 'So Sean and Dexter … '

Sedo raised an eyebrow. 'Ah. The lovers.'

'You think so?'

'I've watched their Tuesday chess games.'

'Chess games?'

'Every Tuesday. Same suite at the Dorchester. SIS keeps the room permanently. I observe. Sometimes I play.'

'What's curious,' he added, 'is how they always sit at right angles to each other. Not across, not side by side. Always that precise L-shape, like they're avoiding confrontation but craving proximity. Their knees touch under the table, constantly. Most chess players lean back. These two lean in.'

'And?'

'They talk about pawns. Sacrifices. Sometimes journalists. Occasionally governments. Always themselves.' He paused. 'They call it "strategic recycling". Say it's what the Americans do, why shouldn't we get in on the game?'

'They cackle about money,' Sedo continued. 'Dexter mostly, he's the one with the budget. But Sean's always there, laughing along. It's a shared game for them, propping up some exile with fake legitimacy – media training, NGO fronts, puff pieces. Then selling him back to his old regime like a used car. Dictators pay well to make problems disappear.'

'And the money?'

Sedo smiled thinly. 'Dexter's still paying off that fake Georgian townhouse in Clapham. Never made it to Oxford, so now he drinks champagne and hires Oxbridge interns to call him "sir". Sean's got debts in Amsterdam: boats, girlfriends, a shop for his wife she never opens. The wife's the decoy. The real entanglement's harder to trace. They spend on fast cars they don't drive, encrypted phones, club memberships and holidays in countries with no extradition treaties. Sometimes they just enjoy watching the balance grow. It's not about need. It's about arrival.'

He sipped his tea. 'They work in shadows, but they dream in sterling.'

Amol sat back. 'Jesus.'

'Dexter watches Sean's white, bony wrists move like pieces. Like a schoolboy eyeing a prefect.'

'And they sleep there?'

'Sometimes. Who's the dominant one, you think?' Amol didn't answer.

Sedo leaned closer. 'They'd gobble you up, Amol. Body and soul. Feast on your principles, your charm, your little brown integrity. And when they're done?' He flicked his fingers. 'Gone. Spat out. Just another story filed too late.'

He paused, then added with dry amusement, 'Dexter watches Sean like a man hypnotized. And Sean? He plays up to it. Lets Dexter pour the wine. Lets him linger in the silence. Power is a perfume, Amol. And in that room, it smells like old secrets and something unspoken.'

He stirred his tea again, slower now. 'It's not about sex, not really. It's about control.

Intimacy as leverage. They sleep in the same room because trust, real trust, is rare in their world. Rarer than love.'

Amol swallowed.

'They also talk about Philby,' Sedo went on. 'And Mossadeq, toppled for daring to nationalize Iran's oil. Lumumba, murdered after trying to free Congo from colonial claws. Old coups. New regrets.'

'And now?'

'Now it's the Americans who run the show. SIS takes the crumbs – the crumbs left behind after Baghdad, Caracas and Kigali. Dexter calls it "strategic alignment". I call it begging.'

'You sound bitter.'

'I sound alive. Bitterness is what's left when you stop pretending.'

Amol looked out at the rain.

'You know the difference?' Sedo said suddenly. 'Between us and them? The Brits pay.

The Americans pay more. But we? We protect our own. We never betray the ones who stand with us. Never.'

He gave a small shrug. 'My grandfather used to say we were meant to be a light among nations. Maybe we've fallen short. But I never betrayed a friend. Not once.'

Amol looked at him, unsure whether to feel honoured or warned. 'You think they'll keep trying?'

'To use you? Always.'

A silence passed between them, but inside Amol something shifted – not loudly, not dramatically, but with the tectonic weight of revelation. All his life, he had worked between empires: the British, the American, the Arab, the Soviet relics, the UN's illusion of neutrality.

He had survived on instinct, charm and a wary journalist's distrust of any flag too proudly flown. Now, to realize that Mossad, the most feared of them all, had been quietly guarding his back, not for leverage, not for headlines, but because he was, in their eyes, decent – it undid him. It felt like something private had been seen, something sacred had been protected. He wanted to laugh, or weep or lash out.

He did none of those. Instead, he sat still, absorbing the unbearable truth: that amid all the users and betrayals, it had been the one Service he never chased, never charmed, never asked for – that had honoured him.

It felt biblical. And unbearably lonely.

Sedo studied him for a moment, then said with a faint smile, 'You're what we call a Righteous Gentile. There aren't many.

But the few there are, we remember. You may not die rich, but somewhere a tree will be planted in your name. Someone will whisper your name in a prayer. Angels will nod.'

He said it without drama, as if he were describing a routine security protocol. That was what caught Amol off guard. Something caught in Amol's chest. Not pain, not joy – just weight. The sudden gravity of being seen not as useful, or clever or brave, but as *good*. It left him speechless.

For once in his life, the words didn't come. And yet, Sedo had spoken with ease. Perfect English. Perfect timing.

The poetry of someone who had spent a lifetime speaking in code, and was now choosing to speak plainly. It wasn't that Sedo had become fluent – it was that Amol was only now seeing him clearly. The mask had always been there. He just hadn't seen it.

But the silence inside him was crowded – with images, with doubts. His grandfather's hand on his shoulder in Delhi, quoting Gandhi in Urdu. Layla's voice in a candlelit room in Beirut, reading Rumi. A rabbi in Jerusalem once asking him, gently, what he believed in. And now, Sedo, sipping tea like a priest dispensing absolution.

Was this what it meant to be chosen? Not by race or creed, but by conscience?

He had spent years outrunning allegiance. Sidestepping labels. Playing the observer. Nowhere was someone who had seen the whole dance – and quietly decided he was worth saving. Amol wondered if this was the true cost of neutrality: that eventually someone would mistake it for virtue and honour you for it. And you would have to live up to the honour. He wasn't sure he could.

He felt like a man conscripted by grace. Unwilling. Unready. And yet, already enlisted. He thought, too, of Layla. Neither of them had been believers, not really. Agnostics by instinct, allergic to zealotry. And yet, together they had climbed Mount Sinai and speculated about the burning bush, the opening of the Red Sea, like the Old Testament claimed.

As in Bethlehem, where she sang beneath the moonlight, she had guided him not with belief but with wonder. He could still taste the sweet tea they'd shared on the mountaintop, the hush before dawn when Layla had whispered, 'Maybe it really did part, just this once, for someone worthy.'

They had absorbed what Muslims say about the Prophet ascending to heaven on a white horse. They had listened open-mouthed to Christian stories about Jesus weeping for the future when he sat where the Church of the Tear Drop now stands.

They had stood by the niche at the Church of the Holy Sepulchre, where Christian women come to pray before death. It was all in the past and yet so real, so present. Echoes of belief they could never quite claim, but never quite leave behind.

Amol's eyes dropped to the dregs of his coffee. For a moment, he saw Layla, barefoot in their Beirut flat, sunlight tangled in her hair, her laugh wrapped around a line of poetry.

What would she say to this? That Mossad had honoured him? That he was, in their eyes, a righteous man? She'd have mocked the phrase and then, perhaps, wept at its truth. Her loyalties were shaped by siege and sorrow, but her heart – her heart had always known the rarest virtue was not partisanship, but grace. She would have placed a hand on his chest, smiled softly, and said: 'You earned it, habibi. Just don't let them break you.'

He let the silence stretch. The city outside blurred into a wash of grey. Somewhere, a police siren keened, distant and indifferent. The moment was too large to hold and yet it had to pass.

Eventually, he exhaled. Not relief, not surrender – just breath. The kind you take when the ground has shifted and you're still standing.

He looked out at the grey blur of the city, thinking of ways to change the dialogue.

Then, softly, almost without thinking, he asked, 'Why do newspaper editors go to Vauxhall Cross for lunch?'

It wasn't a real question, not anymore. Lunch at Vauxhall Cross wasn't an invitation, it was a branding. Only the most obedient editors, the ones who filed clean copy and looked the other way, ever made it through the gate. For cabinet ministers, it was rarer still, a summons disguised as honour.

An audience at Buckingham Palace was theatre. Vauxhall was the dress rehearsal for power. The Queen might knight you; SIS let you feel like a co-author of history. But it was theatre too, the kind where the script was already written and your name was printed on the bottom line as 'reliable asset'. You didn't get invited because you were powerful. You got invited because you could be used – and would be. The reward was access, not truth. A flattering briefing here, a state secret there, just enough to make you feel chosen, but never enough to act freely.

The foreign dignitaries invited to meet the spooks were even more impressed. They came expecting heritage, secrecy and seduction, and were rarely disappointed. From what Sedo had heard, and now relayed to Amol, some genuinely believed James Bond was real. The richest asked to meet 'Q' or buy Bond's Aston Martin at any price. The sharper ones dismissed caricatures like Oddjob in *Goldfinger* as too far-fetched and never mentioned Moneypenny. She was too thin and far too intellectual for their tastes.

These were the same potentates who had no time for the older generation of British spies, the ones who could pass for locals, speak Arabic or Farsi, quote Hafiz and travel on camelback for weeks without complaint. Lawrence, Shakespeare, those types had been written off as impractical romantics. Their replacements were former military contractors, ex-city fixers with defence connections and deskbound men who'd migrated into espionage for the danger pay and early pensions sanctioned from fifty-five.

They came in tactical fleece and discreet earpieces, slightly overweight, gap-toothed or yellowing at the gums – but deadly accurate with American rifles tricked out with British optics and suppressors. None could conjugate a verb in Arabic, but all could deliver a kill shot and a quarterly report.

Their successors had been moulded in a different, more morally compromised image. When foreign dignitaries arrived for their briefings, they were ushered into Range Rovers with blackened windows, driven through the Home Counties to government-controlled firing ranges.

There, under the rhythmic snap of gunfire, they sipped Blue Label Scotch – cleverly concealed in protein flasks. The targets before them were wooden silhouettes, but the true targets, they knew, were not just the figures in the distance. They were the fading remnants of honour, ethics and professionalism that had once defined the Service.

Before the shooting began, they were handed packages filled with the names and details of London's most notorious strip clubs. The performers were ranked like spies, their names as familiar as those of foreign diplomats. A disturbing silence filled the air, broken only by the occasional clink of glass, as these men and women – trained to protect their country – were instead conditioned to engage with a world that had long since abandoned its moral compass.

Between volleys, they compared multi services on offer: luxury exclusive escort services and discreet shopping for the finest luxury goods. A conversation about indulgence rather than intelligence.

And as they took aim at the wooden figures, they weren't just learning to kill; they were learning to drown the last vestiges of integrity in a glass of whisky, blind to the decaying world they were helping to sustain.

One Gulf prince, Sedo said, had even offered to fund a new wing at Vauxhall in exchange for a poison that left no trace, a product bearing a British patent. He called it 'gentle persuasion', as though the quiet death it would deliver was merely a business transaction, no more sinister than any other commodity.

Another time, Sedo said, a young idealist from the Political Directorate tried to gently correct a visiting Central Asian Deputy Minister who had asked to meet James Bond. 'Sir, Bond is fictional – a creation of Fleming, not a serving officer,' the idealist explained carefully.

The visitor waved him off. 'Of course, of course. But I heard him on the BBC last week, talking about Montenegro, the technique he used at the card table to beat the villain. What was his name? Le Chiffre! And that American friend of his, Felix, helped him escape, no? Very professional.'

The idealist had said nothing. Later that week, he requested a transfer to DEFRA (the Department for Environment, Food & Rural Affairs), where the only secrets involved badgers and bees.

It was no longer clear where the myth ended and the machinery began. Perhaps, it never had been.

The SIS chief's brief was never to say yes, and never to say no. His instruction was simple: stay charming, keep them guessing. What a responsibility. What a performance. All that silk and silverware, all that civility, masking conversations about murder.

It was theatre on both sides of the table. The visitors believed the myths; the hosts believed the mystique. Everyone left flattered, and no one told the truth.

In Boris Johnson's Downing Street, they wouldn't have noticed the difference. The whole machinery of state had become a parlour game – half illusion, half indulgence – where everyone played along, believing they still mattered.

Sedo commented with a smile.

Because they think they're still running the country. They get the wine, the wink, the whisper of a knighthood. Enough ceremony to keep them docile, enough flattery to keep them coming back. Sometimes a contract for the wife's PR firm. That's all it takes. A man who once stood up to prime ministers now writes editorials from briefing notes. They don't even notice the leash.

They're fed roast lamb and secrets in the small private dining room on the fifth floor. Told they're patriots. That their silence keeps the nation safe. By the second glass, they're suggesting headlines themselves.

And now? The committee meant to oversee them is broke, muzzled and on life support. Top-notch oversight, they call it. Three billion pounds vanish into black budgets every year, and no one's watching. Not one prime minister's met them in a decade. The watchdog's housed inside the kennel it's meant to guard. Even they admit it's constitutionally wrong. But no one's listening. Why would they? The fog suits everyone.

It's tradition. Goes back to the Cold War. Editors dined at Vauxhall and printed what they were told – 'unnamed sources', 'Western officials', 'concerned diplomats'. The only thing that's changed is the font.

They go in thinking they're players. They come out played. By the time they realize, their paper's hollowed out, their conscience outsourced, their name already printed on a pension file marked 'asset'.

They sat there, two ghosts in a corner booth, while the coffee machine groaned like an old engine and the rain kept falling on a city that had long since stopped caring who ruled whom, or why. But Amol no longer felt quite so weightless. He felt anchored – not by power or promises, but by something older. By memory. By grace. By an invisible ledger in which, somehow, his name had been quietly written down. He did not believe in angels. But if they existed, he thought, they might walk like Sedo – slightly bowed, slightly amused, with no need to explain anything at all.

He did not know if God existed. But if He did, He would be like this: cryptic, unsentimental and sparing with His praise. The kind who showed up late, uninvited, in a damp café near King's Cross – and left you changed.

Amol left a tip on the table and stepped into the soft edge of evening, unsure if he would see Sedo again. Halfway across the street, he paused and glanced back at the café. No sign of him, just empty plates, the hush of clearing up.

Under his breath, not quite smiling, he said: 'L'chaim.'

He wasn't sure if Sedo had heard. He wasn't even sure Sedo was still real. And somewhere far off, he thought, a tree was already being planted. To life, even now.

It happened in a corridor most people never used, too far from the lifts, too close to the fire exit. The carpet was newer than the walls, the walls newer than the secrets.

Sean was standing by a tea station with one hand in his pocket and the other wrapped around a mug he had no intention of drinking. He looked up as Sedo approached unexpectedly, surprise flaring briefly, then something colder settling in.

'Didn't think you were still on the guest list,' Sean said.

Sedo didn't answer. Just stopped a few feet away, adjusted his scarf. No coat, just that faded navy blazer, the one that made him look like a disillusioned professor.

'You've been busy,' Sean added.

Sedo tilted his head slightly. 'And you've been sloppy.'

Sean flushed. 'Is that meant to scare me?'

'No. Just to remind you. Amol's not alone.'

Sean scoffed. 'He's a journalist, Sedo. Not a saint. He'll come around. They all do.'

Behind them, a door opened softly. Peter Dexter stepped into the hallway, adjusting his tie. He didn't interrupt. Just stood by the wall. Watching. Listening.

Sedo didn't even glance at him. His eyes were fixed on Sean. 'Amol came with no strings. You tried to tie him up. That's your failure.'

Sean stiffened. 'He's the one who refused help. Spat on every chance we gave him.'

'Then maybe you should stop offering poison and calling it wine.'

The corridor held still. Sean's jaw twitched, but he said nothing.

Dexter spoke now, voice low and amused. 'Still playing the priest, are you?'

Sedo turned his head slowly. 'No. Just making a final courtesy call. Next time you try to burn a man like that, make sure his friends don't carry matches.'

A long silence.

Then Sedo walked past them both. No salute. No threat. Just the soft drag of worn shoes on expensive carpet.

Sean muttered, 'Ungrateful little shit.'

Dexter didn't reply. He just stared after Sedo, eyes narrowed, like a man reading a file he didn't write and didn't trust.

18

The Other Side of the Coin

The message came just after midnight.

No name. No text. Just a number Amol hadn't seen since Naxos – Macedonian code, bounced through a Balkan gateway, pre-paid. The kind of number you kept in your notes, half as a joke, half as insurance.

He stared at it for a long moment. It had been months. Maybe longer. No calls, no traces, not even rumours. He'd half convinced himself Sedo was dead – or worse, buried alive inside the machinery he once served. But now, this.

Amol rose, pulled on his coat and walked out into the Islington dark.

They met near the canal behind King's Cross – a pedestrian underpass with poor lighting and poorer CCTV. The kind of spot Sedo liked. Unwatched, but not too quiet. London was good at that.

Sedo stood by the railing, hands in his coat pockets, face barely visible under the streetlamp. He looked older. Or maybe just still.

'You told me about Layla,' he said.

No greeting. No preamble.

Amol nodded.

'I think I should tell you something in return.'

They walked. Past closed cafés and locked bicycles, their footsteps muted by the rain-slicked path. 'You already know I'm a Kurdish Jew. What I didn't tell you is what that actually meant. I wasn't born Sedo,' he said. 'That name came later – when the paperwork began to multiply. New borders, new comrades, new uses. But before that – '

He glanced at Amol, testing the space.

'My real name was Eli. Eli Ben-Sasson. We didn't speak Hebrew at home – not much – but we said the prayers. Lit candles on Fridays. My grandfather wrote Aramaic poetry. My mother kissed the mezuzah, even after the mobs came. She said it was better to die with your name than live under someone else's.'

He gave a dry laugh. 'I didn't agree. I took the new name because I wanted to live. And fight. Sedo sounded Kurdish. Eli didn't.'

A pause. Then: 'But it was never really a lie. Just camouflage. You once said names are sometimes the first thing we surrender, Amol. You were right.'

Amol said nothing.

'I was born in Diyarbakir,' Sedo said. 'Our street backed onto the military zone. My grandfather was a clockmaker. He once fixed a Swiss watch without opening the case. My father read newspapers in three languages. And my mother, she … baked bread with caraway. You can smell that kind of memory. Even when it's gone.'

His voice didn't change, but something slowed in him. Like an engine lowering its hum.

'We weren't special. Just unlucky. Wrong side of the border. Wrong kind of name. One winter, the soldiers took my father. No trial. Just a truck in the night.'

They passed a woman pushing a pram with headphones in. Sedo waited until she was gone.

'I joined the PKK the next year. I was sixteen. They gave me boots, a name and a purpose. I learnt to wire explosives from a Libyan who said nothing but quoted verses. I got good. Precise. We blew bridges, not people. At first.'

Amol exhaled quietly. The cold hit harder now.

'I met Öcalan once. He told me war was a form of love. I didn't believe him then. I do now.'

They reached a bench under a broken lamp. Sedo sat.

'Later, I helped negotiate between the PKK and Syrian intelligence. We needed allies. Assad's men needed deniability. I learnt to listen. To pretend. That's how I met Mossad.'

Amol flinched – not visibly, but enough.

Sedo noticed. He always did.

'I wasn't recruited. I was loaned. One of those arrangements no one writes down. Kurdish enough to pass. Jewish enough to be useful.'

He finally sat. Crossed one leg. Gloved hands still clasped.

There had been tenderness once – a kind Amol rarely let himself remember. Sedo had nursed him through multiple seizures, cradling his head as if protecting something more fragile than skull or bone. Later, in the marshes, in the alleys of Baalbek, he'd appointed himself bodyguard without ever saying so aloud. That kind of care wasn't spoken. It was built into presence. Into showing up.

'I don't say this for pity,' he added. 'You think you're the only one who got used?'

Amol didn't answer.

Sedo nodded once.

'I became the bomb-maker because it gave me control. I could choose the wire, the fuse, the timing. No chaos. Just cause and effect. Just accountability.'

He smiled faintly. Not warmly.

'Back in Tel Aviv they thought I was loyal because I was bitter. I wasn't. I was just ready.'

A pause.

'Amol, you're not the only one who got used.'

The canal gurgled softly. A bottle clinked somewhere out of sight.

'What you told me about Layla. That matters. But don't imagine I came through this untouched. We all lose something.'

Amol stared at the dark water below. 'So what does this have to do with Layla?'

Sedo took something from his coat pocket – a crumpled photograph, edges torn. Amol leaned in slightly. It wasn't of Layla, or even of Sedo himself, but the fragments of a device – scorched wires, twisted casing, a blurred date marker. The kind of thing only an expert would recognize. A blueprint of guilt, captured in aftermath.

In those early days, Amol had asked. Gently, then urgently. But Sedo had only looked away, eyes heavy with something close to shame. Now, at last, the silence was breaking.

'I built the prototype in 1989. Not the actual device that killed her – that came later – but the mechanism. The mercury tilt switch. The nested relay. I taught it to the wrong man. Or maybe he taught someone else.'

'You're saying you recognized the signature?'

'Yes. I saw the fragments in the post-blast images. I knew it instantly. That was the second time I changed my name. The first was in Diyarbakir, before the soldiers came.'

'And now?'

Sedo gave a tired laugh. 'Now I carry it like everyone else – a burden with no grave.'

Amol looked at him. 'Why tell me this?'

'Because you loved her,' he said. 'And because I didn't see – not until too late – that she mattered more than any cause I'd ever served.'

They were silent again. But the air between them held something gentler now – not forgiveness, not absolution, just recognition. A shared weight that needed no translation.

'No apology would bring her back. No explanation makes it cleaner. It wasn't personal – but that's the worst part, isn't it? I'm not asking for forgiveness,' Sedo continued. 'Only that you write it down, somewhere. That it mattered. That it wasn't just smoke and noise.'

Amol felt the shift. This wasn't just confession. It was legacy. The same shift he'd felt in himself once, long ago, when he first spoke Layla's name aloud. Sedo wasn't trying to be understood, he was trying to be recorded.

'There's a reason I'm telling you all this now,' Sedo said quietly. 'Some stories can only be told after the fuse burns down. My uncle ran a bakery in Heliopolis, a once-cosmopolitan suburb of Cairo. He sold date-filled bread, coffee, cigarettes. Until 1956. Then the mobs came.'

'Because he was Jewish?'

'Because he wasn't Arab enough.'

A pause.

'They left with one suitcase. A loaf of bread. No bank account.'

'You know what people forget?' he said. 'That once, the Arab world was full of Jews. Not foreigners. Not settlers. Jews who spoke Arabic better than most Arabs. Who wrote contracts in cursive script. Who ran textile mills in Aleppo and studied medicine in Cairo and sang in Baghdad before they spoke in Jerusalem.'

'You know why we stayed in the Kurdish zones, even after Baghdad turned?' he asked. 'Because the Kurds weren't Arabs. Yes, they were Muslims. But there's no recorded history of Kurds hunting Jews. Not like in the cities. No pogroms. No edicts. My grandfather kept his books in Sorani and Hebrew side by side. And when the time came to flee, it was the Kurds who gave us the road out. They didn't hate us. They didn't need to.'

He shrugged. 'We still changed our names. Just in case. But we knew where we were safe.'

He glanced across the canal. 'We weren't Ashkenazi. We didn't speak Yiddish or eat gefilte fish. We came from the sun – not the snow. My uncle read the Torah in Arabic and then walked across the alley to listen to a *khutbah* at the mosque. It wasn't strange. It was the neighbourhood.

'But history decided that didn't matter. After '48, the mobs came. First the graffiti, then the fire. The synagogue in Heliopolis? Empty. The one in Jobar, Damascus? A shell now. Plaster on stone, bullet scars in the lintel. It used to echo with prayer and girls giggling through the curtains. Now it's a ruin with a fence.'

'And it wasn't just abandonment,' he continued. 'Sometimes they didn't wait for us to leave. They made sure we couldn't stay. In Baghdad, they called it the Farhud. June 1941. Two days of slaughter. Jewish babies thrown off balconies. Mothers raped in front of their sons. One hundred eighty dead, while the army stood by and took notes.

'In Libya, mobs came with petrol and knives. In Morocco, they waited outside synagogues. In Aden, they killed eighty in a single day. Torah scrolls trampled, old men beaten with broom handles. All before the first Israeli flag ever flew.'

He looked away. 'We weren't caught between states. We were erased inside them.'

'And while we ran, the Grand Mufti of Jerusalem – Haj Amine al-Husseini – was in Berlin, shaking Hitler's hand. Pledging to take the Final Solution to Palestine. Promising to bring Auschwitz to our doorstep, just in Arabic.'

Amol had only heard fragments – the occasional whisper in foreign briefings, half-formed reports, the outline of something darker. Nazis slipping through post-War cracks. Damascus. Cairo. One or two names. Nothing firm. Nothing usable.

Sedo, though, knew the rest. And for once, he didn't withhold.

'And while our synagogues emptied,' he said, 'the regimes that drove us out found new tenants for their basements. Cairo, Damascus – they became safehouses for Nazis. Real ones. Not just engineers with shadows. Men who'd sorted train lists. Signed orders. Stood beside pits.

'They weren't sheltered out of sympathy. They were tools. Egypt wanted rockets. Syria wanted methods. The Germans built missiles at Abu Zaabal by the early '60s. The Israelis caught wind of it, sent Mossad to lean – not for justice. For trajectory range.

'Alois Brunner – Eichmann's assistant – lived in Damascus under state protection while my mother's cousin swept bakery floors in Tel Aviv, careful not to speak Arabic too loudly. Brunner trained Syrian interrogators. Taught them how to vanish people without a trace.

'Europe wanted to forget. The Arabs wanted to recycle. And we – we just disappeared. Unless someone needed a translator. Or a technician. Or a scapegoat.'

Sedo glanced across the canal. 'We stopped talking about family after that. Too many ghosts. Too many silences pretending to be choices.'

Amol stared at the water but didn't really see it. There were echoes of his own father in Sedo's voice – the same quiet, the same reluctance to look back. But this was something older. A sadness that went back generations, that didn't ask for sympathy, only space.

Layla had once asked if he ever felt out of place. He hadn't known what to say then. Now he did. This wasn't about the past. It was about how silence travelled, passed down like heirloom shame. Like the silence Amol's father carried. Like the silences he'd inherited without even knowing it.

Sedo's mouth tightened – not a smile, just something close. 'Because you spoke first. In that café, back when you didn't know if I was bluffing. You told me about Layla. And about your father. That mattered.' Amol waited.

'And?'

'And because you never asked for leverage. You just listened. And when you asked me to come to Beirut – I came. You didn't beg. You didn't explain. You just said, "I need you to hear this." And I did. That mattered more than you know.'

He glanced away, then back. 'You're not the first journalist I've crossed paths with, Amol. But you're the only one who didn't fumble the trust. Everyone you've spoken to – the old hands, the retired analysts, the ones still circling in Brussels or Herzliya – they've all reported the same thing. You don't trade. You absorb.'

A pause.

Then, quieter: 'What you brought back from Natanz – that wasn't just reporting. That was confirmation. Clean, uncoerced and painfully precise. You mapped things no one else could access without triggering alarms. That doesnt go unnoticed.' He looked at the canal, then back. 'No one else would've heard this. Not from me. Maybe that's a mistake. But it's mine to make.'

He watched the canal for a beat, then turned slightly towards Amol. 'You think I'm being sentimental?' he asked. 'I'm not. This isn't softness. This is calibration. A test of conditions. A reading of the weather.' He looked at Amol directly. 'The real game isn't what we know. It's who we trust with the knowing – and when.'

'You think it's strange I'm telling you this,' he said quietly. 'A *goy*, a reporter, an outsider.' He gave a small shrug. 'Maybe it is. But I'm not Ashkenazi. I was never invited to the inner sanctum. I got used for my language, my face, my reach. You know what that feels like.'

A pause. 'They trust you more than they trust half their own. Not because you're one of them, but because you're not pretending to be. You walked away from leverage when most would've sold it. That counts for more than you know.'

A night bus rumbled past overhead. Neither of them moved.

He gave a half-nod, as if confirming something to himself. 'You listen, and that's rare. Rarer still in our line of work. Maybe that's why I'm telling you more than I should.'

Then his gaze drifted. The light from the canal flickered across his face. 'But don't mistake this for softness. I became a weapon because it was cleaner than being a target …'

Amol finally spoke. 'And now?'

Sedo looked at him – hard, direct, as if weighing the question more than the answer.

'Now, I'm what they call a national asset. Quiet. Strategic. Familiar with both the maps and the margins.' He glanced up at the bridge.

'They turned me into a weapon because I knew how not to flinch', Sedo said. 'You build a bomb, you control the terms. You choose the fuse, the casing, the time of detonation. It's the opposite of chaos.'

A beat. 'I'll be where they need me soon enough. They just haven't said it out loud yet.' He looked back at the water. The lamp behind them flickered, then steadied. 'The same week they start murmuring about Tel Aviv and promotion, the PKK calls it quits.'

Amol said nothing. He didn't need to.

'Forty years of fire,' Sedo went on, 'and they fold after one message from Öcalan's prison cell. They say it's historic. A new page. But that's what they always say when the ink hasn't dried.'

He shook his head. 'Half the commanders will disappear into party suits. The other half will broker deals from exile. And the foot soldiers? They'll become contractors. Or corpses. I trained the men who trained the boys who now want budget lines and bilingual signage.'

He let the silence settle. The only sound was a gull scraping against the wind. 'They call it peace,' he said. 'I call it paperwork.' He stood. 'There's no such thing as disbanding. Not really. Just a reshuffling of names and guns.'

He looked at Amol. 'You'll understand that soon enough. You're not done yet,' he added, voice neutral. 'Even if you think you are. You loved her, Amol. That's not just grief. That's momentum.'

And then he was gone – not quickly, not slowly. Just absorbed into the dark, like someone who had never once needed a headline. Amol stayed where he was. Watching the water. Trying to work out if he'd just heard a warning, a confession – or an invitation. He wasn't sure. But it felt earned.

Later, walking home along the canal, he felt it again – that charged quiet, as if someone were watching. He sometimes caught himself scanning crowds, imagining a lean figure just beyond the streetlamp. Not a threat. Just unfinished business.

19

The Poisoned Room

That evening, Amol's phone rang twice, then stopped. The late spring air held a faint chill, unusual for the time of year.

When it rang again, it was Sean. Unusually polite. Unnaturally warm.

'We've missed you at the office,' Sean said. 'Dexter called, he wants to catch up. He says there's a story you'll want to hear.'

Amol felt the same coldness he'd felt in Taif. The sense of being watched, herded, pre-selected. He didn't ask which story. He already knew it would be poison.

They met him at Simpson's in the Strand. Sean grinned too widely. Dexter poured the wine. The city lights flickered through a hazy dusk.

'We've got something rather good for you,' Dexter said, the way a prefect offers you poisoned cake.

'Exclusive access,' Sean added. 'A defector from the Algerian secret police. Explosive stuff. All yours.'

Amol, unsmiling, left his glass untouched. He already knew it was fiction. The only question was whether they would let him live to regret it.

'We've got more like that coming, by the way,' Sean added smoothly. 'Stories that need telling. Carefully. Helpfully.' He opened his briefcase lying by his side, pulled out a slim folder and slid it across the desk.

'This one's from Milan. Some chatter about a Pakistani diplomat and a German arms buyer. Lot of smoke, very little fire – but the right fire, if you know what I mean. The desk can write it up, but it'd carry more weight if it came from you.'

Amol flipped through the folder. Badly written notes. No sourcing. The kind of story that got quietly pulped at responsible papers ten years ago. 'What's the hook?' he asked.

'Proliferation,' Sean said, eyes gleaming. The mid-90s geopolitical shifts made such stories timely, if often contrived.

'The Iranians love these types. So do the Saudis. Makes the West look muscular again. We frame it right, we get everyone nodding. Bit of democracy dust on top.'

Amol closed the folder. Didn't take it with him.

'And what's in it for us?' Sean grinned, as if that was the real question.

Sedo, meanwhile, had vanished.

No messages, no warnings – just absence. The kind that felt protective, not negligent.

Amol had learnt to read the silences. This one was strategic. He suspected there had been a confrontation. Maybe in a corridor at Vauxhall, or some deniable café near St James's.

Sean would have been petulant. 'After all we've done for you.'

Dexter would have said nothing – just looked at him the way he sometimes looked at Amol: like a man cataloguing risk.

If Sedo was quiet now, it was only because he knew what was coming.

'Well,' Sean continued, 'we're under water again this quarter. Print ad revenue's a disaster. But certain departments,' he tapped the desk twice, lightly, 'they've been known to be … supportive. Quietly. If we're playing the right tune.'

He didn't repeat the suggestion of a CBE or any other honour, but there was always plenty of talk about money. He looked up. 'And you – you'd be compensated. Not officially, of course. But you'd be looked after. Let's call it a consultancy. You'd be amazed how many people are already on that sort of thing.'

Sean produced another folder from his drawer, this one thicker, and fanned out a few stapled packets like he was dealing cards. Look, you don't have to run them as they are. Dress them up. Get creative. No one's asking for stenography.'

Amol picked one up.

He scanned the headlines – black ops fantasies, anthrax conspiracies and a recycled smear about Uday Hussein pushing fake medicine into Jordan. Half of them read like rejected Le Carré drafts. The other half sounded worse.

Amol looked up. 'You're serious.'

Sean grinned sheepishly. 'Well, they're drafts. But the idea is sound. Keeps the pressure on the right people.'

'It's fiction,' Amol said. 'Cheap, clumsy fiction.'

Sean shrugged. 'These days, fiction's what gets funded. And these are the stories we're expected to carry if we want to keep lights on.'

Amol stood. 'You're selling your paper by the square foot to people you won't name, for stories you don't believe.'

'And you think the others aren't?' Sean shot back. 'You think the Americans aren't pumping crap through their think tanks and calling it "regional insight"? You think the Saudis aren't paying for puff pieces in the FT?'

'I don't care what the others do,' Amol said quietly. 'I care what we do.'

Sean leaned back again, arms crossed behind his head.

'Well,' he said. 'Someone still thinks you're valuable. Dexter wants a word.'

Sean had barked and needled, all bluff and bait. Dexter, by contrast, moved like an old schoolmaster – precise, ironic, soft-voiced. But the outcome was the same. One lured with money, the other with meaning. Two faces of the same persuasion machine.

Reaching for his jacket, Amol almost missed the card in his pigeonhole.

No envelope. Just a battered postcard of Mosul's skyline – minarets like broken teeth under a sulphurous sky. The back was blank except for a line in slanted, careful script: 5 March 1994.

He walked away. No name. But Amol knew the hand. He'd seen it scrawling wire lengths and detonation angles on hotel notepads.

There'd been chatter about a new device buried under a Mosul road, surgically timed. Western analysts said it didn't match local signatures.

If Sedo was alive, still building, then someone had failed to contain him. Or someone had used him again. And if Sedo could surface, Amol knew, so could everything he had carried on his behalf: the sketches, the whispers, the lie that the past could stay buried.

For years, Sedo had been their monster in the cellar – buried, denied, never mentioned. If he was walking again, it wasn't just Amol who was exposed. It was everyone who had used him. Everyone who'd profited from forgetting.

He slid the postcard into his coat.

Then he went to lunch with Dexter.

They met, as they often did, at a quiet restaurant off the Embankment. Linen napkins, overpriced fish, a view of the grey Thames. Dexter had a favourite table in the corner, always facing the river.

He rose as Amol arrived.

'Good of you to come,' he said, offering a hand Amol didn't take. The waiter brought sparkling water and bread, neither of them touched. Dexter smiled, polished, unhurried, as always.

'I hear you've had a productive run. Naxos, especially, we all remember that one. Sean's been beside himself with pride. Thinks you've grown into the role.' Amol said nothing.

Dexter adjusted his cufflinks.

'You know,' he said, 'when I first met you, I thought you were too principled. And now … ' he let the thought trail off.

'And now?'

'Well, now I think you're principled in the way we can work with. Steady. Discreet. Never eager, but never naïve.'

Amol sipped his water. 'You're wasting your compliments,' he said.

Dexter smiled again. 'Never. Compliments are just facts with manners.'

They talked for ten minutes – about nothing. Restaurant reviews. Regional politics. A recent reshuffle at the British Council in Cairo. Then Dexter folded his hands.

'We're still very interested in your work,' he said. 'Your access. Your perspective. Your ability to be in places we're no longer welcome.'

'I'm not a courier.'

'No. You're something better. You're credible. And in our line of work, that's rarer than gold.'

He paused, then reached into his jacket and produced a card. Blank except for a single number.

'You'd have an account. Tax-free. Ten thousand dollars a month. Paid through a research institute. No one will ever look.'

Amol left the card on the table. Dexter didn't flinch.

'I don't understand,' Amol said. 'You're making the same offer Josling made. But cruder. Do you not know?'

Dexter blinked. 'Josling?'

'You know – Jerusalem. The daughter. The pitch in the garden.'

Dexter raised an eyebrow. 'I'm afraid I don't follow.'

Amol studied him. He wasn't lying. Or if he was, he was better at it than Josling.

That's when it clicked: they didn't know about each other. Parallel teams. Competing briefs. No cross-reference. A game so old it had outgrown its own memory.

Dexter sipped his wine. 'Whatever you think this is,' he said quietly, 'it's not coercion. It's continuity. You're already part of something. We're just helping you define the shape.'

Amol stood. The Thames below was slick and brown. 'You don't even know what shape you're in,' he said. 'You're a bureaucracy recruiting from a graveyard.'

Amol thought that might be the end of it.

The folders, the free lunches, the subtle threats – maybe they were finished trying.

But then came one final message.

Dexter. Again. This time at a café near Westminster. No folder. No polish. Just the lowest pitch yet.

Amol arrived late, on purpose. Dexter was already seated, reading *The Times* – tie loosened, acting as if this was a conversation between friends.

He waved the waiter over. 'You'll have the flat white, yes? You always do.' Amol said nothing.

Dexter opened his notebook with the practiced elegance of a man who only ever wrote what others would redact. He didn't speak at first. Then reached into his bag and pulled out a thin envelope, the kind used for internal memos or delicate evidence. From it, he slid a single black-and-white photograph across the café table.

Amol looked down.

It was him – undeniably him – suited and booted, walking a baby's pram along the Gaza promenade. The child inside was Arafat's daughter. Four armed guards flanked the group at the front, another four at the rear. Sunlight glinted off the waves behind them. His face was turned slightly, but the image was crisp, deliberate. Professional.

Amol said nothing. Didn't ask who had taken it. Didn't ask from where.

Dexter smiled faintly. 'You're already in the room.' He tucked the photograph back into the envelope, as if it were merely a prop, and waved the waiter over.

'We've got something delicate,' he said. 'Sean's on board. He thinks it's in your wheelhouse.'

That phrase again – your wheelhouse. As if journalism were a racket. As if moral judgement came in packets.

'We want to send you back to Gaza,' Dexter said. 'Just for a week. Nothing overt. Something human. A portrait piece on the Arafats.'

Amol looked up. 'What kind of portrait?'

Dexter didn't hesitate. Nothing fancy, but while you're with them, find out if Suha Arafat breastfeeds her child.'

The words sat there between them, damp and obscene.

Amol blinked. 'I'm sorry?'

Dexter stirred his coffee. 'It's the kind of detail the Americans love. Adds texture. Makes her real. They eat that stuff up.'

He looked almost amused. 'If we get it and pass it along, it boosts our street cred. Shows we've got depth. Not just missiles and maps. Just like Naxos, remember?'

Amol stood. Chair scraping against the tile. 'You're disgusting.'

He stood there, the chair still trembling behind him, and saw it finally for what it was.

This wasn't about Suha Arafat, or journalism or even the Americans. It was about what they always did: turning grace into leverage. Wrapping filth in silk. Giving ugliness a name that sounded like poetry.

Like 'The Purple Swan'.

They had called it that not for its beauty, though it had that too, but for how it moved: clean, silent, devastating. A bomb dressed as metaphor. Elegant, rare, designed by men who quoted Yeats as they soldered wires. A killing machine made beautiful so that those who ordered its use could sleep at night.

He thought of Sedo.

Yes, Sedo had helped build it. But Sedo was never the enemy. He carried his past like a wound, not a boast. He had done terrible things and then tried quietly, without performance, to make them right. Sedo never lied about what he was. He never tried to dress it up.

The real rot came from men like Sean, with his pints and his poison. From Dexter, whose smile always preceded a fall. From Josling, who filed death as a footnote on an expense claim. And even from Douglas Keir, soft-voiced and avuncular, who had once sat at his grandfather's Delhi table, nodding through stories of empire and blood.

They were always the same, these men.

Among Hindus, they would be recognized as '*khoon-choos rakshasas*' – blood-sucking demons reborn each generation, fanged and familiar, feeding on the innocent and marching always towards their final aim: to turn the world into a living Hell.

They smiled as they betrayed. They named torture 'interrogation'. They called executions 'pacification'. They hanged unarmed men from trees and wrote poems about the view.

These were the kinds who once shot helpless Indian teenagers in the back, then signed off reports in perfect copperplate. The ones who pressed boot to neck and told you it was for your own good.

They hadn't disappeared. They'd just learnt to talk softer.

Now they requested breastfeeding schedules like they once asked for troop movements.

These were the ones who sent journalists to their deaths and called it 'access'.

They turned cradle into theatre. Mothers into surveillance targets.

And always, always, they expected you to thank them.

How he despised them. Not for their power, but for their ease. The calm with which they dirtied everything and called it duty.

In that moment, Amol thought of the rare ones. The men who didn't twist the world into shadows. His father, David, so gentle he'd barely survived it. Tolkien, who used language to build wonder, not obfuscation. They were one in a million. And they were gone.

The Purple Swan wasn't just a device. It was the lie they wrapped in grace. A thing of beauty, turned inward. A name that betrayed the very idea it claimed to honour.

And he had seen it now. Clearly. Finally.

It was never about information. It was always about power. And about the pleasure these men took in wielding it.

Dexter didn't flinch. 'You're the man to do it, Amol. You're trusted. You're already in the room.' Amol leaned in, quiet and cold.

'I was never in your room. You just can't tell the difference anymore.'

And then he left. No coffee. No deal. No reply.

The Editor's office smelt of carpet glue and forgotten meetings. He didn't look up as Amol entered.

'Right,' he said. 'You've got something to say about Sean.'

Amol sat. 'I've been approached – repeatedly. First in Jerusalem. Then again in London. They've offered money, travel, women, power – whatever currency they thought I'd take.'

The Editor leaned back. 'They?'

'SIS. Through Gallagher. Through a handler named Dexter. Josling in Jerusalem.'

He slid a copy of the blank card across the desk. The one Dexter had left with the number. Another printout of the fake story proposals.

'They've tried to make me into something I'm not. Something I've never been. And Sean – he's either helping them or he's too dim to realize they're using him. Either way, he's not fit to be a senior editor.'

The Editor didn't blink. Didn't reach for the paper. 'We take your point.'

'You're being used,' Amol said. 'Your paper's being bought in instalments. Do you understand what that means?'

A long pause. Then: 'You've always been dramatic, Amol.'

Another pause.

'But yes. We'll look into it.'

Which meant they wouldn't. Not really.

Maybe a quiet word with Sean. Maybe nothing at all.

But Amol stood and left anyway – lighter, if not clean. He had done the one thing they couldn't manage.

He'd said no.

The newsroom pretended not to know. By early afternoon, tension simmered beneath the hum of printers and ringing phones.

But by the end of the week, everyone knew. It started with a single A4 sheet pinned to the corkboard above the cafeteria toaster – where job ads and birthday cakes were usually announced. No headline. Just a grainy photo of Sean Gallagher sunning himself on the deck of a yacht docked somewhere close to Amsterdam.

Beneath it, typed in 14-point Times New Roman: 'How did he pay for this?' No signature.

Someone has scribbled underneath, 'Government grant' and drawn a small anchor. Below that another hand added, 'sunk costs'.

By lunchtime, a second sheet appeared – pinned neatly beside it. This one was longer.

A Note from Friends

Sean Gallagher has been keeping files on his colleagues at the request of Peter Dexter, formerly of the Foreign Office. He is known to have submitted at least five stories sourced directly from SIS talking points.

He receives a monthly retainer through a front consultancy. He has used his position to suppress dissent, steer assignments and push manufactured copy under the guise of investigative journalism.

All of this appears to be coordinated by SIS – on British soil. Why is this happening on home ground?

Why is MI5 silent?

No one claimed responsibility.

By 3 p.m., copies of the letter were posted in the toilets, slipped into desk drawers, tucked into the margins of story proofs. No one spoke about it openly.

But by then, it didn't matter.

Something had cracked. The summons came by intercom.

Not email. Not in person. Just a flat voice over the newsroom PA: 'Batty. Editor's office. Now.'

Amol climbed the stairs to the top floor. The usual door was open this time. The Editor stood behind his desk, jacket off, sleeves rolled up like a man doing real work.

He didn't offer a seat.

'What the hell did you do?'

Amol raised an eyebrow. 'I wrote a letter. Quietly. To you.'

'Well, it's not quiet anymore, is it?'

He slammed a sheet of printer paper onto the desk – one of the anonymous notices, the one signed 'friends'.

'Is this you?'

Amol didn't answer.

The Editor stepped back. Ran a hand through his hair. 'You have no evidence, Amol. You understand that? No recordings. No receipts. No emails. Just your word against Sean's.'

He leaned forward.

'And mud sticks. You might think you're the principled one, but this mud's going to end up on all of us. Especially now that every damn intern's whispering about SIS and yachts and black ops in the teacup room.'

He picked up Amol's letter from his desk drawer. Held it up like it was radioactive. 'This? It never happened.'

Amol crossed his arms. 'So that's it?'

'No,' the Editor said, almost kindly. 'That's survival. And I suggest you remember which side of the river you live on.'

A pause.

'Sean's not going anywhere. Not yet. And unless you want to start looking for freelance gigs in Belgrade, I'd advise you to stop playing hero.'

Amol turned to leave, reflecting: Fleet Street morality, measured in column inches and deniability.

By then, the panic had reached Vauxhall Bridge, that fortress of glass where the secret agents whispered and the shouting meant failure.

The conference room on the ninth floor had been soundproofed for discretion – but even so, the shouting carried. Dexter slammed a dossier onto the table, scattering clipped photos and a printed copy of Amol's letter.

'Do you understand what he's done?'

Sean shifted uncomfortably in his seat. 'We can still contain it –'

'Contain it?' Dexter spat. 'That half-caste bastard has lit a fuse under a half-dozen projects, poisoned a newsroom and made us look like paedophiles with notepads.'

He turned, pacing. Raging. 'All because you couldn't manage one bloody byline.'

Then, quieter now, almost to himself: 'He turned us down. Took everything we offered: access, protection, comfort and walked away like it was filth.'

His voice thinned. 'I see it in his face. That look I used to have. Like he still believes in something.' He paused. 'Belief like that? It doesn't survive long.'

Sean's face darkened. 'Don't pin this on me.'

'I am pinning it on you, you idiot. You were supposed to guide him. Groom him. Not – Jesus – let him write a letter to the editor like some bloody school prefect.'

They stood in silence for a long moment. Then Sean cleared his throat. 'There's a way to fix it.'

Dexter looked up.

'Send him out again. Somewhere we can't be blamed if things go wrong. Somewhere that looks like a legitimate assignment.'

'Where?'

Sean grinned slowly. 'Bosnia.'

Dexter narrowed his eyes. 'Sniper Alley.'

They exchanged a long, cold glance.

Sean shrugged. 'It's a war zone. Plenty of freelancers die. If he's too noble to play ball, let him bleed for his principles.'

Dexter nodded slowly.

'And if he doesn't get killed … ' Sean raised an eyebrow.

' … We have our own people who can do the job,' Dexter finished.

'Just punishment,' Sean said, already reaching for his phone.

That afternoon, in a private room off Pall Mall, Dexter slapped a cable on the table.

'You said Sedo was neutralized.'

Sean scanned it. 'Berlin? Christ. He surfaced?'

'Briefly. Asked after Amol.'

Sean exhaled. 'So now they think he's still in play.'

'No,' Dexter said. 'They think Amol is.'

A pause.

'If he leaks what happened in Naxos – or the bomb design – we're finished.'

'You want me to lean on him again?'

'No,' Dexter said softly. 'I want you to end it. Neatly, if you can.'

The summons came late in the day. Sean's email was unusually short.

'Quick word re: Balkans string. My desk. 4 p.m.'

When Amol arrived, Sean was already halfway through a KitKat, crumbs on his collar. He didn't look up.

'Big story bubbling,' he said. 'Sarajevo. Ceasefires breaking down. Rumours about ethnic cleansing, artillery outside Mostar.'

Amol raised an eyebrow. 'We already have two stringers in the region.'

Sean shrugged. 'One's drinking through it. The other's in love with a UN translator. We need someone reliable. Eyes open, boots on the ground.'

He slid a slim folder across the desk. 'Sniper Alley's where the juice is. Central Sarajevo. Hotel Holiday Inn still standing – for now. You'll file from there.'

Amol flipped the folder open. It was thin. No fixers. No insurance details. Just a one-way ticket and a brief marked 'high-value bylines'.

'No return date?'

Sean smiled. 'Depends how fast you write.'

Amol stared at him. Something brittle passed between them.

'This wasn't your idea,' Amol said quietly.

Sean leaned back. 'You're the one who said you were a journalist, not a spook. Well, here's a story. Go prove it.'

Amol stood. 'This is punishment.'

Sean didn't deny it. 'It's war,' he said. 'Everyone gets what's coming.'

Amol didn't pack. Instead, he walked.

Down to the Thames just before dusk, when the city held its breath and the water turned gunmetal grey. The cold stung his cheeks. He lit a cigarette and stared into the current, waiting for clarity or some shadow of it.

And then – they came. Not ghosts. Not hallucinations. But presence.

On his left, Layla, barefoot on the embankment stones, eyes dark and patient. On his right, his grandfather, in a woollen shawl and old Delhi spectacles – watching him as if he were still ten years old and reading newsprint upside down.

They didn't speak – not at first.

He turned towards her. Her face was exactly as he remembered – intelligent, amused, unflinching. The kind of beauty that had nothing to do with surface.

'You still walk too fast,' she said softly.

He blinked against the wind. 'I miss you every day.'

She nodded. 'Then stay. Breathe. Let them fail without you. Don't go.'

Then his grandfather: 'You don't owe them your death.'

Amol swallowed hard. 'But what do I do?'

The old man nodded slowly. 'Call your friends. The ones who owe you.'

Amol found the number buried in an old address book, in a drawer of clipped wire reports and fading press cards. Miro. Tall, broad-shouldered, always in a jacket two cuts too fine for Cairo. A Serb with a conscience. And, just maybe, a little reach.

Amol called from a payphone in Paddington, the kind that still took coins.

Miro answered on the second ring.

'Batty,' he said warmly. 'Still alive?'

'Trying,' Amol said. 'I need a favour.'

He explained the Sarajevo assignment. The folder. Sniper Alley. Dexter. 'I must not go, Miro.'

There was a pause. Then Miro, quiet: 'Leave it to me.'

The call came the next morning. 9.07 a.m.

Sean didn't even say hello. 'The bloody Yugoslavs have rejected your visa application.'

The news arrived just as spring was beginning to thaw the bitter winter.

Amol held the receiver in silence.

'They say it's a "security concern." Total bollocks. You've got clean credentials.' Then, lower: 'This is a setback. You understand? Dexter's not going to be happy.'

Amol smiled faintly. 'I'll live,' he said. 'That's the point, isn't it?'

Sean hung up without a word.

Islington. Just past midnight.

The hallway was cold when he got home. The kind of cold that doesn't come from broken heating – but from something else. Something that waits.

An envelope lay on the floor. Cheap paper. Thin enough to see through. No stamp, no postmark.

Block capitals, smudged ink from an old typewriter or a bad ribbon printer. Inside, a box the size of a matchbook. Plain cardboard. No logo.

When he opened it, the cardboard gave a soft wheeze – and inside, nestled against a square of kitchen roll for padding, was a single bullet. Silver. Real. At the base, crudely etched as if by hand: AMOL

That was it. No note. No explanation. Just the metal. And the name. He stared at it for a long time.

Not the bullet, he'd seen worse. But the letters. The pressure. The pause. Someone had taken just enough time to mean it enough to want him afraid.

He sat on the edge of the couch, coat still on. Across the street, a cat darted through the bins. Somewhere, a bottle broke.

But inside his flat, there was only the hush of it.

The kind of hush that comes before something breaks. He didn't call anyone. Not the police. Not the paper. Not even Sedo.

But somewhere in the back of his mind, he felt it – the faintest flicker of presence.

The kind Sedo left behind like aftershave: sharp, subtle, unmistakable. If he was still out there – and Amol knew he was – he'd seen the envelope too.

Not because he was tracking Amol. Because he was tracking them.

Later, in the half-light between sleep and waking, he speculated if they were destined to gather somewhere beyond – not quite dead, not quite gone.

The watchers, the plotters, the men who never blinked.

There were so many of them lurking beneath the timelines. What would they say about, and to, each other? Did they realize they were never chasing history, merely fleeing oblivion?

Curran, Blee, Rositzke – long gone but still whispering in bureaucratic eternity. Keir with his clubland smile. Efimov as Miro, always dressed for a funeral. Josling polishing his offers like a used car salesman. And Dexter with his leering schoolmaster's charm, talking pensions and Krug while plotting death. They didn't haunt corridors or case files anymore; they had their own afterlife.

A kind of spectral reunion in Cairo's City of the Dead – tombs turned to meeting rooms, mausoleums hosting briefings, the air thick with cigarette smoke and undeclared wars. Some were fading.

Others, it seemed, had been absorbed into a kind of dark matter – still present, still exerting force, but never seen. A private hell of clever men, playing pitiless rounds of 'Catch Me If You Can', not with each other, but with the lives of everyone else. Years had passed since those secret meetings, but the shadows they cast lingered still.

And sometimes Sedo was there too, but always apart – not seated at the table, not playing their game. Watching. He had the same tools, the same damage, but something extra the others had long discarded: a moral core, bruised perhaps but unbroken. A *sabra*, like the Israelis say – tough skin, soft heart.

Amol never knew if he admired Sedo or pitied him. Perhaps both. Perhaps it didn't matter. What mattered was this: when it counted, Sedo had told the truth.

And the others – the spooks without souls – never did.

20

Winners and Losers

Amol's exile began not with a sacking but with a suggestion.

'You've been going non-stop,' the Editor said, eyes darting from desk to floor, 'Middle East, Iran, Sudan, Jerusalem, all of it. Maybe it's time to take a breath. Recharge. You've earned it.'

Spring was when they called it extended leave. Framed as a gesture of goodwill – a pat on the back disguised as a push out the door. Not quite disciplinary, not quite voluntary. Just time off. Paid, technically. Open-ended, ambiguously phrased. 'No pressure, of course. Just some space.'

Space, he learnt, is where people are sent before they're erased.

In the first week, colleagues messaged him – cautious, supportive.

'Let's catch up.'

'Still on the masthead in my heart.'

'Classic tactic – stay cool.'

By the third week, the messages stopped. No assignments came in. His inbox was silent. His pass no longer opened the building.

It wasn't that his stories were being spiked. That would have required action, decision, responsibility. It was worse than that. They were simply being allowed to drift away. This was how the

British did it. Not with batons, not with censorship stamps or midnight raids – but with a kind of elegant apathy. Nothing ever needed to be denied. It was simply not pursued.

The Americans had congressional hearings. The Russians had show trials. The British had meetings that weren't minuted and policies that weren't printed.

He remembered the line Keir had offered him in the garden all those years ago – the Lubyanka was honest. You knew what it was. But here, the floor was quiet, and the carpet thick, and you didn't notice the trapdoor until you were already falling.

It wasn't that they punished you. They just let you fade. The worst part? They made you wonder if it was your own fault. Maybe the piece hadn't been that strong. Maybe you'd misjudged the tone. Maybe it was you.

That was the genius of the system. It never told you no. It simply arranged the silence.

He left the office early, feeling like a man who'd just sat down to dinner and found the table already cleared.

The following month, his name vanished from the forward planning sheet. Then from the email distribution lists. Then, entirely, from the newsroom wall – that grid of headshots once filled with foreign correspondents frozen in heatwave khakis, now reduced to PR rewrites and desk-bound opinion.

He heard whispers. From loyal friends. From people trying not to be seen speaking to him.

'They're reviewing overseas roles.'

'There's pressure, someone upstairs doesn't want your byline anymore.'

'It's not just Sean. Dexter's name keeps cropping up too.'

By early 1995, the redundancy letter arrived.

One Friday, an envelope appeared through his letterbox. Thick, cream bond paper, the kind they reserve for weddings, promotions and professional executions.

> As you know consultations have been taking place for some time about staffing levels,' it read. 'It had been hoped to achieve the necessary reduction in staffing through voluntary redundancy. Unfortunately, there has been very low take-up of this offer. We have therefore advised that it will be necessary to make some posts compulsorily redundant. Selection criteria have been agreed with your trades union and, as a result of the application of these criteria, your post has been identified as one of those which is redundant.

There was no meeting. No phone call. Just a handwritten and somewhat ambiguous note from the Editor:

> Amol, I wrote this to look generous-hearted, but I fear it only made things worse. I named your sources and said we'd have to agree to disagree about the advisability of taking briefings from the secret services. You've become a difficult case. I wish it hadn't come to this.

A difficult case. What it meant was: You crossed a line.

First, by exposing Sean's arrangements with Dexter. Then, by sabotaging the Bosnia assignment, the one designed to bury you under sniper fire.

Around the office, the truth dripped out in half-sentences and footnotes.

One colleague wrote: 'Sean has, idiotically, taken us towards a stage of hysteria and phoney war.'

Another confessed: 'Sean provided a very detailed dossier from his spook friend. I was very jumpy about being manipulated so directly.'

A third: 'I don't know how he persuaded Dexter to supply us with stuff and whether there was any quid pro quo demanded ...'

None of it mattered. None of it offered protection. Because the question had shifted from who said what to who was expendable.

Amol had become a liability, someone who wouldn't play along. Someone who remembered. Someone who refused to forget.

So they closed the book on him.

And then, like a bell tolling across the city, came the question no one dared ask aloud but everyone felt gnawing inside their bones: Who were the winners and losers in this hideous cat and mouse game?

Between the spooks and the media? Between the vultures operating from their Stalinist headquarters in Vauxhall and the young Fleet Street minnows still fighting for the underdog, for the rights of free speech and the freedom of the press?

At times, it looked as though SIS was deliberately experimenting with the lives and fates of reporters, seeing how far they could be manipulated, corrupted, bought off. Like Soviet commissars, they ridiculed the very idea of a Fourth Estate, of journalism as a counterweight to power, as something nobler than a mouthpiece.

Amol had resisted. He had fought, not with guns, but with memory, with truth, with stubbornness. And so, he vanished. Quietly. Predictably.

And yet, as the dust settled and the months slipped past, it was Sean who seemed to emerge unscathed.

After a brief silence, word trickled back. He'd resurfaced, of all places, in Papua New Guinea. A sinecure with a British-registered NGO, nominally focused on 'post-conflict reconciliation' and 'press development'.

No one asked how the role was funded. But those who knew how to read the Foreign Office website's footnotes saw the fingerprints.

A Foreign Office grant. A partnership with an aid consultancy run by a former ambassador. Quiet money, tucked into the folds of benevolence. He gave the occasional lecture to earnest interns about 'ethics in conflict zones', sipping from a mug marked 'Press Freedom is Not Negotiable'.

From the tropics, he posted the odd sunset photo. A filtered shot of him holding a machete near a mango tree. A blurry frame of him on a boat with a line about 'finding peace, finally'. The captions read like aftershave ads.

But it got worse for Amol. By the time the complaint came, he was already out, removed, shut down, erased. The redundancy had been confirmed, his desk cleared, his pass cancelled. No severance worth the name, no leaving drinks, no farewell email.

He assumed that was the end of it, that they'd buried him quietly and moved on.

Then one afternoon, as the rain-soaked Holloway Road and the air stank of burnt oil and wet concrete, his phone rang. An unknown number. A curt voice.

'Mr Batty? This is Kentish Town police station. We need you to come in for a voluntary interview under caution. A complaint's been filed against you.'

No explanation. No solicitor arranged. Just a time. A tone. He went alone.

The station was cold, fluorescent and slow – the kind of place where minutes became hours. They made him wait on a hard plastic chair beneath a peeling poster about hate crime and community safety. Eventually, a constable led him to a small room with a recording device already blinking red.

The allegation came from Bonny, Sean's ex-girlfriend – a woman Amol had spoken to only once, briefly, at a crowded bar years ago. He hadn't seen Bonny since that evening years ago – Sean's leaving party at a Fleet Street bar, noisy and forgettable. He remembered the night: a leaving do for a sub-editor. He'd asked her where she was from originally, and, in passing, mentioned that 'Asians and Africans feel the cold more, don't they? Something to do with body fat'. It had been a throwaway line, based on nothing more than half-remembered science and a vague attempt at small talk.

Now it had returned as a formal complaint. Bonny had gone straight to the police. She claimed the remark was 'a racial stereotype', 'deeply offensive' and made in a way 'that conveyed hostility'. The complaint continued, 'I was shaken up, distressed and frightened.'

The phrase 'racially aggravated harassment' was read aloud, slowly, as if it belonged to someone else's life.

Amol blinked. The room seemed to darken around him. It was a single line, pulled out of context, turned into a legal threat and a career-ending slur.

This wasn't the first time the system had laughed in his face.

Swansea. Years ago. He'd gone to cover a minor strike: local unions, a cold weather protest. Nothing dramatic. But by nightfall, he had nowhere to stay. Every B&B he passed had a sign in the window: No dogs. No Niggers. No Indians.

He ended up sleeping on a wooden bench under a streetlamp, coat zipped to his throat, trying to look like a man waiting for a late train. In the morning, he filed his copy from a greasy spoon and pretended it hadn't mattered. But it had.

That was Britain too – just as violent, just quieter. Not a mob with bottles, but a list of exclusions, printed and laminated.

He explained the context. That he hadn't meant it that way. That he himself was of Indian origin. That it had been a single, unmemorable exchange. That he hadn't seen her since.

It didn't matter.

The officer nodded sympathetically. Wrote nothing down. Closed the file.

'You're being released on unconditional bail,' he said. 'The CPS will review and likely move it to Crown Court. Trial date will be set in due course.'

No arrest. No charge – yet. Just the slow machinery of accusation set grinding into motion.

He walked out into the drizzle and stood under the overhang of a shuttered betting shop. The rain was sideways now. He couldn't move. Couldn't feel his hands.

He was alone. Utterly alone.

This wasn't just professional ruin. It was personal annihilation.

The slow, clinical unmaking of a man – reputation, history, intent – replaced by a single phrase taken out of context and weaponized in the void of everything else. The absurdity of it might have been funny, had it not been so deadly serious. A stray remark, twisted by silence, now echoed in a courtroom with terrifying weight.

As for Sedo, there was no word, not a shadow.

It was unlike him. And yet, perhaps it wasn't.

One Israeli contact, a reliable old fixer from Tel Aviv, had mentioned a quiet reshuffle at the top of Mossad.

'A new broom,' he'd said. 'Not just ruthless, radiant. They're calling him Eli Ben-Sasson again. But it's the same eyes.'

The cadence in the reports, the phrasing of the directives. Amol recognised Sedo's mind, even behind the new identity. He didn't need the name to know who it was.

A younger version of Isser Harel, someone murmured, not in stature or style, but in intensity, in the conviction that intelligence wasn't about information, but memory and menace.

Amol didn't need the name. He imagined Sedo in the glare of an interrogation room, or at the head of a table in Herzliya, not wearing a suit but radiating command. He'd always belonged to fire, not ashes. He wouldn't be allowed near Amol now – too compromised, too loyal.

Still, it stung. After everything. The café. The canal. Layla. A man who had once cradled his head during seizures and stood between him and gunmen now disappeared into silence, protocol, the clean gleam of official forgetting.

But in his darker moments, Amol sometimes imagined him there, just beyond the reach of CCTV, coat collar turned up, matchbook in his pocket.

Watching. Waiting. Ready, if the fuse ever needed lighting again.

It was in that mood, furious, betrayed and out of options – that he did something he hated himself for.

He wrote to the outgoing head of SIS.

'Dear Sir Richard,' he wrote, 'I am embarrassed to reach out to you, never having previously initiated contact with your office. However, I have interacted in the past with some of your former colleagues – without compromising my personal integrity – who told me never to hesitate if I was ever in trouble and needed a bit of help.

'I don't know if he is still active or now retired, but one of them was Keith Josling, former SIS bureau chief in Tel Aviv, who offered his support when my girlfriend was killed in a bus bomb near Jerusalem.

'I am currently being charged with "racially aggravated harassment" because of a casual comment I made in a London bar about how some Asians and Africans are more vulnerable to the cold in this country.

'I know you don't have a magic wand, nor can you interfere with due process, but I nevertheless wanted to bring this to your attention in the hope that you might be able to put in a good word for me with relevant officials.'

He posted it without ceremony, already regretting the impulse. Days turned to weeks with no reply.

Bonny never responded to his messages. Nor did Sean, who had by now fully disappeared into his tropics-funded exile, curating his virtue while the knives he'd left behind did their quiet work.

Amol understood then that character wasn't just assassinated in public. It was worn away – drip by drip – until nothing was left to defend.

And yet, the same question repeated, echoing louder than before: Who were the winners and losers in this hideous cat and mouse game?

From the outside, it looked as though the winners were thriving. Sean, secure in his post-colonial paradise, funded by Foreign Office slush and pious mission statements.

As for the Editor and his cronies, they rose ever higher. Promotions disguised as restructures. Title bumps, consultancy bonuses and sudden speaking gigs at panels on 'journalistic integrity' and 'the media in a multipolar world'.

Their expenses were rarely questioned. Oyster and Krug. Michelin stars and Cotswolds weekends. The Editor's new Jag parked proudly in the loading bay, right next to the delivery van marked Newsprint Ltd.

And each December, the elite of this crooked ecosystem gathered at The Ritz. The end-of-year champagne party hosted by SIS, a tradition so openly corrupt it had become folklore.

Dexter, before his quiet reassignment, had joked: 'The more you drink, the better it is for us. It all rolls into next year's budget.'

The party continued. Laughter, Krug, the same tired jokes. Amol's name never spoken, but never quite forgotten.

The ruling gang had buried the nuisance, preserved their networks and monetized the machinery. They had survived the scandal that never quite happened.

They had, in their own eyes, proven themselves untouchable. And yet, something dark flickered just out of reach. A faint current, imperceptible at first.

Because justice – true justice – is not bureaucratic. It does not arrive with memos or legal notices. It does not knock politely or announce itself in calendar invites. It waits. But before justice flickered, before the wheel turned, life took another nosedive.

Bonny's complaint was followed by a summons to Highbury Magistrates' Court one rain-lashed morning. The charge: racially aggravated harassment was repeated, along with a description.

'I would describe Batty as brown skin colour, receding hair line, black curly hair, distinctive glasses orange/red in colour, F6, medium build, jeans or trousers, t-shirt or shirt, light jacket,' Bonny wrote. 'I cannot recall the colours of the clothing. If I see Batty again, I would be able to recognize him.'

Other details were flimsy. The context ignored. The phrase about the cold, now enshrined in legalese, weighted with implications. He stood in the dock as if in a dream, his name mispronounced by the clerk, his protestations barely noted by the duty solicitor who glanced through his papers with all the urgency of someone ordering lunch.

The magistrate was stern but efficient. 'You will be granted unconditional bail,' she said. 'The matter will proceed to Crown Court. Estimated trial date: twenty-one months.'

Two years. Two years of limbo. No career. No clearance. No right of reply. Just the stain of a charge and the waiting silence that followed.

He left court with the press snapping no pictures – he was no celebrity, no MP, no tabloid bait. Just a name on a docket, already fading.

After that, London closed in.

His friends drifted. His phone barely rang. The Editor, when pressed, issued a statement affirming the paper's commitment to 'inclusion and accountability'. Sean remained silent.

Amol began to walk at night – long, senseless walks across the city, from Camden to Chelsea, crossing bridges without knowing why. The Thames became a kind of silent witness to his despair.

There were even times when he considered ending it all,

finding a convenient building in East London's Canary Wharf, from where he could hurl himself off an unguarded balcony when nobody was looking.

The alternative was to jump onto the rail tracks at one of London's many underground stations. Baker Street was the obvious choice for that. So many Tube lines converging in one wedged space. So many choices, but then, miraculously, it all passed. And then one day, on an impulse that felt like instinct, he used the freedom of his bail to go.

First to Beirut. The city greeted him not with questions, but warmth. He wandered Hamra in the early evenings, letting the sea breeze and diesel air wash over him. One night, as he passed the old Commodore Hotel, a memory cut through him like broken glass – Layla, barefoot on the hotel balcony, arms wrapped around her knees, laughing at some half-translated line of poetry he'd recited.

He almost turned back then. Almost caught a flight home, via Istanbul. But instead, he walked the Corniche at dawn and let her ghost keep pace beside him.

People remembered her. A driver nodded and said, 'The French girl, no? The one who wrote about the camps.' A café owner near Ain el Mreisseh still kept a magazine where her article had run. Her byline blurred now, but still visible. She was everywhere, not in mourning, but in colour. The lilac scarves in market stalls. The brass bangles in Mar Mikhael. The sound of Fairuz playing through car windows.

From Beirut, he went to Jerusalem. Talpiot was in bloom. The view over Al Aqsa shimmered with spring light. He stayed in his old flat, now let short-term to foreign students. They didn't mind sharing the space – one recognized his name and brought him strong coffee in the mornings without asking questions.

At night, he walked to the edge of the city, where she had once planned to photograph a bus station that no longer existed. He stood there now, reciting lines she used to love – Keats, Neruda, Gibran. He whispered them into the dry wind like prayers for the vanished.

One afternoon he drove himself to the Mediterranean shore near Caesarea, where he had once scattered her ashes. The waves rolled in as they always had, indifferent, eternal. 'You're still here,' he said aloud, unsure whether he was speaking to her or to himself. 'You never left me.'

Later in the year, he arrived back in Delhi.

In Golf Links, his aunt greeted him with long hugs and rosewater cakes. Neighbours remembered his grandfather. Some responded to his previously unspoken memories of Layla, too – how she used to ask for sugarless chai and always wore the same perfume.

Delhi embraced him without explanation. In its heat and dust, in its sprawling chaos and sudden tenderness, he felt something unspoken settle inside him. As if part of his soul had been reabsorbed.

In each city – Beirut, Jerusalem, Delhi – he lived backwards through time. Not in mourning, but in memory. With Layla. With purpose.

He still didn't know what the future held. Whether the Crown Court case would proceed. Whether someone would resurrect the smears. Whether he would ever be cleared.

But for the first time in a long time, he felt less afraid.

Eventually, Amol returned to London. There was no fanfare, no indictment, no redemption. Just the same cold streets, the same wet wind curling around the embankment. The same weight of waiting – for the Crown Court date, for some signal from the world that he had not been entirely forgotten.

He had no work. No bylines. No contact with the paper.

His solicitor advised patience. 'The system's slow,' she said. 'But things shift in silence. You'd be surprised.'

So he waited. Kept to himself. Spoke to no one.

Each morning, he walked the same route along the Thames – past Cleopatra's Needle, past the London Eye, over the river and back again. London's rituals rolled on around him: joggers with headphones, mothers pushing prams, tourists pressing fingers to maps. He moved through the crowd like a man waiting to be remembered.

21

Interlude

And then, one restless night, the dream came.

He was back in Jerusalem, on a hill near the city walls. The sky was thick with stars, not the pale pinpricks of polluted London skies – but bright, burning constellations. He stood alone at first, and then she was beside him, barefoot, her hair caught in the wind.

Layla.

Not younger. Not older. Just herself.

She smiled, without words, and touched his arm. 'They will forget what they did to you,' she said. 'But you must never forget who you are.'

'I'm tired,' he whispered. 'I lost everything.'

In his dream, he wept uncontrollably as Layla looked at him gently with that half smile he had once chased across three countries, and touched his hand. 'Not everything. You still walk.'

She leaned closer and whispered something – a line of poetry, or prayer or nothing at all. He woke with the sound still echoing, a fragment of breath more than words.

Later, walking by the river, it all returned to him.

'Fade far away, dissolve, and quite forget

What thou among the leaves hast never known –
The weariness, the fever and the fret …'

It had been one of her favourites. Keats, quoted one dusk on a balcony in Beirut, her voice half lost in the sound of the sea. He whispered the words again, as if repeating them might keep her near.

The morning light was weak, the sky already closing in. He pulled on his coat, hugging it close and continued walking.

The wind stung his face, but he didn't flinch. It almost felt like blessing.

He turned towards the river, hands in his pockets, collar up and began to walk.

Alone. Branded. Forgotten. But still walking.

22

Epilogue

Late Spring, London

By the mid-'90s, London felt quieter, the Cold War ghosts receding. The knock came just after dawn, when London was still wrapped in a grey shawl of mist, the kind that muffled footsteps and blurred intentions. The streetlamps still flickered. Birds tested their morning scales, hesitant and half hearted.

Amol opened the door in his dressing gown, coffee in one hand. The postman nodded – businesslike, familiar. A padded parcel was passed over with a clipboard to sign.

Three oversized stamps caught his eye, brilliant blue peacocks dancing beneath the word 'HELLAS'. Greece. Ornamental, seductive and blind to the havoc they carried.

Like all decoys, they drew the eye away from what mattered. The real swan slept inside.

Back inside, he placed the parcel gently on the kitchen table and peeled away the tape with the care of an archaeologist unearthing a relic.

He didn't open it. Just stood there, hands on the cardboard. Something about the weight of it – literal and otherwise – made him pause. If this was from Sedo, and if he was alive, walking, visible, the game wasn't over. It was just beginning.

Some men carried passports. Sedo carried detonators in his head, in his past, in the sketchbooks they thought had been burnt.

He poured the rest of his coffee, staring at the stamps: blue peacocks, dancing, blind to the havoc they carried. For a moment, he considered leaving it unopened. But the spell broke. He reached for the scissors.

—

Beneath the bubble wrap lay a square metal box. Matte finished. Compact. Sinister. Etched in tidy sans-serif were the words: 'TOTAL CUSTOMER SATISFACTION'.

Beneath that, in smaller font: 'Cylinder 3593, 16, 35'.

Soulless. Clinical. But humming with dormant menace. Three trigger switches accompanied it. One with a thick red lead. One silver. And the third – most ominous – twin plugs joined by four wires: red, yellow and two black. Like arteries in a mechanical heart. It was a complete Purple Swan prototype.

He thought of the bus in Jerusalem. The seared metal, the bodies unnamed. They'd said it was homemade, untraceable. But now, staring at the precision of this box, he wasn't so sure. Maybe Layla had died not by accident, but by export. A test run, or worse, proof of concept.

Amol had only ever seen fragments of it before, sketches Sedo had made in Naxos, ink-stained and feverish, his fingers trembling with urgency and fear. Now it was here. Whole. Real.

There was a letter atop the device. Folded neatly. Sedo's handwriting was unmistakable – confident, angular, always slightly leaning forward, as if the words couldn't wait to reach the end. 'Heard you were in trouble, my old friend. Don't let the bastards get you down.'

Beneath the letter, a photograph. Amol paused.

There they were: Three men in half-shadow, arms awkwardly crossed. Dexter, mid-gesture. Sean, trying too hard not to smirk as he held a Purple Swan aloft like a trophy – part weapon, part souvenir. And to the side, a younger, sharper, utterly unmistakable Sedo. Not just alive. Witness. Witness to all of it – the meetings, the cover-ups, the manipulations they later disavowed.

Beneath the photo, pencilled faintly in the same angled script as the postcard: 'You weren't wrong.'

So Sean had known everything. From the beginning. Not just the outlines. Not just what Amol had reported. But the full arc, the device, the design, the bargain Sedo had offered. And still he'd lied. Coaxed. Manipulated.

This wasn't just betrayal. This was theatre. A long con dressed as journalistic process.

He turned back to the letter.

'They renamed them. "White Doves", the British called them. Easier to explain in Parliament. More palatable for our friends abroad. But they're mine. Ours. They took what we made and turned it into an export model. First to Israel. Then to India. Maybe elsewhere.

By my count: over a million units. Gaza. Kashmir. The Line Actual Control. You know what that means, don't you?

'They made billions off what we built in a cave and you brought to light on a beach.'

Attached were London and Cayman account numbers, underlined in thick black ink.

Amol sat down heavily. The letter trembled in his hand. He looked again at the box. Cold. Final. A totem of the war they never admitted they fought.

Revenge wasn't always an explosion. Sometimes it was evidence. Exposure. The refusal to let a lie pass into history uncontested.

Redemption? Not from institutions. Never from them.

Renewal? That was harder. It demanded something of the soul.

He turned to the Remington. His grandfather's old typewriter sat like a monument on the desk. It had travelled from Delhi to Oxford to Jerusalem to London. The ribbon was faded, but the keys still struck with weight and rhythm.

He rolled in fresh paper. Began composing a message to Peter Dexter.

Dexter – the brush salesman-turned-spook. Badly pressed suits and false modesty. He had once praised Amol for passing six 'tests' – loyalty, risk, courage, congeniality, compassion and technical competence. But it was a crooked kind of praise. Recruitment by flattery. Now Amol had his own message.

He attached photocopies of Sedo's letter, the photo, the additional memos containing underlined numbers of bank accounts in London and the Caymans.

His own handwritten message noted: 'Your ghosts are leaking. You think the curtain won't rise again, but it already has. I kept the original. This copy is just a courtesy.'

He addressed the envelope to the last known safehouse in Pimlico. Then dropped it into a red postbox on the Embankment. A drizzle had started; he walked home in it, unbothered.

Within days, the pressure around him evaporated. The police notified his solicitor: 'No Further Action'. The racial harassment charges had vanished. Bureaucratic silence. No apology. But it was over.

At the paper, the fallout was volcanic. The Foreign Office grant was suspended. The consultancy was shut down. PR budgets slashed. Columns disappeared. Journalists were laid off. The Editor issued a statement about 'realignment with core values'. One day, the doors were padlocked. A note on the wall read: 'Due to circumstances beyond our control. The free lunches stopped. The Bollinger dried up.'

Rumours circulated about how Sean was in Bahrain now, 'advising' the crown prince on media strategy, others insisted he had relocated to Mauritania of all places. Still others swore he'd changed his name, grown a beard, disappeared into diplomatic fog. But in a bar in Mayfair, a junior Foreign Office aide once whispered: 'You didn't hear this from me, but he still has a file on you.'

Then came the news from Paris.

Sean's body in the Seine on a wet Tuesday morning. No passport, no wallet. Just a rumpled linen blazer with a London tailor's label and a soggy copy of *Le Monde* folded into the inner pocket. The French said suicide. The British offered nothing. A two-line notice ran on the agency wires: 'Former British journalist, long-time Paris resident, found drowned. No foul play suspected'. That was all.

Amol sat dry eyed. The idea was laughable. Sean had tried to have him killed. Had filed lies, watched others bleed, taken money to corrupt what was once a trade of truth. He died like the tool he was, discarded the moment he lost utility.

Was it suicide? Maybe. Or maybe the Service just cleaned up the mess. One push, one slip, a polite silence on the wire. That's how these stories ended. Not with a bang. With red roses and no signature.

Spies die three deaths, an old editor had once told him: the one in the papers, the one among friends and the one only the Service knows. Sean got all three. And none of them with honour.

Amol didn't cry. Why would he? The man had tried to get him killed. Had watched colleagues fall, fed lies into the bloodstream of his profession, sold off its last shreds of truth.

No, there were no tears. The thought of Sean in a pale, swollen mask should have brought something up from the pit of his gut. But nothing came. Not sorrow. Not fear. Not even rage.

Instead, and for no reason at all, he began to hum an absurdly paraphrased version of 'Sous les ponts de Paris'.

'The reason why they sing this song is easy to explain. It tells what happens all along the bridges of the Seine … '

His voice was low, tuneless, almost tender. The words floated over the water, absurd in their softness.

'They want to hold you tight, Far from the eyes of night

Under the bridges of Paris with you – They'll make your dreams come true … '

He didn't know where it had come from. Only that it had been lodged in him for years. A tune from a film, maybe. Or a joke someone once told in a Paris café. Now it bubbled up like something half-remembered from a previous life. He stopped humming.

The river moved on.

He did watch the rain for a long time that night, listening to it pool in the gutters and run down the windows. Water always finds a way out.

But all of it – Sedo's bomb, Sean's betrayal, the collapse of the paper – was gradually overtaken by a different kind of energy. Not triumph, but clarity. A purpose that sharpened with each memory recalled.

He didn't feel triumphant. Just unfinished. There was still something left to write. Not as a weapon. As a witness.

The past never disappeared. Not completely. Layla still hovered in the shadows of his mind, as did others. Sedo too was ever present, a shining star urging him never to forget.

He owed the truth to both. To Layla, who taught him love. And to Sedo, who taught him how to survive it. He thought that was the end of it. But the world wasn't finished.

The process of remembering raced through his mind and fingers. Writing. Piecing it all together. With Sedo's material and his own notes, he began to sketch a novel – part memoir, part reckoning. It traced the shape of lives lived in exile, under shadows, between betrayals. It was called *The Inheritance.*

The book ignited. Reviews called it 'a masterpiece of moral clarity' and 'a spy novel that indicts its own genre'. Translations followed. Awards. Invitations. The same people who had once erased him now queued up to praise his prose, clapping with the same hands that once signed his exile.

In Israel, the book became an inexplicable publishing sensation. No one could quite account for it. A foreign correspondent's memoir – ambiguous, digressive, morally tangled – was suddenly everywhere.

Bookshops in Tel Aviv sold out within days. Columnists dissected passages as if decoding state secrets. A well-known

Israeli novelist – reclusive, respected – was photographed in a Dizengoff bookstore, thumbing through the translation with a look of troubled recognition.

Amol received invitations from Israeli universities, think tanks, a late-night chat show. He declined them all. He never mentioned Sedo by name. Not once. But those who needed to know, knew.

Perhaps it was nostalgia. Perhaps guilt. Or perhaps the nation was simply learning to treasure the kinds of stories it once preferred to ignore – stories where the borders between betrayal and loyalty were not so much crossed as inhabited.

When a friend sent him the Israeli cover, Amol laughed out loud.

Friends Never Forget.

He knew better than most: Some friendships haunt, not just endure.

One festival – at Amalfi, Jaipur, he couldn't recall – he saw them.

Two men near the catering tent, seated close together, baseball caps low over their brows. The way one tilted his head, the way the other gestured mid-sentence with his bony white fingers – it was uncanny. They could easily have passed for Sean and Dexter.

But Sean was dead. Wasn't he? A body fished out of the Seine, no passport, no wallet, no answers. Dexter had vanished too, into one of those long corridors where old agents go to collect pensions or favours.

Much further behind them, almost swallowed by shadow, stood another figure. Alone. Still. The silhouette was angled just enough for Amol to catch a glimpse of the jawline, the collar turned up against the breeze. Something in the stance – a tension held in check, a history carried lightly.

Then the figure raised a glass. A slow, deliberate motion. A silent toast. Towards Amol.

He blinked.

Was that Sedo? But Jews don't drink, do they?

Or maybe that was just another myth. Another thing learnt too late.

By the time Amol turned for a clearer view, the silhouette was gone. The chairs were now empty. The space between them filled with harmless chatter and the clink of cutlery.

A trick of light? A spectre shaped by guilt and memory? Or something more deliberate? A final message.

Amol stood by the trellis as the applause swelled and broke behind him. One of the hosts called his name again. Louder this time. He didn't move.

A waiter passed behind him. Or maybe it wasn't a waiter. The footsteps slowed. Then paused.

Something in his chest stirred – a ripple, not panic, but not peace either. Instinct. Memory. Ghosts.

He drew in one more breath. Held it. Let it settle.

The moment stretched. Heavy with unfinished things. Then the breeze shifted.

And the presence, whatever it was, moved on.

Later, back in his hotel room, he tried to laugh it off. Festival fatigue, too much sun, too much sentiment. But then, buried inside the organizers' gift bag – beneath the pens and leaflets and branded notepad – he found a napkin. Folded with care.

On it, drawn in dark ink: a single dancing peacock. Purple. Not blue this time.

The colour had changed. The meaning too. What once disguised now declared.

Perhaps it was Sedo's way of saying: I made my choice. You made yours.

Peacock or swan? Hard to say now. Both moved with grace, both wore their plumage like warning.

If it was him, the gesture wouldn't have come lightly. Sedo never did anything lightly. It may not have been a toast. Perhaps a farewell. Or a warning. Or a reckoning.

Amol folded the napkin. Twice. No more.

Purple now. Not blue. Placed it back in the bag and slid it under the bed.

He lay with his back hard against the pillow, fingers resting lightly on the old notebook beside him, bare ankles protruding from his pyjama bottoms. His back ached, just a little, as he absorbed the sparsely furnished room, the predictable hotel carpet and an exit door offering the illusion of escape.

Naxos lurked among the quiet memories, folded into the pages of that same notebook, beside the half-chewed pen, the small box of unopened painkillers, his mobile and the watch he always took off at night.

The bedside lamp stayed on. A watery light paused over it all. Sleep welcomes those jostling memories, splitting and swarming without logic through the long hot night.

So when the phone buzzed at 5 a.m., he didn't answer right away.

'Hell,' he muttered. Then: 'Hello.'

Silence. A line still open … but no voice.

Was this how it was meant to end, or was this a beginning?

Glossary of Acronyms and Terms

BBC – British Broadcasting Corporation
CBE – Commander of the Order of the British Empire
CID – Criminal Investigation Department (UK police)
CIA – Central Intelligence Agency (US)
DEFRA – Department for Environment, Food & Rural Affairs (UK government)
FCO – Foreign and Commonwealth Office (UK)
FIFOT / FIFOTS – 'Failed in the Foreign Office, Try the Spooks' (Oxford slang for spook recruiters)
HQ – Headquarters
ID – Identification
IRA – Irish Republican Army
MECAS – Middle East Centre for Arab Studies (UK government Arabic training institute, formerly in Lebanon)
MI5 – UK domestic security and counterintelligence agency
MI6 – UK foreign intelligence service (also known as SIS)
NATO – North Atlantic Treaty Organization
NGO – Non-governmental Organization
PA – Palestinian Authority
PFLP – Popular Front for the Liberation of Palestine

PKK – Kurdistan Workers' Party (militant Kurdish separatist group in Turkey)
PLO – Palestine Liberation Organization
PR – Public relations
PROVO – informal nickname for the Provisional Irish Republican Army active in Northern Ireland from 1969 to 2005
RAF – Red Army Faction (German Left-wing militant group)
RAW – Research and Analysis Wing (India's external intelligence agency)
SAS – Special Air Service (elite UK military unit)
SIS – Secret Intelligence Service (UK foreign intelligence agency, also known as MI6)
TV – Television
UDBA – Uprava državne bezbednosti (Yugoslav State Security Service)
UN – United Nations
UNHCR – United Nations High Commissioner for Refugees
US – United States
QE2 – Queen Elizabeth 2 (ocean liner)

Acknowledgements

Writing *The Quiet Correspondent* has been a long journey through memory, invention and the blurred line between the two. I owe deep gratitude to my editors at Juggernaut Books, Swati Chopra and Krishna Sawant, for their patience, rigour and generosity of spirit.

To Peter Buckman, for his belief in the manuscript at a crucial moment, and to John Sweeney, for his camaraderie, candour and fearless example in the craft of journalism.

I would also like to thank Paula for her help and support. And Deirdre for her meticulous reading and comments that kept me alert to tone, rhythm and restraint. To colleagues and friends in London, Delhi, Jerusalem, your conversations, kindness and steady companionship over the years sustained me more than you know.

Above all, I remember James Cameron, whose blend of courage and compassion defined to me what journalism could be, and should still aspire to be.

A Note on the Author

Shyam Bhatia is a foreign correspondent currently living in London and previously operating out of Cairo, Beirut, Jerusalem and Washington, D.C. He has been the Middle East correspondent and diplomatic editor of *The Observer*, the US correspondent and foreign editor of the *Deccan Herald* and editor of *Asian Affairs* magazine. In 1994, he was selected as Foreign Journalist of the Year in the annual British Press Awards. He is currently the London correspondent for *The Tribune*. He is the author of *India's Nuclear Bomb* (1979), *Nuclear Rivals in the Middle East* (1988), *Brighter Than the Baghdad Sun* (1999), *Goodbye Shahzadi* (2008) and *Bullets and Bylines* (2016).